"Was I …?" Elizabeth swallowed. "What you hoped for?" she finished in an agonized rush. *Was I an unspeakable disaster compared with your incomparable first wife?* She stared into the darkness, waiting.

"Elizabeth Malinder." There was no condemnation here, only lazy humor in the use of her new name. "Have you so little courage? I did not think you a coward."

Was he laughing at her? "I am no coward! I did not dislike it!" Elizabeth clutched the linen covers to her neck in sudden defense.

"Thank God! An honest woman!" Richard stretched out to push aside her hasty covering and drew one long, smooth caress from shoulder to wrist, finally capturing her hand and raising her palm to his mouth as he had once before. "It will improve, lady. Now, come here."

He pulled her close again, holding firm when she would have struggled for her freedom. It was no contest. Elizabeth found herself pinned against that toned body she had so admired. And Richard felt all the tension drain from her, felt her smile against his chest.

* * *

Chosen for the Marriage Bed
Harlequin® Historical #1022—December 2010

Author's Note

My heroine, Elizabeth de Lacy, was born out of the dramatic tale of Ellen Gethin, wife to Thomas Vaughan, Lord of Hergest in the Welsh Marches. The story tells that Ellen's brother David was murdered by her cousin. In a desire for revenge, at an archery contest Ellen took up a bow and arrow, aimed at her villainous cousin and slew him. Whether she had to answer for her crime before the law is not told, but she earned the title Terrible Ellen.

It is a true romance of a headstrong, spirited lady, and I was determined to write about her. Ellen can be seen today, a carved figure on a magnificent alabaster tomb in Kington Church in Herefordshire, where she lies beside her husband. She has a calm serenity in her face that I imagine she did not have in life.

So I wrote my romance of the Wars of the Roses. Ellen became Elizabeth de Lacy, the Black Vixen, who of course needed a husband purposeful and driven as she. Richard Malinder had the measure of his willful bride, even though he had to come to terms with her pride and her unsettling knowledge of witchcraft. Thrust into a marriage neither of them sought, I knew it would be a difficult journey for them—yet their love was to prove stronger than fear and suspicion, bloodshed and grief, the viciousness of civil war and cold-blooded murder.

I like to think that the spirits of Elizabeth and Richard still linger in Herefordshire today. I hope you enjoy their romance.

CHOSEN *for the* MARRIAGE BED

ANNE O'BRIEN

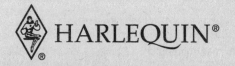

TORONTO • NEW YORK • LONDON
AMSTERDAM • PARIS • SYDNEY • HAMBURG
STOCKHOLM • ATHENS • TOKYO • MILAN • MADRID
PRAGUE • WARSAW • BUDAPEST • AUCKLAND

Recycling programs
for this product may
not exist in your area.

ISBN-13: 978-0-373-29622-4

CHOSEN FOR THE MARRIAGE BED

First North American Publication 2010

Praise for
Anne O'Brien

The Disgraced Marchioness
"O'Brien makes the themes of secret identities, secret
babies and misunderstandings tense and believable in the
tightly woven plot of her novel of manners."
—*RT Book Reviews*

The Outrageous Debutante
"Delightful characters light up the pages of this poignant,
emotionally moving love story. The well-drawn
Regency backdrop includes not just ballrooms
but a darker side of the era, as well."
—*RT Book Reviews*

The Runaway Heiress
"Charming, sensitive historical romance writer O'Brien
captures the modes and morals of the Regency era."
—*RT Book Reviews*

To George, as ever, with love

Chapter One

⁓⁓⁓⁓⁓

The Welsh March—1460

In Llanwardine Priory in the Welsh March the little room had stone walls, a stone-flagged floor and a ribbed roof. Damp cold clung to every surface, a nasty gleam in the light from the single lantern. It had the air of being long unused, except for now at the dark of the night. Two women and a cat shivered from the chill and lively apprehension. The door was barred, windows close shuttered against any who might show an interest in their activities.

The women sat facing each other across a rough plank trestle, the cat curled to one side. Both figures were dark cloaked. One, the elder, was Mistress Jane Bringsty, round of face with ample girth and the plain garments of a serving woman; the other was Elizabeth de Lacy, daughter of one of the foremost aristocratic families in the March. Pale and thin, she was young, and in the black robe, white veil and wimple of a nun. In silence, Elizabeth took from a sack four crude tallow candles and set them in a square before her serving woman. Jane placed a pottery dish in the centre, poured in water from a stoppered vessel, then lifted her eyes.

'Are you sure, my lady?'

'Yes.' Elizabeth's teeth chattered against the cold.

'If you say so.' Jane angled a glance at the cat, that immediately turned its back, to wash its paws and its ears with studied indifference. On a sigh of resignation the woman searched and took from a pocket a number of small packages, then lit the candles from the lantern. They gave off thick and acrid smoke as much as they provided further light. 'Scrying is dangerous.' Jane shuffled her bulk on the stool. 'What if we were followed? Or just discovered here?'

'We were not. The infirmary is empty.' Elizabeth placed her hands flat on the table, palms down, fingers spread. No rings adorned her red and swollen knuckles. Her lips were pressed unflatteringly into a thin line.

'Even so…' The older woman narrowed her eyes in appraisal of her mistress's sharp features. Hollowed cheeks and shadows, deep as bruises below her eyes. The frame of the severe nun's wimple did nothing to enhance the young woman; rather, the gloom and flickering flames drew attention to her shortcomings.

Elizabeth frowned in quick irritation. 'Just do it, Jane. You are far clearer at divination than I.'

'More practice, that's all.' From one of the packets Jane Bringsty drew a handful of dried mugwort leaves and set herself to read the future for her mistress.

First she crumbled some of the herb into the candle flames to give off a pungent aroma. With closed eyes she inhaled deeply and then sprinkled the rest on to the surface of the water in the pan.

'Whatsoever is wrought by me with thee, may it have good and speedy effect,' she intoned, a bare whisper. With the index finger of her left hand, Jane began to stir random patterns from the centre, shifting direction without conscious plan, for the length of six deep breaths, then set herself to watch and interpret as the water and the scattering of leaf settled.

'What do you see?'

'Hush. Wait.'

Elizabeth clasped her fingers to still them. 'Well?' She could wait no longer.

'Murky business, my lady. Clouds. Bloodshed.' Jane looked up. 'Death.'

'Mine?' A sharp edge.

'Not so. For you—a journey, perhaps. A dark castle, but whether there is a welcome or a rejection there, friend or foe, I know not.'

'Thank God!' Elizabeth breathed. *A journey.*

'Hush, my lady. Not wise to call on His name here.'

Elizabeth nodded in acceptance of the mild reprimand, but continued to interrogate, leaning forwards as if she too would see the images in the dish. 'When will the journey be? Soon? Or shall I be old and grey and beyond hope? Or—'

Elizabeth de Lacy stopped on a quick intake of breath, eyes fixed on what she saw. There in the swirling water a face emerged, a face with a whip of dark hair as if lifted by some unseen wind. Grey eyes, dark and stormy, looked back at her with formidable power. An extraordinarily handsome face to her mind. Straight nose, carved cheekbones, firm chin—he was beautiful. And as she acknowledged the symmetrical perfection, it was as if she fell into his gaze, so that she felt him slide beneath her skin, sink into her bones. A tight knot formed within her chest. Was this a possession, an owner-ship? Elizabeth blew out a little breath, discovering that she had been holding it against the intrusion. Was it perhaps the work of the Devil? Was this connection between the unknown man and herself of good or ill? An awareness prickled along her skin as a film of sweat touched her upper lip despite the clammy damp of the room. She touched her hand to her lips, which suddenly felt tender as the face looked sternly back at her. She could not imagine those firm lips curving into a warm smile. There was no warmth there, merely a hard, calculating cynicism.

'Who is that?' she whispered. 'He is a man who could trouble my dreams.'

The eyes looked steadily back, holding her own as if he would dip into her mind and read the secrets of her heart, so that she felt her cheeks flush. And perhaps those lips curved, infinitesimally, into a smile. Or perhaps it was merely a movement in the water. Elizabeth passed her tongue over her own dry lips.

Then the servant shrugged and sat back from the table, abruptly passing her hand over a mere dish of water and herbs to close down the visions, and he was gone. 'I cannot tell. It is all grey and insubstantial tonight. But I see two men, shadowed, on the edge of your life.'

'Two?' Elizabeth queried, reluctant to let the image go. 'I saw only one.'

'Two,' Jane Bringsty confirmed. 'Both dark. One is to be trusted. The other will prove to be a bitter enemy.'

Elizabeth rested her chin on her clasped hands, her thoughts still with the vivid features. 'All very well, but how do I tell which is which? How will I know?'

'Use your head and your heart, my lady. What else?'

'I will if I ever escape this place.' A depth of despair was allowed to creep into her voice. Elizabeth bowed her head as any nun might, but not in prayer. She sounded tired to the bone. When she looked up, there was a dullness in the dark eyes. Her servant reached out, touched her fingers in silent compassion and Elizabeth squared her shoulders. 'Jane. Did you bring what I asked of you?'

'Yes. Not difficult. The nuns watch me far less than they watch you.' She unfolded the other packets on the table. 'This is what you wanted. Celandine.' The metallic golden petals and heart-shaped leaves of this earliest of flowers lay wilting and sad.

Elizabeth nodded, but without discernible pleasure. 'Excellent. To escape unwanted imprisonment or entrapment of all kinds. In Heaven's name, I need it. What are the rest?'

Jane unwrapped the remaining packets to reveal a dried mixture of ugly roots and faded leaves. 'Vervain—to aid escape from enemies. And woodruff to ensure victory.'

Elizabeth picked up a piece of woody stem. 'Comfrey for safety and protection on a journey. It seems I shall need it if your vision is true.' For the first time there was a slight curve of the lips, a genuine warmth in the dark stare that fixed on the servant.

'It does no harm to give fate a nudge, my lady.' Jane tucked the whole into a small leather bag with a drawstring and pushed it across the dusty wood. 'Wear it next to the skin, my lady. Be sure to keep it from prying eyes.'

Elizabeth lifted it, pushed it beneath her robe, her expression cold and flat. 'I will wear it. And pray to God and His Lady Mother that it works. Or I shall assuredly go mad in this place.'

'I suppose it does no harm to call on all powers to come to your aid, my lady.' Jane quickly doused the candles with a rapid gesture of her hands and stood. The cat rose and stretched, keen to leave. 'Let us return before one of the sisters notices your absence and flexes her right arm in the name of Holy Obedience.'

'Amen to that!' replied Elizabeth with feeling, already knowing the bite of the whip against her flesh.

In her heart and in her mind, Elizabeth de Lacy—not *Sister* Elizabeth, she would never be *Sister* Elizabeth—seethed with anger and rebellion, and all but shook with bitter frustration. Her life at Llanwardine was beyond tolerating, from the unpalatable food to the bone-chilling cold of endless nights. To the freezing water in which it was her task to scour the cups and bowls used by the elderly nuns. As she lifted the remains of the candles, her sleeves fell back from her hands and forearms. The bones of arms and wrists were too fragile, too delicate, as if they might snap at the first provocation. She had never been a robust child, but now the pale skin of her face was almost translucent, the violet imprints beneath her eyes far too deep. Her fingers were rough and red from hard work and chilblains. She must eat more—she knew it—but it was difficult to do more than force a little of the hard bread past the lump in her throat, washing it down with a spoonful of the greasy broth. It was an ongoing battle between her mind and her belly, but the grease of the broth coated her mouth, the rancid vegetables turned her stomach.

Was the rest of her life to be spent in this place? Would she grow old and die here?

No. And, no! No, she could not believe that life would hold nothing for her but this trial of poverty and obedience, deprivation and hardship until the day she died. She was only just one year past her second decade and, before God, she had no calling to be a nun, as He must know. Surely He would see and understand her sufferings and not commit her to such a fate, despite the determination of her powerful uncle, Sir John de Lacy, to keep her here until she bowed in obedience before him.

And, no, she could never wed Owain Thomas, to achieve yet another Yorkist alliance for her family in the March. Never! She shivered at the memory of Sir Owain, the tall, spare knight with thinning hair, elderly enough to be her father, his fingers dry and rough against her hand when he bowed over it with clumsy greed. His eyes when he had agreed to wed her had been as damply cold as a reptile. She swallowed against the remembered scratch of his hand on hers. Whatever life held in store for her, at least she had escaped that!

Elizabeth de Lacy turned her steps towards the priory kitchens, where she would once again plunge her hands in the icy water. Into her mind came the austere face of the scrying, the level stare of the dark-haired man that sent a shiver through her body. It was not from the bitter draughts that fluttered her robes. Within her belly a heat bloomed.

Richard Malinder, Lord of Ledenshall, head bent, frowned over the sword blade he was cleaning, making a pleasing picture if he had either known or cared. His build and temperament were those of a soldier. Faint lines of determination and a certain inflexibility were clear to be read on the vivid face. In the direct gleam of his eyes there was an uncomfortable cynicism. He was dark, black of hair, dark grey of eye, with a straight, high-bridged nose made for arrogance. Lean cheeks, a well-moulded mouth, capable of a disgraceful degree of charm, but now stern. A handsome man, so women would say and frequently did, but high-tempered and imperious, not a man easily dealt with. One of the Black Malinders, who could charm and attract, but whose character could be as forceful as his appearance. Now his frown deepened over the stark announcement made by the de Lacy messenger not an hour ago, news that had had the shock of a lightning bolt.

Maude de Lacy, the ten-year-old daughter of Sir John de Lacy, the girl who was to have been his wife, was dead of a fever.

He had had no premonition of it. How should he—she was only ten years old. He was sorry, of course, had expressed appropriate words to be carried back to the girl's father, Sir John de Lacy, Lord of Talgarth. The death of Sir John's only child was an occasion for grief, even though Richard had to dredge through the depths of his memory to bring up any more personal detail of her than a small girl with chestnut hair and a deep blue gown, with laughter on her face as she chased a hound puppy through the courtyard of her home. The only occasion he had set eyes on her, when their betrothal was sealed.

But beneath his regret ran a guilt-ridden torrent of relief.

This had been an alliance that in his heart he had never wanted, a political alliance in which the child Maude had been simply a pawn to be used in the struggle for power in the March. It was very clear in Richard's mind. Sir John had wanted to tie him into an unbreakable union with the de Lacys, presumably to dominate the March between them. But Sir John would be an uncomfortable ally in the present circumstances. The de Lacy loyalties to the House of York did not tally with those of Malinder's support for the Lancastrian King Henry. Nor did Richard relish the prospect of Maude as a betrothed. She was far too young to be a bride.

And yet he needed to marry again after the death of his wife Gwladys. It was high time that he sired an heir to the Malinder estates. On a thought, his black brows twitched together as he applied the soft cloth to the blade's edge. As long as Sir John did not try to remedy this sudden collapse of the negotiations by offering another de Lacy bride. What if Sir John proposed his unwed niece, Elizabeth de Lacy, to take the place of his daughter in the Malinder marriage bed?

Richard abandoned the blade on the table beside him and leaned back against its edge. Elizabeth de Lacy. A difficult girl by all accounts, with more than a passing interest in the Black Arts. He knew the woman by repute, rumours being quick to spread the length of the March. Nothing good was said about her. A brittle, angular girl—in fact, no longer a girl—with a brittle tongue. Short of temper, short of beauty, short of any softer feminine emotions, she had when still a young girl taken control of her family home at Bishop's Pyon and the upbringing of her younger brother on the untimely death of her father, and was still unwed despite her advancing years. Add in her forthright speaking and her dabbling in witchcraft arts as well… Richard grimaced—no, she was not an appealing bride.

But, in truth, he doubted that Sir John would offer her anyway. Rumour said she had been sent away to Llanwardine

Priory to take the veil under the authority of Lady Isabel de Lacy, her great-aunt, who was the Prioress there. Sir John might claim the girl had found a vocation, but gossip suggested that she had been shuffled off out of Sir John's way.

'Well, I don't want her either,' Richard informed the hound at his side as he made for the door. 'Whatever the reason for Elizabeth de Lacy's sudden calling to the wilds of Llanwardine, all I can say is thank God!'

In a circular tower room in the great de Lacy fortress of Talgarth further to the north, a man donned a black magician's robe over tunic and hose. Nicholas Capel, renegade priest, necromancer, caster of horoscopes and personal adviser in all unorthodox matters to Sir John de Lacy of Talgarth lit a single candle. Master Nicholas Capel was a man of overweening ambitions and cunning perversion. By his reckoning it was all about to bloom into spectacular fruition.

Power! What more could a man desire? The power to manipulate, to bend men to his desires as pieces on a chessboard. The power to destroy if need be.

He moved to sit behind a table in a high-backed armed chair, painted with strange symbols, with blood-red naked swords on each of the four stout legs. He drew the velvet cover from a crystal. Spread his hands, palms flat against the wood, and looked deep into the crystal's heart.

'What is the future here?'

Beside the crystal rested three torn pieces of parchment with Capel's distinctive angular lettering. Three names. John de Lacy, his temporal lord—or so that fierce magnate believed. A little smile warmed Capel's eyes. De Lacy would never be *his* master. Richard Malinder of Ledenshall, whose growing power in the March was a thing to be envied. And it would grow further if steps were not taken to harness or appropriate it. Then there was his own name, or the one that he was known by. Nicholas Capel.

'Our fates are connected.' He moved his palms to cover the three names. 'I know it. But how? Show me the future!'

Then grunted, startled. In the crystal a female figure emerged. Dark haired, tall and slender.

'Who are you?'

The figure turned full face. Capel strained closer.

'Elizabeth de Lacy?' he whispered. 'This is unexpected.'

Within the crystal sphere the figures flowed silently as if in the steps of some complicated dance. Until he and John de Lacy faded away into nothingness and, in the very centre, Elizabeth de Lacy stood beside Richard Malinder. Silently, smoothly they turned to each other as if drawn by some invisible cords. They smiled. Malinder stretched out his hand. Elizabeth placed her fingers there so that he might kiss them with silken grace. He held out his arms, she stepped into them and they curved around her, enfolding her. The scene shimmered with power as he bent his dark head to take her mouth with his own. She allowed it, clinging to him, so close it was as if they were one being. Her dark robe wrapped around his thighs, the mass of her hair lay on his shoulder, his hand wound and clenched within its heavy weight. The kiss was endless, infused with a striking depth of passion.

Capel frowned at the intensity of the scene.

'So you too will play your part, Elizabeth de Lacy. It seems you are destined to become lovers. Now, that does surprise me. Perhaps it is not wise after all for you to be left to dwindle into obscure unwed old age in Llanwardine Priory. Perhaps I must ignore your wilfulness and find a new path for you.'

The scene changed. Richard retreated. Elizabeth stood alone. In her arms lay a new-born child, dark of hair. Massed clouds of danger threatened an imminent storm.

Capel smile widely to show his teeth, leaned back in his chair after casting the cloth once more over the crystal and blowing out the candle, consigning the lovers to oblivion. For a long time he sat and thought in the dark shadows. Separating the strands, weaving them together until the final tapestry suited his purpose. He would use his powers in the service of John de Lacy for as long as it was in his interest to do so. There was an advantage to being the power behind the mailed gauntlet where no one would look or suspect. And then? Well, then all would be revealed.

But of one thing he was certain. Richard Malinder and Elizabeth de Lacy must be brought together. They would provide the path to his greatness.

Chapter Two

Elizabeth de Lacy stood outside the iron-studded door of the Prioress's private chamber, defiantly twitching her skirts into more seemly order, smoothing the novice's wimple around her shoulders. She had been summoned and her nerves raced beneath her skin, even though she could think of no sin she had committed for which she had not already been punished. She knocked lightly. Entered on command, then came to a halt on the threshold, eyes narrowing in astonishment, then deep suspicion.

'Come in, Sister Elizabeth.'

She obeyed the calm, beautifully modulated voice. Bowed her head to the Prioress, hands folded before her and eyes downcast as she had been taught, before curtsying to her uncle, Sir John de Lacy.

Elizabeth gave no thought to the tasteful comfort of the room, in stark contrast with the rooms of the Priory that she inhabited. Her whole attention was centred on the man who stood beside the Prioress's chair. And the second man who hovered at his shoulder. Now what?

'You have a visitor, Sister Elizabeth.'

Elizabeth felt the power of his presence as Sir John cast an eye over her. His energy filled the room, as his figure did not. Not over tall, light-framed, wiry with dark hair and light blue eyes, proclaiming more than a hint of Welsh blood in the de Lacy family over the generations, Sir John was all controlled energy. Face heavily lined with impatience but deliberately impassive, he stated the reason for his visit.

'You look well, my niece.'

Elizabeth inclined her head with arrogant composure as her only reply. Her only protection against those searching eyes. She knew what she must look like and it could not be a pleasing picture, her black habit unflatteringly leaching any colour from her cheeks, and it would be even worse without the disguising folds of her robes and veil. She would not smile or bid him welcome.

Nor would she even acknowledge the man who travelled with her uncle. Nicholas Capel. Tall, impressive with his sweep of hair to his shoulders, he was a familiar figure at Talgarth. What was he to her uncle? Adviser? Servant? Elizabeth did not think the man served anyone but himself. Some said he was a priest, defrocked for unnamed sins. Jane, tight-lipped, swore he was a necromancer who served the Devil. Clad in black from collar to hose, his bottomless dark eyes all but stripped the flesh from her bones. Elizabeth shuddered.

'I have made a decision on your future, Elizabeth.'

Elizabeth's heart leapt in her breast within the confines of the rough black cloth that rubbed her skin raw. A sudden beat of hope that shook her whole body. Surely everyone in the room must be aware of it? But she allowed none of it to register on her face.

'And what is your decision, Sir John?'

'You are to come home.' Elizabeth allowed the briefest of glances at the Prioress, but found no enlightenment there. 'Or not home, exactly. But you are to leave the Priory.'

'I see.' But she did not.

There was a light knock on the door, which opened

to admit a young man whose presence brought the first genuine emotion to Elizabeth's face and a quick flush of bright colour.

'David…! I didn't know you were here.'

'I've been seeing to the horses…'

Once she would have run across the room to greet him. Once she would have flung her arms around the young brother whom she had raised from childhood, holding him close in delight at his presence. Once she would have laughed her pleasure at his familiar, lively features and kissed his cheek, ruffled his dark hair. Now under the stern gaze of the Prioress, her uncle's untrustworthy watchfulness, Capel's sinister stare, she stood her ground and waited.

'Elizabeth!' Regardless of protocol, David strode across the room to grasp her rigid shoulders and salute her cheek, studying her face with the sharp blue eyes of the de Lacys. 'I couldn't stay away.'

'You look well. How is Lewis?'

'When does our brother not thrive?' David swept her query away. 'Has Sir John told you?'

'No. He has told me nothing.' Elizabeth returned the grasp of his hands, a quick fierce pressure, then released herself. It would be too easy to allow emotion to hold sway. She must take care to show no weakness. She had still not been told of the plan for her. 'So what do you want of me, Uncle?' she asked Sir John. 'Why must I come home—but not home, exactly?' Better to know now, however much she might dislike the outcome.

'My daughter Maude is dead.'

'I know.' Her face softened a little. 'We had heard. I am sorry.'

The Prioress was quick to intervene. 'We are not so closed off here that we were unaware. We have offered our prayers for the little maid's soul, Sir John.'

He nodded, but continued to address his niece. 'It is

intended that you take Maude's place in the negotiated set-
tlement with Lord Richard Malinder of Ledenshall. That *you*
will honour the marriage contract.'

Startled, Elizabeth took a breath as she considered the
statement. Release from Llanwardine. But at what cost? She
was once more to be a player in the ongoing de Lacy scheming
to achieve even more power in the March. But with a difference. Dismay gripped her. 'I should have known, shouldn't
I? I am to be a bride again. But this time I am to be married
to a *Lancastrian*, not a Yorkist. I am to be wed to the enemy.
Your plots would seem to have taken a turn for the devious,
Uncle.' She ignored her brother's strangled cough, keeping
her direct gaze on Sir John's suddenly heated countenance. He
might prefer that their differences not be aired before Lady
Isabel, but what did she care?

'You will find Malinder a more congenial prospect than
Sir Owain. His politics need not trouble you.' The harsh reply
dared her to disagree or to continue her public washing of
family linen. 'It will be arranged that you have an escort from
here to Ledenshall, Malinder's home.'

'I am not to go home first. To Bishop's Pyon.' Elizabeth's
query hid a wealth of hurt.

'Surely, Uncle...' David added, 'would it not be more
fitting...?'

'It is better if you travel straight to your new home, my
lady,' Master Capel observed, smooth, conciliatory. 'The wedding ceremony can take place as soon as you arrive.'

Better for whom?

Elizabeth merely dropped her gaze. What did she think
of this unexpected development? A handful of months ago it
had taken only the space of a heartbeat to reject the prospect
of Sir Owain Thomas as husband, to dare to run the gauntlet
of her uncle's displeasure. But having spent the intervening
months here at Llanwardine, she had learnt a harsh lesson.
Surely this new offer would be better, more satisfying than

life here. She had thought so often enough, when the bell for
Prime dragged her from her bed into the frozen spaces of the
Priory church. When her hands had stiffened with cold as she
dug the iced and unyielding earth to liberate the final winter
roots in the kitchen garden.

But Richard Malinder? What did she know of him? Tales
of him were rife, of his growing authority, the increasing
power of his blade and his fist in the name of Lancastrian
King Henry. Black Malinder, who had lost his first wife to
a tragic pregnancy that had claimed both mother and child.
Would she want this man as her husband? He was the enemy.
A Lancastrian, giving his misguided allegiance to the man
who claimed the throne as Henry VI, whereas she had been
raised to follow the superior rival bloodline of the Plantagenet
House of York. How would it be if she were wed to a man
whose political leanings were directly opposed to her own?
The dismay deepened. Would he insist that she change her
allegiance? Could she do that?

And then another thought. Black Malinder, he was called.
Was he the beautiful face in the scrying dish? Was he one of
the dark men of Jane's scrying, who might be either friend
or foe? There was no knowing. All the men in her life were
dark. Her brothers Lewis and David. Sir John himself. Even
that dreadful creature Nicholas Capel, who was smiling at
her as if he could see into her very soul. Jane's reading of her
future had given her no help at all.

So Elizabeth must decide if she wanted this marriage, and
quickly. Sir John was already scowling at her. Well, why not
accept the offer? All men were untrustworthy, ambitious,
self-seeking. Richard Malinder would only want her as guar-
antee of peace between two potentially warring families in
the March. And to carry his heir to the Malinder inheritance,
of course. She could accept that. But at least he was not as
dried up as a beech husk and he was not old. In the end,
she realised, it was an eminently simply decision to make.

This marriage would be for her an escape, a key to an otherwise locked door, and fate might never give her another such chance before her final vows were made, chaining her for ever to rules and enforced obedience. Sir John's control over her life would finally be at an end. By the Virgin, she would do it! Despite all her reservations, the Lord of Ledenshall's hand in marriage would give her status, authority, a measure of independence, and would open for her that all-important door from her own captivity.

It really was not a difficult decision to make at all.

'Very well, Sir John. I will wed Richard Malinder.'

Sir John's lips curled in sleek satisfaction. 'So be it.'

'Does…does Lord Richard accept my hand, sir?' She found a sudden need to ask, to know his reaction to taking her rather than her cousin Maude. Maybe he would not find her too disagreeable.

'It's not been finally arranged.' Sir John waved the query away, a matter of no importance. 'There'll be no difficulty. He'll take you. You'll be so well dowered he'd be a fool to refuse you.'

You have not asked him, have you? He does not even know!

'Then of course he will take me if you are prepared to buy his compliance.' Elizabeth felt the inexplicable hope that Richard Malinder might want her for herself die in her breast. 'How foolish of me to ask.'

The visitors were gone, leaving Elizabeth alone with her great-aunt.

'You have many talents, many gifts to offer Richard Malinder,' Lady Isabel assured her.

'Talents? Gifts? I have no evidence of that. My father showed no affection towards me. Owain Thomas wanted me for my de Lacy blood.' Elizabeth swallowed against the hopeless self-pity that threatened, refusing to give in to it. 'Now I am desired only as a replacement. For Lord Malinder's dead wife. For my cousin Maude. Not for *myself*.' The reply came with a spark of temper, with heat from the heart. 'And what hope is there for happiness for me, or even tolerance in such a marriage, where we shall be enemies before the rings are exchanged?'

'There is always hope.' The Prioress was stern, yet Elizabeth felt an understanding there. 'Before you leave us, I would say this to you. And mind me well, Elizabeth de Lacy. If you are ever in need of help, you will know where to find a safe refuge. At present the March is quiescent. I think it will not always remain so. If the war erupts again between York and Lancaster, you will be caught up in the maelstrom, as will we all. If danger threatens, you and yours will always be welcome here. Come. Soon the bell will ring for tierce. We shall include an Ave Maria for your safe delivery to Ledenshall.'

Some few days later, sounds of arrival at Ledenshall, of the clatter of hooves on cobbles in the courtyard below, caused Richard Malinder to abandon a sheaf of documents to stride across the room, deflecting the hound from his path with a passing caress of its ears, to lean from the window. What he saw below—who he saw—made his face break into a smile of delight that warmed his eyes, a lightening of expression not often seen of late on the face of the Lord of Ledenshall. He took the stairs at a ground-covering lope to welcome the Red Malinders below as the man at the head of the cavalcade dismounted and began to help the lady from her mount with words of impatient encouragement. Their escort was engaged in leading away horses, unloading baggage from pack animals and a small wagon.

'Rob! Have you perhaps come to stay with us?' Richard looked askance at the small mountain of boxes and packages which was now growing steadily on the cobbles beside him.

'Come for the wedding, of course.' Robert Malinder, clearly

a Red Malinder, grinned over his shoulder, then turned back to growl a suggestion that the lady remove her foot from the stirrup this side of nightfall if she expected his help.

'News travels fast.' Richard's brows rose. 'It seems that you must have known of the happy event before I did!'

Then the cousins came together, gripped right hands in recognition of family and friendship and political allegiance. Robert Malinder. Tall, broad of shoulder. Russet haired and green-eyed. Fair of skin, now pink and glowing, nose more than a little red from the brisk cold. Nothing like the Malinders at Ledenshall except in height and frame, but unmistakably one of the Red Malinders of Moccas.

'It's always as well for us to know what the de Lacys are planning,' Robert explained unnecessarily. 'We have our sources.' He hesitated but, typically, only for a moment before making his abrupt acknowledgement. 'We were sorry to hear of Maude's death.'

Before he could make a suitable and equally typical non-committal reply to the blunt commiseration, Richard discovered his attention to be quite deliberately sought and captured.

'Well, dearest Richard. Will you not welcome me? When I have travelled all this way just to see you?'

He felt a gentle touch of a hand on his arm, a tug on his sleeve. He turned with a smile of welcome, looked down. For a moment his breath backed up in his lungs. The muscles of his gut clenched, the smile of welcome faded, leaving the flat planes of his face taut. *Gwladys!* was all that he could think, when he could think at all. His wife's image filled his mind, before common sense and brutal reality took control. Of course not. Gwladys was dead. He blinked at the face at his shoulder, feeling foolish, hoping that the girl had been unable to sense his initial reaction to her. But the resemblance was there, stronger than was comfortable. Red-gold hair, neatly braided, mostly hidden by her travelling hood. The same heavy-lidded green eyes, dark as emeralds, framed by long lashes. Well-marked brows, a straight nose and flawless skin. Cream and rose, in comparison with Robert's ruddy cheeks. Anne Malinder was a beauty. But of course, Gwladys and Anne Malinder had been cousins, both carrying the family traits strongly.

'Anne. I have not seen you since…' Since he had wed Gwladys, when his eyes had been only for his beautiful wife and he had seen Anne still as a little maid. No longer so. 'Since before you grew up!' Richard, disgusted by his lack of a suitable greeting, surveyed Robert's sister, whose head now reached quite neatly to his shoulder.

'I have grown up. I am now old enough to be wed.' The heavy lashes veiled the brilliant eyes, the perfect lips curved ingenuously. 'I persuaded my brother to bring me. I thought your new bride might like some company. Of her own age. Although I think she is a good few years older than I.'

'That was kind of you.'

'Of course. We must make her welcome, even if she is a Yorkist and older than most new brides.' Anne tilted her chin with an appealing flash of green eyes.

Richard's glance sharpened, but the girl's face shone with innocuous pleasure. Her hand still on his sleeve tightened its hold with quick pressure from pretty white fingers. Even her hands were Gwladys's—small and slender, made for jewelled rings. Richard bent his head and kissed Anne's cheeks in a cousinly salute.

'Welcome to Ledenshall, Anne.'

'I had to bring her.' Robert's grimace was rueful. Horses and men-at-arms had all finally vanished in the direction of warmth and comfort, the baggage disappearing into the living accommodation with smooth-running efficiency. The cousins, after admiring the quality of the Malinder horseflesh, followed into the Great Hall.

'No matter.' Lord Richard signalled to a hovering maid-servant to replenish the ale and bring bread and meat.

'My sister threatened to come on her own if I did not escort her, and pestered our mother until she agreed. Anne can be a nuisance when she's bored or denied.' Robert stripped off gloves and cloak, cast them on a bench, and began to unbuckle his sword. He cursed fluently at his clumsy and icy fingers where painful feeling was beginning to return. 'She lacks female company of her own age, I suppose. And with the promise of a wedding on the horizon—well, I had to bring her.' He stamped his feet and winced. 'Poor weather for travelling!'

'She'll have enough company and more over the forthcoming days.' Having recovered from the initial shock on seeing the girl, Richard had thrust his discomfort to the back of his mind. He poured ale into a tankard and handed it to Robert, who took it and drank deep with appreciation. Steam began to rise from his damp clothes and boots.

'That's better.' He groaned and ran a hand over his wind-scoured face.

The serving maid bustled in with platters of food and added logs to the fire with an arch look at the newcomer. The hound sank once more with a sigh to its place by the hearth, now that the excitement of arrival was over.

'A quiet journey?'

'Very.' Robert wiped the back of a large hand over his mouth. 'The Welsh seem to be lying low, for once. And the weather, of course. No one's stirring.'

'Come and take the weight off your feet.'

Robert grunted his appreciation, was silent for a moment as he drank, still hugging the fire. Then, having thawed out to his satisfaction, he threw himself into a chair with graceless ease and propped his feet on the opposite settle. 'Tell me all. You're to align yourself with the de Lacys, in spite of Maude's death.'

'Yes. Sir John's niece.'

Richard stared into his ale. The name of Elizabeth de Lacy had been swiftly substituted for that of Maude in the betrothal contracts. In the interests of peace in the March, the proposed Malinder–de Lacy marriage would stand if he, Richard Malinder, would agree. Richard exhaled slowly. It was very difficult to like Sir John, a man driven by self-seeking ambition. As for Master Capel, his obsidian eyes had gleamed with conspiratorial interest throughout the proceedings. The man might have remained silent, carefully deferential, but there was about him something that touched Richard's spine with a slither of distaste.

'I suppose you know what you are about.' The lift in Robert's voice made just a question of the statement.

'Yes, I do.' Richard's brows rose, but he kept the tone light. 'And, yes, I've heard the gossip, but there can't be so much wrong with the girl. I didn't want her—swore I wouldn't take her, but I've changed my mind. Sir John's enthusiastic and I see no reason for delay.'

'As long as you keep your eyes and ears open to de Lacy intentions,' Robert advised, suddenly serious. 'Watch your back, Richard. Sir John must have an ulterior motive—he always does. When's it to be?'

'Soon. It's intended that she—Elizabeth de Lacy—travel here directly from Llanwardine Priory. She's well born, of an age to be wed and raised to be a competent chatelaine. I need just such a wife because I need an heir. And she's extraordinarily well dowered.' Richard eyed his cousin, an unexpected flicker of amusement in the cold depths of his eyes, then strode across the room, flung open the lid of a heavy oak coffer, to rummage to the bottom to extract a roll of ancient and tattered vellum. Now he smoothed it out, anchored it with tankards and his own poignard. Then, hands splayed on the table top, he bent to study its content with reference to one of the sheets of the marriage contract.

'Come and look at this, Rob.'

It was a roughly drawn plan in coloured inks, now much faded, of the extent of the Malinder possessions. It was formidable when seen in a swathe of indigo blue. There were the lands of the Black Malinders, forming a substantially solid block through the east and central March with Ledenshall situated towards its western rim. And there the acquisitions of their cousins of the red hair, principally into South Wales. The Malinders were a powerful family.

'It's formidable,' Robert agreed. 'Black and Red Malinders together.'

'It is. And thus understandable why de Lacy should fear our influence and wish to clasp hands with the Malinders. But look at the girl's dowry. Sir John said that the titles came to her from her mother's family, the Vaughans of Tretower, a family with strong connections in the March. So she would bring with her that estate there.' Richard referred to the stipulated estates on the contract and pointed at the location of the lands on the plan. 'And there. And also there. As well as this stretch of land.' He ran his finger along the proposed estates that the bride would bring with her, splaying his hand over them thoughtfully when he had traced the full extent. 'I would say that Sir John chose them most carefully.'

Robert nodded. If Elizabeth's lands were subsumed into the Malinder holdings, Richard's land ownership would sweep in an impressive block, almost unbroken, along the March. 'More than generous.'

'Too generous?' Richard pushed himself upright and allowed the vellum to re-roll, scooping it up and replacing it in the coffer. He then sat on the lid, forearms braced on thighs to pin his cousin with a speculative stare. 'It would appear to me to be foolhardy in the extreme. To consolidate *my* power in the central March at the expense of his own. Sir John's no fool. So why has he done it? Because he values my charm and place at his table as a member of his family?'

Robert grunted. 'I can think of nothing less likely.'

'Nor I. He's very keen to draw me in. This offer is far more advantageous to me than when I agreed to wed Maude. So why?'

'Is it simply that he's keen to get the girl off de Lacy hands?'

'No. Not that.' Richard pushed impatient fingers through his hair to clasp his hands behind his head and lean back against the wall. He frowned down at his crossed ankles as if they would give him the answer to the riddle. 'He's given too much away. If the problem is the girl, why not simply leave her in Llanwardine Priory where she's an irritant to no one but the Lady Prioress? No. Sir John has some scheme in mind that demands an alliance with me. Is it simply that I don't look too closely at what he's up to in the March? He could have bought my compliance with much less—I've no overt quarrel with Sir John unless he steps on my toes, in spite of his allegiance to York. So there's something here that I'm not seeing.' The sun caught a sharp glint in Richard's eyes as he turned his head. 'To my mind, Sir John sees Elizabeth and her estates as the bait in a trap.'

'With you as the unsuspecting rat?' Robert hitched a hip against the table, emptied the tankard.

'Hmm. Not so unsuspecting. But what's the trap? That's what I can't see.'

'As I said—watch your back, Richard.'

Richard's reply was cool and contemplative. 'So I shall. Because another question is, do you suppose that the bait— the cheese to catch the rat, Elizabeth de Lacy herself—is an innocent party to this? Or is the undesirable Elizabeth part and parcel of Sir John's dark and devious scheming?'

Richard let his own question hang in his mind. He had no liking for such murky doings, and yet there were definite advantages to this match. A high-born wife with an enviable parcel of land. As long as he kept his wits about him he would be in no danger. So the girl was neither amenable nor passingly attractive. Would it matter so much? As long as she could hold the reins at Ledenshall in his absence and bear Malinder sons, then she would be an acceptable wife.

'I'm just surprised you would even seek an alliance with a family that would overthrow King Henry and raise up the Duke of York in his stead,' Robert remarked.

'To my mind it could be to an advantage, Rob. Better to have some small window through which to spy into the intent of our enemies than to be taken by surprise. So if Sir John is in truth plotting against me…'

'Elizabeth de Lacy is to be that window.'

'Then why not?'

'Then the girl has my sympathies.' Robert held out his tankard. 'An object of intrigue from both sides of the alliance.'

Richard stood to refill Robert's empty cup with a rueful smile. 'I doubt it will ever come to that. Enough of this. The contract is signed. The lady seems to consider marriage to me at least preferable to life as a nun or to the embrace of Owain Thomas. I should feel duly flattered and honoured!' A touch of steel in eye and voice. 'As long as she realises that once she has crossed this threshold her loyalty will be to me and not to her family. I will not tolerate any desire to cleave to de Lacy politics.'

Robert raised his tankard. 'Then, if you are set on it, let's drink to the success of the enterprise.'

And Richard raised his tankard. 'Amen to that! To my fruitful union with Elizabeth de Lacy.'

Chapter Three

Elizabeth arrived at her new home in the middle of a thunderstorm. The expected guests erupted without ceremony, horses and riders, into the outer courtyard in a chaotic flurry of hooves and mud and a downpour of rain. Richard turned his face up to the heavens. Grey clouds pressed down. If he had been a man of superstition, he thought, he would have seen this as a sign of ill omen. All he needed was a pair of passing ravens to croak their disapproval.

Then the gates creaked and thudded shut behind them. Servants emerged to see to the comfort of the travellers. Two young men, unrecognisable in cloaks and hoods, issued orders. Elizabeth de Lacy's brothers, Richard decided. They swung down from their horses and would have gone to the aid of the women, but Richard forestalled them. His eye had sought and found the younger of the two female forms, well muffled against the storm. As a gesture of greeting he waded through the wet to help his betrothed to dismount.

'Come, lady. Hardly the welcome I would have wished for you. Let me help you…'

She did not reply. Her face was shadowed by her deep hood. He stood beside her weary horse, raised his arms to place his hands firmly around her waist to lift her down from the saddle. Only to be answered by a sharp hiss from within her cloak. A flash of dark fur and lethal claws. A shallow but bloody scratch appeared along the length of Richard's hand.

Startled into immobility, Richard stared at the blood, his hiss of surprise as much as pain echoing that of the cat sheltered within the folds of Elizabeth's cloak. He looked up, to find two pairs of eyes fixed on him. One feline and definitely displeased, golden and unblinking from the confines of the cloak. The other dark and watching him equally intently from within the hood, as a wild animal might watch a hunter, he thought, from the safety of its lair. Wary, uncertain, but with a strong streak of defiance, both mistress and cat surveyed him.

Elizabeth de Lacy found her voice first. 'Forgive me, my lord. You surprised her.'

Richard's words of welcome had dissolved in the deluge. '*I* surprised *her*? You're travelling from Llanwardine with a *cat* in your lap?'

'I had to bring her. There was no other way.'

For a long moment their gazes held, his astonished, hers defensive. Then Elizabeth blinked the rain from her lashes and the contact was broken.

'Never mind,' Richard forestalled any further conversation as thunder rolled overhead. 'Let's all get in out of this infernal weather. Including that animal. If you could prevent her from mauling me further, I would help you down.'

Grasping Elizabeth de Lacy firmly—and the struggling cat—he lifted and deposited her on her feet, aware of her lightness, relieved when the girl thrust the cat into the arms of her serving woman. So Richard took her arm to lead her into the Hall where there would be a small reception awaiting them. He was conscious of her drawing back, a definite reluctance, but why? She had seemed neither shy nor lacking in confidence in that first brief connection. Her eyes had met and held his with not a little self-worth, so why hang back now? This was not the reaction of a forthright, headstrong young woman, as Elizabeth de Lacy had been painted. Richard Malinder frowned. She would be his wife and Lady of Ledenshall so he would not allow her to succumb to foolish reticence, but pulled her forwards into the light and warmth. Servants removed and carried off sodden cloaks. A fire was burning towards which all gravitated. Wine was brought.

For better or worse, his bride had come home.

But first things first. Richard sought out Elizabeth's elder brother in the throng. It was not difficult. The de Lacy stature and colouring was clearly marked on both of Sir John's nephews. Richard drew Lewis, a rangy young man in his early twenties with a not-quite-hostile expression on his face, aside. Now was the time to build some bridges between the two families.

'I owe you my thanks for escorting your sister here.' Richard clasped the hand of Lewis de Lacy, forcing a courteous exchange.

'I was given no choice, my lord. Sir John ordered it.'

'But you are safely here. A bad day for such a lengthy journey.' Both were uncomfortably aware of the political divide between Malinder and de Lacy, but for the occasion it was pushed aside by tacit and common consent. 'Some refreshment, I think.' Richard beckoned one of the maids, who promptly handed a tankard to the young man.

Lewis accepted and drank, dry humour surfacing under the influence of the warmth and ale. 'My sister will be relieved to have arrived. Postponing the journey was not something we discussed. I doubt I could have persuaded her to remain at Llanwardine another night. Perhaps I should introduce you formally,' he suggested.

'I have had a painful meeting already!' Richard responded

to the humour, pleased to see the boy relax, and flexed his hand where the scratch stung. 'I'll live. Not sure about the cat though.'

'Ha! Vicious and unpredictable—but much loved by Mistress Bringsty and so untouchable.'

'Do you say?' Richard smiled.

'*I* would not risk it! But Elizabeth is more amenable than the cat,' Lewis ventured, before adding with a quick and engaging grin, 'or most of the time. But I would watch Mistress Bringsty, if I were you.'

Richard's brows snapped into a dark bar as he followed the direction of Lewis's glance across the room towards the woman who stood at Elizabeth de Lacy's shoulder in a position of support and protection. Then his mouth curved and his eyes warmed in reply. 'The voice of experience. I'm grateful for the warning.' He began to move in the direction of the two women, until a hand grasped his sleeve.

'One thing I must say. And I dare say you won't like it, Malinder.' Richard turned, seeing that Lewis was serious again, tense as if needing to draw on inner depths, but determined none the less. 'Elizabeth will deny it, but her life has not been an easy one. Our father, Philip de Lacy, had no affection for any of us, whilst Sir John sees her as a means to an end. It was despicable to send her to Llanwardine. Elizabeth deserves some contentment, some measure of happiness. She's had precious little in her life so far.' His bright level gaze held Richard's, suddenly older than his years. 'If you hurt her—I'll hunt you down, Malinder or no.'

Richard looked at the impassioned features, unconcerned with the threat, astounding in itself, more taken with the fierce loyalty of the young man and the glimpse that had been unexpectedly opened into Elizabeth de Lacy's previous existence. He found that he liked Lewis de Lacy no worse for that fierce loyalty.

'The lady will receive all consideration at my hands. I can

free her from de Lacy control, if that's what you mean. I hope she can be happy and content here.' He kept the tone light as he felt the heat of the fire in Lewis's regard.

Then Lewis nodded. 'That's what I want for her. So come and meet her. Elizabeth…' Lewis walked to her, touched her arm. She turned slowly to face the two men. And so Richard Malinder gained his first true impression of his bride.

His inner and very candid reaction to her appalled him.

A drowned rat would have presented a more appealing picture. Despite the heavy cloak, she was soaked to the skin with unflattering consequences. The dark gown, not a nun's habit, but no more attractive with its sodden folds and mired hem, clung to her figure, clammy and revealing. She was tall—her eyes almost on a level with his—but too thin, too angular. He noted her wrists as she held a mug of steaming ale, the bones pressing against translucent skin, the sharp collarbones where the neckline of her gown revealed them. The drenched wimple clung to her head and framed a face notable for its hollow cheeks and thin, straight nose. Her hair was completely covered by the unflattering cloth. Her skin was sallow, colourless, the faintest smudge of mud on one cheek where she had wiped away the rain. She looked stretched and strained from lack of sleep. Her mouth might be full with a generous lower lip, probably enhanced by a smile if she was ever moved to give one, but instead it was taut and uncurving. Dark unfathomable eyes watched him warily, the brows, beautifully arched, raised a little. She awaited his response with what? A certain confidence? Or a deep disquiet, well concealed? Whatever feelings she hid, she was not a prepossessing presence.

As he approached, and as Elizabeth de Lacy turned to acknowledge him for the first time, Richard saw her eyes widen, a flash of light in their depths. Her fingers tightened on her cup, high colour slashing across her sharp cheekbones, her colourless lips parted as if she would express some immediate thought. Then she pressed them together, at the same time veiling her thoughts with a down-sweep of lashes.

Her reaction to him—was it shock? Fear? What was she thinking?

But then that question was obliterated by a slight movement to one side of Elizabeth. Richard's attention was caught. Anne Malinder had approached to stand quietly there, as if to give Elizabeth some companionable support on this tense occasion. Gowned in rich blue damask, a profusion of braided red-gold hair covered with a transparent veil and delicately tinted cheeks, she was rounded and feminine and astonishingly pretty. A fleeting image again leapt unbidden into his mind, of Gwladys, who had also enjoyed wearing blue. It provided an unfortunate and terrible comparison with Richard's new bride.

His heart sank.

Richard, his manners impeccable, deliberately turned his eyes from Anne and back to Elizabeth de Lacy, careful to show none of his inner turmoil. Taking her hand, long fingered and cold, he found himself wondering whether there was any warm blood to be found anywhere in her body.

'Welcome to Ledenshall, Elizabeth de Lacy.'

He raised her hand to his lips in a brief formal salute. Her fingers were as icy against his mouth as he had suspected, the skin roughened, the knuckles ugly and swollen.

Recovered from whatever had disturbed her, Elizabeth inclined her head, the tiniest of movements. 'Thank you, my lord Malinder. I am honoured by your desire to wed me.' Her eyes remained direct beneath his searching gaze. 'I am most pleased to be here.' Her voice surprised him a little. Low and soft, it had a husky depth that was most appealing. His heart sank even further. It was the most attractive part about her as far as he could tell.

Elizabeth allowed herself time to admire the room that would be her own. Timber-ceilinged, plaster-walled, painted in floral patterns now faded into delicate soft colours with the years, a patterned tiled floor—it all wrapped her round in an aura of wealth and comfort. A fire burned in the stone fireplace and beeswax candles had been lit in tall candlesticks to push back the shadows. The bed—oh, glory!—had patterned silk curtains and tester, the canopy attached by tasselled cords to the ceiling beams. After the deprivations of Llanwardine, she could imagine the sheer luxury of lying there, beneath the silk cover where she could see the luxury of a feather mattress and cool linen sheets. An oak chest, a box chair, a stand with pewter ware. Elizabeth took it all in with a silent sigh of delight. The Malinder household had taken pains to make her feel welcomed. The bands of tension around Elizabeth's heart loosened a little; her fingers, which had been clenched into fists at her sides, slowly opened.

Before she could express her thanks, her attention was truly caught because there before the fire stood a bound wooden tub. And buckets of steaming water brought in by servants. Elizabeth looked at it longingly, with unspeakable gratitude, as she tugged at her gown where it clung unpleasantly to her hips. Her appearance on her arrival could not have been worse. She hated to think what she looked like. She *knew* what she looked like. What a shock it must have been for Richard Malinder to see his betrothed for the first time, as if she had just been dragged from a river. At least she could only improve. A cynical twist touched the corner of her lips, quickly hidden as she recalled her first unfortunate reaction.

Richard Malinder was definitely the man of the scrying bowl. The same astonishingly attractive features, the same fall of black hair. And when those grey eyes had looked at her she had felt her bones melt, and was almost compelled by some inner force to reach out a hand to touch him. Not that she had, but surely he was everything a woman could want in her husband if physical beauty mattered.

How tragic that she could not match him with a beauty of her own.

Yet she must remember. Elizabeth, unaware, frowned at her new surroundings. He was a Lancastrian, and therefore her enemy. It would be unwise to be seduced by the magnificence of a man's face. And what was it that Jane had said in warning? Two dark men, one friend, one enemy.

If Richard Malinder was to prove to be her enemy, then she must be on her guard.

She had seen the tightening of his muscles when he approached her, until good manners had forced him to play the gallant. It was the moment she had been dreading. She had to summon all her inner resources to present a blank and unresponsive exterior, anything but reveal the fear in her heart. And he was so cold and formal—he must dislike the match more than she thought. A pity she had nothing to recommend her to change his mind. Not compared with the decorative little cousin who was even now watching her, head tilted, with a slyly amused light in her eyes.

Elizabeth's meagre belongings had already been brought in. Never had a bride from so powerful a family been so poorly prepared. Jane Bringsty deposited the cat, which took up a position on a corded box and watched the proceedings with half-veiled hostile eyes. Then as warmth pervaded, it stretched and began to wash its damp fur with intense concentration. If only it could be as easy for her to settle into these new surroundings.

Jane Bringsty, aided by a suspiciously willing Anne, began to open the packages on the bed, intent on discovering a suitable gown. An impossibility, Elizabeth acknowledged, knowing the contents. Meanwhile with cold stiff fingers she unpinned and removed the heavy wimple. As she held the coarse cloth in her hands, Elizabeth sensed and heard the reaction. And knew why. She herself had grown used to it—almost.

'Oh.' Anne's eyes danced. 'How shocking!'

'The nuns,' Elizabeth found herself explaining, 'believe that long hair encourages vanity and distracts a woman from her vocation and the true meaning of life. At least they did not shave my head. It could be worse.'

'Not much worse!' Anne answered with devastating frankness.

True enough, even though the comment was pure malice. The shortest of dark hair covered her head. Soft and short, raggedly cut, it hugged her skull, hardly a covering at all.

Knowing that she had no control over the next few minutes, Elizabeth tensed against what must follow, grateful that the candles in the room were few, the light dimly shadowed. Her gown was removed and then her chemise until she stood, clammy and damp in shivering flesh beside the steaming tub. A little draught touched the skin of her neck and shoulder, as of a door opening, and with it a sudden presentiment. Elizabeth lifted her head, quickly glancing over her shoulder, to see that the door was indeed partially opened. There, unmoving on the threshold, was a dark figure. He must have knocked and, receiving no answer, opened it to ask after her needs. This was far worse than any of her imaginings. Richard Malinder, shockingly aware of the most intimate of her secrets.

Elizabeth stood immobile, as unmoving as he, her eyes wide and lips parted in dread, appalled at what she knew he must see. His face might be expressionless, but she could imagine the thoughts clamouring in his mind. To her horror his gaze moved from hers to slide over her shoulders, her back, down to buttocks and thighs. Then back to hold hers again. Light, insubstantial his appraisal might be, yet she felt that his keen eyes had taken possession of every inch of her skin—and presumably found her undesirable. How mortifying! Elizabeth shivered in awareness at the chill in that direct judgement, the only blessing that the flickering of the candles might mask the worst of the scars.

And that was not the worst of it. By the Virgin! Would he come in? Would he find a need to comment, to draw even more attention to her with its ensuing degradation? And if he did, would she be forced to abandon what dignity she had left to snatch up her robe to cover herself and her shame? Elizabeth prayed he had enough sensitivity to retreat and not inflict any more humiliation on her. Was it not bad enough that his beautiful cousin should see her punishment revealed?

Even as the thought crossed her mind, as if hearing her silent plea, as if reading the dismay on her face, Richard Malinder bowed, and withdrew before the others in the room knew of his presence, closing the door softly. Leaving Elizabeth to claw back her control. The whole had only lasted a matter of seconds, yet it had seemed to Elizabeth a lifetime of raw exposure, to be scrutinised and judged.

Meanwhile, Anne Malinder, unaware, looked at Elizabeth with emerald-eyed interest.

'What did they do to you?'

In her mind, Elizabeth saw herself as Anne would see her. As Richard Malinder must have seen her. She carried no extra flesh. Her ribs could be detected beneath her skin, as could the press of bones at hip and shoulder. Her breasts were small and undeveloped. Almost a child's body in its slightness, despite her age and obvious womanhood. She could almost hear the condemnation. If Richard wanted a wife for child-bearing, he had not chosen well. Overcome with shame, as if her deficiencies were all her own fault, Elizabeth turned her back on her unwelcome audience to pick up a bedgown and so hide herself from this too public view and inspection. An action that allowed the candlelight to glimmer along silver welts. Healed but visible. As she realised what her action had revealed to Anne Malinder, Elizabeth stiffened again, but it was too late.

A fraught silence descended. Until the sharp tension was broken by a quick and attractive gurgle of laughter. Mistress Anne covered her smiling mouth with her hands in what Elizabeth instantly recognised as a parody of regretful sympathy. Her eyes shone brilliantly.

'What *do* you suppose Richard will say when he sees you?'

For the first time Elizabeth truly looked at the girl who stood beside the bed with one of her desperately unattractive and unfashionable gowns in her pretty hands. And immediately recognised in Anne Malinder a danger. There was no friendship offered in those sparkling green eyes.

But was Mistress Anne Malinder not accurate in her observation? Elizabeth decided Anne was everything that she was not. Beautiful, well groomed, compliant, socially at ease in this household. And cousin to Lord Richard. In that one moment of blinding recognition, Elizabeth had no doubts of the girl's intentions. She wanted Richard for herself, and resented Elizabeth's presence. To be so outspoken suggested a child-like naïvety but Elizabeth recognised the sly deliberation for what it was. Recognised the deliberately fashionable clothing that displayed Mistress Anne's figure to perfection, and would highlight her own failings. No wonder the Lord of Ledenshall had looked as if struck with a battle-axe when Anne had so cunningly positioned herself in close proximity to the new bride!

But would Richard care what she, Elizabeth, looked like? As long as he had the alliance he desired and a wife who would bear him an heir, he would not care at all. She was only a replacement for Maude, after all. She must not forget it.

'Forgive me, my lady.' Anne smiled, eyes wide in regret. It could almost have been a simper, but the charm was heavy, as if Anne was aware of her lack of discretion and would make amends. There was no harm in offering an apology after all since the damage had been done. 'I should not have been so outspoken,' she murmured. 'I meant no ill.' But it was difficult for the girl to disguise the glow of triumph in her eyes.

Yes, you did! Elizabeth swallowed the words. Recognising an enemy, swamped with alarm at Richard Malinder's reaction to what he had seen, Elizabeth returned the smile as she pinned the girl with her night-dark eyes in which there was no humour. 'Why should you ask forgiveness? You spoke nothing but the truth, as all here must recognise. Perhaps I will tell you what my lord has to say, Mistress Anne, when he has made his thoughts known to me. And *if* I consider his words to be any of *your* concern, of course. And now—' she turned her back on the girl '—I would welcome that hot water!'

Elizabeth realised that she had stoked the enmity further, but sank into the warm water in delicious relief. So much for a comfortable homecoming as Richard Malinder's betrothed. Elizabeth sighed. She would think about it all tomorrow.

For now, the battle lines had been drawn.

As she tumbled into sleep, one impression remained with Elizabeth. The sleek dark hair, the bold grey eyes, the austere features of Richard Malinder. How much had he seen of her in that brief appraisal? It had been cursory enough, and she had been in the shadows, but was it enough to cause him to regret his decision to take her? She had been able to read nothing on his face, but could well imagine. Dismay at best, but perhaps revulsion, outrage. And what *would* he say when he saw her uncovered and fully revealed in his marriage bed? Their marriage would have, of necessity, to be consummated. He was hardly marrying her for the sharpness of her wit or for her unusual education, was he? What if he touched her only out of necessity, because he had no choice, or even worse out of pity for her deficiencies? The thought appalled her.

* * *

Retreating rapidly from so intimate a female preserve, to stand silently for some minutes outside the door, Richard was forced to consider the impression that had been made on him with the sharp bite of a lance against unprotected flesh. In retrospect he should not have gone there, and had known better than to linger when all had become clear. What was it he had seen in that brief instant, what had taken his eye to the exclusion of all else? A bride with marks of a whip on her shoulders—oh, yes, he was sure of it, as the weals had caught the light, although the intensity of the punishment was overlaid by the poor quality of light. A bride with eyes wide in fear and shock. Had the whip been used to force her into marriage with him? The thought that it had made it necessary for him to breathe deeply. Elizabeth de Lacy certainly gave the impression that the last thing she wanted was to spend a night in *his* arms, as if the act of love would be nothing more for her than an assault, the touch of his flesh against hers simply a matter of loathsome tolerance. Richard prayed wordlessly to God that she would not flinch from him. He could not—really could not—tolerate his wife shrinking from him yet again.

Chapter Four

Ledenshall looked cold and rain-washed from the vantage point of Elizabeth's bedchamber, with a nasty little teasing wind, but she felt no inclination to remain in her bed.

'This is now my home,' she stated firmly to the empty room.

Weeks of rules and insistent bells had awakened her before first light. With the stir of the castle around her as the servants took up their duties for the day, and no urgent need to break her fast, Elizabeth was driven by a desire to explore. She pulled on the first gown to hand, hating the coarse material, but it was not as if she had a choice in the matter, even if the garment had curled Lady Anne's mischievously disdainful lips. She covered it with a heavy fur-lined cloak borrowed from one of the clothes presses. Considerably shorter than Elizabeth's own garments, barely reaching down to her ankles, yet it was fine and luxurious, better than anything she had ever possessed. Elizabeth pulled the collar close around her throat with a little shiver of pleasure at the touch of the soft fur, and would have left to begin her investigations until she remembered, with a little *moue* of distaste. Hurriedly she

pinned a plain linen veil into place to hide her shame from
the view of any interested eyes.

For the next hour she indulged her own whims with no
one to hinder or forbid. From the main family rooms in a
comparatively new wing, she descended into the Great Hall,
remnant of the original castle with its square keep. Here the
windows were still arrow-slits, the roof timbers high above
her head, the spaces vast and the draughts lethal enough to
swirl the smoke and shiver the tapestries that decorated the
walls.

On to the kitchens, where, with a brief smile and a word of
greeting, Elizabeth accepted the offered heel of a loaf, before
climbing the outer staircase to the battlements, to look out
over the bare hills and leafless trees, the muddy track leading
back to Llanwardine. Her spirits lifted. By the Virgin, she
would never return there! Then back down to the stables,
brushing crumbs from her fingers and the damask of the
cloak. The chapel. Pantries and storerooms, a rabbit-warren
of corridors and doors. Aware of the glances and whispered
comment from soldiers and servants who knew this inquisitive newcomer was to be their mistress.

Richard Malinder, another early riser, watched her inves-
tigate. He saw the flutter of movement, saw her emerge from
the Great Hall in a well-worn cloak which swirled some ten
inches from the ground as the tall figure strode across the
inner courtyard. Noted the energy, the light, confident step
as the lady explored his home. Her curiosity, her quick agility
as she ran up the staircase, striding around to inspect the view
on all four sides. And she talked to people as she passed. The
guards on duty. His steward, Master Kilpin, answered some
query with a nod and a wave of his arm. The servant girls from
the dairy. Anyone who crossed her path. It was as if the pale,
damply reserved creature of the previous day had been reborn,

a butterfly, if still a sombre one, so perhaps a moth—his lips twitched—emerging from a dull chrysalis.

He should speak with her. He had agreed to take her in matrimony, had he not? Lord Richard had to resist a sigh after that one vivid memory of her, naked and vulnerable, wary as a wild hare before the hunting dogs. No time for regrets now. He climbed the staircase to meet his betrothed where she leaned on the stone parapet to look to the distant Welsh hills.

Elizabeth turned quickly at the sound of his boots on stone. Solemn, her steady gaze watchful, careful, but unnervingly direct. Waiting, he realised, to gauge his mood.

'You took no harm from your journey, Lady.'

'No. I am quite recovered from the drenching. Thank you, my lord.'

She said no more but stood, motionless, cautious, as he advanced. He held out his hand in invitation. Elizabeth promptly placed hers there with no sign of reluctance. Richard's interest was caught. Perhaps she was not wary at all, simply circumspect, unwilling to give too much of herself away until she had taken his measure. Then she surprised him when she reversed their clasped hands, turning his uppermost to reveal the back of his own wrist. And touched the long red scratch gently with apologetic fingers.

'I'm sorry for this.'

His brows twitched in sardonic humour. 'I take it the animal isn't hidden beneath your cloak this morning.'

'No.' The corner of her mouth quirked in the faintest of responses. The deep blue of her eyes, reflecting the rich hue of the cloak, picked up a glint of gold from the weak rays of the sun.

'Do I call you Beth? Or Bess?' he asked. 'What do your family call you?'

'I am Elizabeth,' she replied gravely.

'Then Elizabeth it shall be.' It told him much of her

upbringing, that she had never been named informally with affection. 'Do you approve?' he asked.

'Of what?'

'Ledenshall.' He gestured to their surroundings. 'Your new home.'

'Of course.' The slightest hint of colour rose from the fur at her neckline, as if in guilt that she had been found out in some lack of courtesy. 'You didn't mind?' A quick contact of eyes, as if she feared a reprimand.

'Of course not. It's your home. You're free to enjoy it.' A contradiction here, he realised, between confidence and vulnerability. He thought about what he wanted to say to put her at her ease, which she clearly wasn't. 'I'm sorry you should have had to face this ordeal alone. Your uncle should have been here to welcome you.'

The heightened colour deepened. 'And I am sure we can deal well enough without him, my lord. Sir John is the last person I would expect to be here to make *me* comfortable.' She closed her lips firmly.

So the tale of the estrangement between uncle and niece was true. He found Elizabeth was now looking squarely at him, head tilted, whilst Richard awaited the outcome, senses on the alert. It was not often that young women appraised him in so serious a manner, without a smile on their lips or an invitation in their eyes. She was definitely taking his measure. Her words surprised him further.

'Let us be frank. We both know it, my lord. I am here as a replacement for my cousin Maude because Sir John wishes it,' she announced gruffly. 'And because for you the de Lacy connection would have its advantages in the March. There's no need for pretence between us. You did not want *me*, I know. But I presume that Sir John was most persuasive with my dowry—my mother's Vaughan lands, I expect. And, of course, you'll need a Malinder heir. I shall do all in my power to oblige.'

Well, here was plain speaking. But if her words took him aback, he hid it and answered in kind. 'That is all true. And I warrant that my offer to take you as Lady of Ledenshall would give you far more satisfaction than the narrow life of a nun in Llanwardine. There are advantages on both sides.'

The colour flared as if she had been struck, and he was sorry for his lack of finesse, but her reply was immediate. 'That is also true. I regret Maude's loss to you. She had the promise of such beauty and spirit.'

What could he say to that? His mind scrabbled for an answer, until it was made obvious that she had no expectation of empty flattering remarks.

'I have studied what I see in my mirror, my lord.' She turned from him to look out over the battlements. 'I shall try to be everything a wife should be. You need not fear for my loyalty, if that would be a concern. I would not wish it to be an issue between us.' Now he was definitely startled that she should pick up so contentious an issue, almost as if she could read his mind. Honesty indeed on such brief acquaintance, even if it proved to be painful. 'My family is Yorkist—you and I have been brought up as enemies from our cradles, and I shall always consider the claim of the Plantagenet House of York to be superior to that of poor mad King Henry. But I swear that my loyalty in marriage will be to you.'

Richard looked at his bride's stern face with a complex mix of astonishment and admiration and decided to be just as forthright. 'My own oath is given to that same King Henry, whatever the state of his wits, because he is the anointed King, whilst the Plantagenets have bloody treachery in mind.' He smiled a little as she stiffened at his accusation. 'I see we shall never agree on this divisive issue—but with such honesty between us, we shall do well enough together.'

'I expect we shall.' She risked a slanted glance 'We are both adult and see the value of honesty and loyalty between man and wife. I dislike pretence and disguise.'

'And I.' How strong she was beneath her pale fragility, how magnificently controlled in the circumstances. But she was not a comfortable presence. He felt it was a bit like negotiating an alliance with a potential enemy with the flags of war still raised on both sides.

'And the marriage ceremony?' Elizabeth asked bluntly.

'Soon. I see no reason to prolong the arrangements.' He leaned against the parapet to watch the play of emotion over her face. 'If that is to your liking, of course—I suppose I should never underestimate the amount of time needed by the females of a household.'

'I have no objection. I have no experience of such matters.' Her flat words were accompanied by a little lift of her shoulders as if she did not care.

Although his hackles rose, instinct quickly told Richard Malinder that it was a pretence. It mattered to her, though she would not admit it. He did not think she would admit anything to him—yet. He took possession of her hands again, turning them over, smoothing them with fingers callused from sword and reins. Hers were no better than his, he mused, no softer, and impossibly red and rough with swollen knuckles and chapped skin, nails chipped and broken. Not the hands of a lady of birth. His lips tightened as he came to understand her life at Llanwardine.

'You will not have to scrub floors here, lady.'

'Thank God.' She looked at her hands with a little frown of distaste. 'This was from digging for roots in frozen ground. And breaking the ice on the water to wash the bowls after meals.'

'Chilblains?' he enquired in some sympathy. He enfolded her fingers gently within his.

Elizabeth sighed. 'I fear so. And my toes. Jane Bringsty urges pennyroyal salve on me, but to no avail.'

'We must look after you here. I cannot have a Malinder bride suffering.'

He looked again at her hands, warmly enclosed within his. They might be damaged and painful, but her fingers were long and slender, the nails pale ovals. They could be beautiful, he suspected. And it reminded him that he must give her some symbol of their union. Not a ring yet, he decided. Not until she could wear it with pride and some satisfaction. But he knew exactly what he would give her.

Elizabeth made no attempt to pull away. When, in a noble gesture of chivalry towards his bride, Richard bent his head to kiss her work-scarred hands, he felt the slightest return of pressure as she tightened her fingers on his. The little gesture of trust tugged at his heart, surprising him, so that he felt compelled to turn her hand to press his lips to her palm. In contrast to her fingers the skin was enticingly soft so that he lingered, his lips warming, then looking up to find her eyes searching his face. He was transfixed by the beauty of their violet depths, a leaping connection that made him want to soothe and reassure her as he would a newly broken mare.

For a long moment they simply stared at each other.

The she pulled her hands free and the moment was broken.

'Let us go down. The wind has too much of an edge here.' He made to lead her down the steps, placing himself unobtrusively between the lady and the increasing gusts. 'Food, I think. And you need to be introduced to those of the household whom you have not already met.'

On level ground again within the courtyard, sheltered from the worst, he pulled her hand through his arm to walk back to the living quarters, in no manner dissatisfied with the turn of events. Outspoken to a fault she might be, she would never be easy to live with—too much obstinacy, too wilful, he had decided—but there was at least a measure of agreement between them.

Whilst Elizabeth de Lacy fought a difficult battle to repress the little spurt of hope that warmed her heart. *Take care!*

she warned herself. It would be too easy to allow this man to break down the barriers so effectively constructed over the years to protect her heart from further hurt. But Richard Malinder was kind. He had shown her a level of understanding that she had not expected, and his arm was strong beneath her hand.

'What is it?'

Glancing across at her as they reached the courtyard, he seemed to catch her line of thought, and smiled at her as he made his enquiry. But Elizabeth, after a little hesitation, merely shook her head and veiled her eyes with dark lashes. How could she tell this man who was concerned for her happiness and the state of her hands that he was so very beautiful? That his dark hair, ruffled to a tangle by the wind, and the stunning lines, the flat planes of his face, brought an uncomfortable flutter to her heart.

A sudden gust of wind blew her cloak, rippled her veil. She raised her hands to hold it secure, conscious of her unsatisfactory pinning of the folds. Aware of nothing but the sheer magnetism of this dark figure who stood so close and to whom she would soon be bound. Aware of nothing but the throb of her blood beneath his touch. The imprint of his mouth on her palm still burned like a brand. She closed her fingers tightly over it.

Before they parted company at the main door, their paths crossed that of Robert, who had unashamedly been watching their approach. Smiling, he bowed to the departing Elizabeth, then cast a wry look towards at his cousin.

'A pity that she…'

Robert lurched to a stop as he read the cool expression, most definitely a warning that dared him to say more. 'No matter. I was always tactless.' And then, irrepressible to the last, 'But she's not a cosy armful, and you can't argue that she is!'

Richard merely stared at his cousin, searching for a suitable reply, only to find himself thinking of Gwladys. Beautiful, desirable in face and figure, any man's dream to own and hold. He remembered as a young man falling hopelessly in love with her undeniable beauty, his physical response to her, his desire to kiss her and caress her into mindless delight. He recalled his pride in her as his wife and his hopes for that marriage. How his breath had caught, his loins stirred whenever he set eyes on her. Now Elizabeth… A complicated woman who roused in him—what? He wasn't sure.

'No, she's not a cosy armful. But at least Elizabeth is honest. I think she might be incapable of dissembling,' he replied, unaware of the snap in his voice until he saw Robert's reaction. 'Unlike Gwladys, who…' Richard shifted, impatient with himself, conscious of Robert's arched stare, his piqued interest at what had been a carelessly thoughtless comment on his part. He should not have made it. But at least he knew Robert would not ask.

And Richard found his thoughts leaping from beautiful Gwladys to Elizabeth de Lacy. It was not as uncomfortable a leap as he might have suspected. *She's not beautiful, but neither is she plain. She talks to people. She has beautiful eyes. She speaks openly without dissembling. Her touch is firm and responsive when I take her hand. She smoothed the wound on my hand as if my pain mattered to her. When I kissed her hand, she responded. What would it be like…?*

What would it be like to kiss her lips?

Richard cursed himself for a fool.

Elizabeth found a refuge in the solar where she could consider, and marvel at Richard Malinder's effect on her. Hardly had she sunk to her knees before a welcome fire than the door opened to admit Mistress Anne, a vision of delectable feminine fashion. A fur-edged side-less surcote fit snugly over a vibrant green cotehardie, falling in dramatic folds from the jewelled belt around her elegant hips, a fashion guaranteed to draw the eye to the girl's soft curves. The transparent veil did nothing to hide the glory of her plaited hair.

'Elizabeth. If you need anything for your marriage, Richard is to ride to Hereford tomorrow,' Anne announced in a glory of self-importance.

'Thank you. I will speak to him.' A little wary.

Anne seated herself comfortably beside the fire in a confiding manner, folded her hands. Smiled. 'He will make time to see Mistress Joanna there, I expect.'

The moment hung in silence, as the dust motes hung in the still air, glinting in the sun. Not at all innocent, but sharp edged and deadly. Recognising it for what it was, a malicious tease, Elizabeth titled her chin, waited.

'Did you not know? Well, of course, how should you!' Anne, brow smooth, eyes wide, was all concern and gentle compassion. 'But best that you should know what everyone at Ledenshall knows.'

'And what is that?' Elizabeth's breathing was shallow. 'Who is Joanna?'

'Richard's mistress, of course. Everyone knows Richard has a mistress in Hereford.'

Ah! 'And you thought, in your concern for my peace of mind, that you should inform me of Richard's liaison?'

'Why, yes. Do you think me insensitive? Forgive me, dear Elizabeth, I presumed you would wish to know. I meant no ill will. I would never deliberately hurt you.' Anne's smile was sorrowful, her eyes not so.

Elizabeth marvelled at her control. She titled her head in speculative interest, kept her gaze steady, her voice supremely composed. When she answered it was with the slightest lift of her shoulders. 'Richard's concerns are, of course, his own. Mine too, perhaps, when we are wed, but certainly, Mistress Anne, they are not yours.'

'Why, no. Of course not. Forgive me my ill judgement.'

But the damage was done. Anne Malinder did not stay.

Alone again, Elizabeth allowed the fury within her to settle from flame to ash. So Richard had a mistress in Hereford called Joanna. Of course she would wish to know of such a liaison, and of course Richard might have a mistress, but she would rather not hear it from Mistress Anne's viperous tongue. Elizabeth's fingers curled into admirable claws. How she had stopped herself from attacking the malicious little creature, verbally at least, she had no idea. Then her nails dug into her palms as she recalled how impossibly beautiful Anne Malinder was with the sunlight on her red-gold hair, gleaming in her emerald eyes.

Her thoughts turned to her betrothed with a sinking heart. She had thought him kind this morning in their meeting on the battlements. Yes, he was, but only because it did not matter to him. He did not need an intimate relationship with her beyond the purely physical to achieve an heir. How foolish to allow that little seed of hopeful anticipation to become implanted in her heart.

So Elizabeth raised her head, lifted her chin, drawing on pride as she had so many times before. She would make the best of this marriage and make use of Richard Malinder as he would make use of her, if that was the best she could do. She would administer Ledenshall Castle with all her considerable ability. She would dress well for the marriage as befitted a Malinder bride. She would challenge Mistress Anne's determination to hurt and wound. She would certainly show no weakness before her or respond to her barbed arrows. If battle lines had been drawn between them on the previous day, Elizabeth now silently declared war.

And it was in this mood that she found herself cornered by Jane Bringsty, who sought her mistress out with deliberate and heavy footsteps, intent on good advice and herbal potions.

'There's one thing that you should do before you spend many more nights under this roof, my lady.' Jane handed over a small pot of a slimy green substance with an unpleasant smell. She saw the frown immediately forming between Elizabeth's brows. 'Use it and don't fuss. It will bring nothing but ease.'

Without comment, because it was the simplest thing to do—and true—Elizabeth obediently began to smooth the salve of pennyroyal into her hands and fingers, her mind occupied with the bright memory of Richard Malinder's cool mouth against her damaged skin.

'What is it that I should do before I stay here longer?' She drew in her breath at the hot itch as her fingers grew warm.

'Get rid of that woman—of Mistress Anne Malinder.'

Elizabeth's eyes flew to her servant's face, to see there not the mild mischief as she had expected, but something deeper, more severe.

'I think we are in agreement, Jane,' Elizabeth replied carefully. 'I cannot like her. But she'll be gone back to Moccas as soon as the wedding ceremonies are over.'

'Tomorrow would not be soon enough. A little belladonna administered in her wine. Not enough to cause harm, but—'

Elizabeth's expression became stern. 'No, Jane. You will not. I don't fear her.'

'Well, you should. She's a danger.'

'Have you been scrying again?' Elizabeth's demanded, her fingers stilled.

'What if I have?' Jane bustled about the chamber, folding the borrowed cloak, then returned to fix her mistress with a stare. 'But I did not need to. Nor do you if you'll be honest with yourself. Mistress Anne is easy to read. I have your best interests in my thoughts and actions. She does not.'

'What did you see?' Curiosity got the better of Elizabeth, even as she silently reproved herself for encouraging such dabblings.

'Not much, but enough to know.' Satisfied, Jane took the pot of salve from her mistress and replaced the stopper. 'The dark man who would wish you ill is still there.' She clicked her tongue. 'Enough of him. Anne Malinder is red-gold and venomous, her green eyes glossed with sly envy and jealousy. She wants him. If you take my advice, a quick bout of sickness would persuade that lady to remove herself to her own home, far away from you and his lordship. I wager she'd not be interested in feasting and dancing with pains in her limbs and in her belly.'

It was an engaging picture. For a second Elizabeth enjoyed it. Then stared aghast at Jane's suggestion and her own momentary compliance. 'Hear me, Jane. I'll not have it.'

'You'll regret it!' Jane's lips closed with a snap.

'Do you suggest that Lord Richard would not have the power or inclination to withstand Anne Malinder?' A flame of disappointment began to flicker in Elizabeth's stomach.

'What man was ever so foolish as to resist so fine a figure and so blatant an invitation?' Jane Bringsty stood with hands fisted on broad hips, sure of her argument. 'Have sense, my lady. She dresses as if to attend a court function with a remarkable show of throat and bosom for so chilly a season.'

'Perhaps.' The image of Anne in a glory of patterned emerald velvet and fur crept unbidden into Elizabeth's mind. 'Her manner of dress is her own choice.'

'Powdered aconitum root would do the trick,' Jane continued, unconvinced. 'It would give her the shivers as if she has the ague. She'd soon wrap up warm within her cloak, enough to hide her undoubted attractions.'

Which made Elizabeth smile. 'I'll not have it, Jane,' she repeated, despite the appeal.

'Very well, my lady.' On which note of reproach, Mistress Bringsty exited with disapproval in her portly step, only lingering in the doorway to state once again, 'You'll regret it. Never say I didn't warn you.' The door swung shut behind her.

The cat stayed to curl on Elizabeth's lap in comfort. Yawned widely, but fixed her mistress with narrow eyes. Not unlike, Elizabeth realised, the sharp green gaze of Lady Anne.

'I know. We are surrounded by influences, generous and malign.' She smoothed her hand over the dense black fur of the cat's head and back, rousing an instant rumble of pleasure. 'I like him,' she whispered. 'Richard Malinder is dark as a crow's wing, without doubt, but he's not the one of Jane's predictions. I saw him in the scrying bowl at Llanwardine. I felt the bond with him even though I denied it.' Her fingers dug into the black fur, causing the cat to arch in protest. 'He is not my enemy. I can't ever believe that,' she murmured. 'But what does he think of me?'

Against all common sense, Elizabeth de Lacy allowed herself to dream.

Chapter Five

Throughout the days before her marriage, Elizabeth found herself fractious, and beleaguered.

The problem was, as Elizabeth freely admitted to herself, she was feeling lonely. Lewis had taken himself off to Talgarth to report her safe arrival to Sir John. David too had abandoned her to join Richard on his visit to Hereford. Even her betrothed had left her, and in the end with such a leave-taking as to shock her to her bones, giving her more than a hint of the Black Malinder beneath the surface charm.

His farewell, in full public gaze in the courtyard, had been formal, hurried and unsettling.

'God keep you, lady. I'll be back for the ceremony.'

A brief inclination of his head, an even briefer squeeze of her hand and he had gone to mount the bay stallion. Was that all he would say? Perhaps it was in the circumstances, surrounded as they were by men-at-arms and baggage wagons, or perhaps the anticipation of seeing his mistress again was strong. But Elizabeth, with narrowed eyes on his splendid shoulders as he gathered up his reins, was reluctant to give him the benefit of any doubt. He was brushing her off as if she was less than important to him. Her stare was less than friendly.

By chance Richard caught the condemnation. For a long moment he looked at her, then tossed the reins to his squire, handed over his gauntlets and strode back.

'That's no suitable leave-taking of a bridegroom to his sweet betrothed.'

Elizabeth coloured at the sardonic words. He must have read every thought in her head. But then he cupped her face in his hands, smoothing his thumbs over her cheekbones, and when she would have stepped back in quick retreat with a murmur of self-consciousness, he took her mouth with his, despite their audience.

Heat and power. A lingering and most thorough possession. Elizabeth could think of nothing at all as the breath left her body, until he lifted his head and, still unsmiling, raised his brows in wry enquiry. Nor could she find a word to say. Was this a wooing? More like a binding to his will. There was a ruthlessness in him, as instantly proved when he took her wrist and pulled her with him towards his mount.

From the saddle he leaned down. 'Smile at me, Elizabeth.'

She kept her face stern, chin tilted.

His own smile was edged. 'Perhaps you will smile when I return.' And then he was gone, leaving her standing alone in the courtyard.

So she felt bereft. And Elizabeth watched for his return, although would have admitted it to no one. Her ears were tuned to the sound of approaching hoofbeats, of raised voices in the courtyard, of warnings from the guards on the gate-house battlements and the raising of the portcullis, her hopes to be dashed again and again when the new arrivals proved to be only more wedding guests.

How could he matter so much to her? She had barely known him for longer than twenty-four hours in her whole life. She sighed as she surveyed the empty road, her fingers clenched against the stone coping. Perhaps he would arrive barely in time to exchange vows at the church door. It could hardly matter to him since this marriage was based on nothing but political necessity. It should not matter to her. She felt her temper rise. It would probably not matter to him even if he were wed in his campaigning gear, travel-soiled, sweat-stained and dusty from a week's riding along the March. Why she should be concerned with her own appearance, she had no idea. Richard Malinder would only care that the alliance be made.

The days passed, the hour of the marriage drawing closer. What was he doing to be away so long? It came into her mind that Anne Malinder had known the truth. That Richard's visit to Hereford involved a long-standing relationship with a woman called Joanna. It was like a cold hand closing its fingers around her heart. Elizabeth hid her anxieties behind an impassively solemn exterior, perfected with long practice. But her temper and her patience shortened by the day.

Meanwhile she was beleaguered by well-meaning attempts to improve her appearance and Anne Malinder's less than subtle hints at her deficiencies.

'I feel like a goose being fattened for a Twelfth Night feast,' Elizabeth grumbled as another platter of little venison pasties, crisp and golden, appeared at her right hand as she sat and set the stitches in her wedding gown. Yet Elizabeth, grateful for the concern, duly tried to eat. She must do so if she did not want Richard Malinder to look aghast at the lack of covering on her bones. If he was able to count her ribs, surely he must turn from her in disgust. Doubtless Joanne was an enticing owner of sensual curves to lure Richard to her bed. So she ate.

She found herself under siege as she rubbed Jane's salves and potions into her hands, as well as drinking, under protest, a bitter decoction of white willow bark to clear and brighten her skin. But it was entirely possible, she decided finally, with a little spurt of pleasure, that the bridal ring would slide easily past her knuckle rather than stick fast.

But it would take a miracle to improve the disaster of her hair. In her worst moments of depression Elizabeth remembered it as it had been. Long and thick and straight. Black with the shining iridescence of a magpie's feathers. As black as Richard's. She imagined, unable to resist a smile, his being able to run his fingers through the length of it, before she shook herself back to reality. It still hugged her head in an unlovely manner, a short fur covering. She washed it in the heady liquid of dried lavender flowers steeped in wine that Mistress Bringsty swore by as a tried-and-trusted remedy, but her hair's growth would be a matter of time that she did not have before her wedding day. It would, she thought, be a matter of devising suitable veiling to cover the worst of the damage. She could not—would not—be wed in a nun-like veil and wimple.

The bridal gown was duly measured, cut and snipped and sewn, the luxurious velvet a deep red, the colour of the best Bordeaux wine, guaranteed to flatter and draw colour into her pale cheeks, a gown to disguise distressingly sharp collar bones and an unfortunately flat chest. And what a miracle, Elizabeth considered cynically, that Richard Malinder should have been thoughtful enough to provide it for her.

'What a lovely gown this will be,' Anne Malinder announced. 'And what a shame you do not have the bosom to carry so fashionable a bodice. I could do so, of course. My own gown for this occasion is fashioned on one of Queen Margaret's herself. Now *her* figure is magnificently proportioned.' Anne allowed her gaze to rest knowingly on Elizabeth, before continuing. 'I believe it is customary to use the bride's hair in sewing the wedding gown, for good fortune,' she informed her as she set her stitches with exemplary skill, the needle no sharper than her tongue, her eyes on her stitches, a smile on her lips. 'I doubt that will be possible, dear Elizabeth. We could, of course, sew in one of mine. It would be perfect.'

Elizabeth might curb her instincts, watch her words through necessity, but Mistress Bringsty sprang to her defence. 'We've no need of such ruses, which smack of nothing less than witchcraft, Mistress Anne. I can think of better charms from nature's own goodness to bless this union.'

So into the hem was sewn leaves of periwinkle and a handful of the flat translucent honesty seeds, to promote a lucky and happy marriage. Elizabeth eyed them ruefully. She feared she would need far more than a handful of seeds to bless this marriage. Particularly if, even now as she waited for his return, her bridegroom was enjoying a heated liaison with Mistress Joanna.

Richard's business in Hereford took longer to complete than he had expected as he had a particular commission of his own, so unavoidably he returned to Ledenshall less than twenty-four hours before the ceremony, which, if he had thought about it, should have warned him of possible consequences. He found Ledenshall in festive and lively uproar, every available space housing some degree of relative or family dependant. He also discovered a bride waiting for him in the courtyard, a bride who had little time for him, spine strikingly rigid, face set, hardly willing to grant him, or her brother David, more than a few words in passing. Certainly not a smile as might be expected between a lady and her betrothed. Much as on his departure, he received nothing but a flat stare.

'Welcome home.' Her tone said it all.

Richard dismounted. 'Elizabeth. We were delayed.'

'I am aware.'

'You are well?'

'Yes. As you see.'

He frowned, displeased with her short reply, her brusque manner. So he would push the issue of their relationship a little more. Stern-faced, his eyes never leaving hers, he held out his hand, palm up in a tacit demand that she respond to him. Instead, his gentle bride thrust her hands behind her back.

Richard held firm, conscious of every eye on the pair of them. Pride stiffened his jaw. He would not be defied in this manner in his own castle by a girl who was not yet his wife. He waited. Until Elizabeth flushed, and, with obvious reluctance, touched her hand briefly to his. With instinctive reactions, he pounced, closed his hand on her sleeve when she would have pulled away. Then raised her hand to his mouth and kissed her fingers with slow deliberation.

'Elizabeth. I have not abandoned you, as you see.'

'No, my lord.' But the tension from her fingers did not ease.

Is that what she had feared? That his absence meant rejection? Surely not. He could hardly refuse to wed her now that she was ensconced in his home as his accepted bride. He swung round at a request from Master Kilpin, to give orders for the disposition of the pack animals and their burden. To discover when he turned back again that the only view he had was of the lady's retreating figure, shoulders still formidably straight as she marched towards the door.

'Well…' He pushed a hand through his disordered hair, admitting to a brush of anger, until he caught David's grin and raised brows. 'What did I say?'

'Nothing.' David chuckled. 'And not for some days. That's the problem.'

'So what should I have done?'

'Got back here before the eleventh hour. Elizabeth has a temper.'

'As I know.' He cuffed the lad gently on the shoulder. 'Should I fear her retaliation, do you suppose?'

At which David guffawed inelegantly. '*I* am not afraid of Elizabeth.'

Richard's lips twitched at the implication. What had he expected from his betrothed? Well, more than he had received. She had scowled at him when he left and scowled when he returned. His tardiness was not entirely his fault, but Elizabeth de Lacy had not bothered to discover the reason before putting him in the wrong. His temper began to simmer again, and Richard Malinder was aware of a level of disappointment that the understanding they seemed to have achieved in their battlement discussion had vanished in his absence.

Since it was not in his nature to leave it like this between them, Richard followed her into his home, catching up with her in the Great Hall. 'Madam!' His commanding voice, brooking no refusal, stopped her as she placed her foot on the first stair. Elizabeth turned.

'My lord.'

With long strides he caught up with her. 'When I return to my home, I expect to find a gracious and welcoming wife waiting for me, not a sharp-voiced shrew. I will not have my people entertained and intrigued by your lack of propriety and good breeding. My lateness was not of my doing, nor should you as my wife question it.' He found his irritation in full flow and did not consider the force or direction of his words. 'I had hoped the tales in the March of your wilfulness and lack of courtesy were mere gossip and exaggeration.'

He saw her hands clench, her lips whiten with pressure, her face grow pale, and watched curiously as she took a breath under the onslaught of his words. Her eyes, suddenly dark with unknown anxieties, held his and he could not fault her courage. Unnerved by the grief, even pain in her face, still he was driven to make his point or what respect would there be in this marriage? 'There is no excuse for rank bad manners in my household, lady.'

Her eyes fell. 'No, my lord. There is no excuse.'

'I expect you to receive me and my guests graciously.'

'Yes, my lord. Forgive me. I was at fault.'

'Then we have an understanding.'

'Yes, my lord. I will not be guilty of…of graceless ill manners again.'

He waited to see if she would say more, surprised by her acquiescence. When she merely stood, head bent, because he could think of nothing more to say and was now perhaps regretting his choice of words, Richard left her.

Through her lashes Elizabeth watched him go. She had been entirely at fault, but how could she tell him of her fears that made her lash out? Of seeing herself in comparison with the achingly beautiful Anne Malinder, who undoubtedly schemed to become the equally lovely Gwladys's successor. Of fearing his attachment to the lover in Hereford. Embarrassment, slick and cold, coated her from head to toe. She had undoubtedly been in the wrong—what was it he had said? A sharp-voiced shrew?—and she had no idea how to make amends. Despair washed through her. Still she forced herself to walk up the stair with magnificent dignity.

To meet Anne Malinder, watching, waiting, at the top, her perfect teeth glinting in a smile of sheer delight.

'I see dear Richard is returned. Have you fallen out with him already?'

'No. We understand each other perfectly.'

The girl leaned close. 'He'll go back to Mistress Joanna soon enough if you quarrel with him.' A trill of laughter. 'His mood is not sweet for a bridegroom. I will go and talk to him for you. I could always wind Richard round my fingers, even as a child. Now I am a child no longer. Don't worry, Elizabeth. I will see to his needs.'

'I am sure you will!'

It was the final straw. Elizabeth brushed past her nemesis and shut herself in her bedchamber, regretting the mistakes she had made, unable to see any way forwards.

Whilst Richard, back in the courtyard, wallowing in the lost sadness in a pair of deep blue eyes, was finding it difficult not to regret his intemperate words. His impatience flared when Mistress Bringsty placed her stout figure in his path.

'I need to speak with you, my lord.'

'I don't have time for this.' He would have stepped past her, but she surprised him with a hand to his sleeve. His glance sharpened. 'Well?'

'Spare her the public bedding, my lord.'

And before he could ask more, the woman had bustled away. But of course he did not need to ask. He had not needed her warning. Or perhaps he had, because in the deluge of demands on his time he had not thought of the repercussion for Elizabeth of the traditional, very public disrobing of bride and groom, had accepted that it was part of the drink-fuelled celebration as much as the vows and the priest's pious words. The memory of silvery weals of the lash on her shoulders jolted him back to what he must do. Whatever the residual annoyance from their recent encounter, he could not inflict an array of prurient and inquisitive eyes on her.

He was sorry to have spoken to Elizabeth as he had. There were depths—uncomfortable ones—to his bride that he had not even come close to discovering.

The door to Nicholas Capel's circular chamber at Talgarth was shut and bolted. There must be no prying eyes to this ceremony. The marriage was imminent; now was the time to take action. All it took was the wax from two stalwart candles, judiciously softened, to fashion two figures. He smoothed, formed, crimped and carved, until two figures lay on the table, male and female. Crudely manipulated yet easily recognisable, naked and sexually explicit.

So the marriage was assured, but it would do no harm to give fate a twist. Capel smote his hands together in a sharp gesture of authority.

'Let us draw the pair together, with or without their will.

Let us ensure the power of Malinder's loins to get an heir on the woman.'

Capel poured water from an ewer into a silver bowl marked with Christian symbols. He murmured Latin words over the water, consecrating it, and then sprinkled the holy liquid to name the two figures.

'I name thee both: Richard Malinder. Elizabeth de Lacy.'

From a fold of parchment he shook the contents. Two dark hairs from the head of Richard Malinder. Two longer, equally dark, Elizabeth's hair from before her departure to Llanwardine. Then, winding the hair around their crude necks, Capel placed the figures face to face, breast to breast, thigh to thigh, and with strong wire he bound them close until they were tight knit.

'May your union be effective and fruitful,' Capel murmured with a vicious satisfaction. And smiled gloatingly.

How trusting John de Lacy was in his innocence, believing that the authority was fast in his own fist. How willing he was to follow advice when power was dangled before him, a juicy plum to fall from the tree into his waiting hand.

Except, Capel rubbed his hands together, de Lacy would not be the one to catch the falling fruit.

Richard offered his hand to his bride. Elizabeth placed hers there, lightly. He gave a little nod, either of acceptance or encouragement, his fingers closing warm and firm before they turned together for him to lead her up the final steps to the waiting priest. And there was something that needed to be said.

'Forgive me my harsh words of yesterday.'

'I do.' Her gaze was solemn. 'I ask pardon for my lack of grace.'

'I give it freely.'

In her new finery Elizabeth felt strong and confident. Even

the weak sun had decided to bless her and to gild her appearance. Its fragile heat comforted her, encouraging her tense muscles to relax. Soon she would be Elizabeth de Lacy no more. She kept her head raised, her chin lifted, secure in her rank and position as Lady of Ledenshall. Why should she not be happy?

She had been quite wrong after all. Richard Malinder had no intention of wedding her in campaigning garments and the dust of four days or more of hard travel. Her heart stuttered, just once, before resuming its steady beat. At her side he looked magnificent. His dark hair had gleamed as he inclined his head to welcome her. Clad in deep green-and-black brocade, patterned in fluid swirls, his knee-length tunic trimmed with an opulent edging of dark fur, his status as a Marcher lord was proclaimed for all to see in the jewelled and gilded belt to secure his sword at his side. There was a glint of costly rings on his fingers. A heavy gold and gem-studded chain of wealth and power rested on his shoulders. Richard Malinder, Elizabeth suspected, could play the role of courtier equally as well as that of soldier and lord of a Marcher fortress.

What woman would not wish to marry this man? Elizabeth raised her eyes to his, soothed by what she read there. For she saw an understanding of what would be an ordeal for her through a long day, but also a gleam of admiration in the clear grey depths. Admiration, it seemed, for her. And it brought a wave of delicately flattering colour to her cheeks.

Richard was aware of nothing but the cool hand in his, and the subtle differences in his bride from the uneasy creature who had exchanged edgy opinions with him on the battlements little more than a week ago. She had been busy in his absence. Tall and undoubtedly elegant, the rich velvet flowing around and behind her, the fluid lines were all grace and softness, completely destroying his memory of a brittle bride without charm or allure. The long, tight sleeves ended in furred cuffs, over which flowed open sleeves, so cut that they flowed down to her hem in sumptuous pleatings. The sun shimmered on the rippling folds of a butterfly veil, arranged to fall to her shoulders over thin wires.

A cosy armful? No, but by God she was not the sodden creature whose cat had left a lasting memento of its dislike. Unobserved, he flexed his hand. Perhaps his bride too could be seduced into retracting her claws.

As they took their place before the priest, everything for Elizabeth settled into clear and vivid focus, not least the fact that a dark cloud settled over all before the vows were fully made so that everyone shivered and pulled cloaks tight. It was not an omen, she insisted. In a clear voice, Richard announced the extent of the dowry that his bride had brought with her. Startled at the extent, she tightened her fingers in his. Of course, it would have been necessary for Richard Malinder to be bought. But so much? It was a high price for John de Lacy to hand over, this important swathe of land through the centre of the March. She hoped Richard would find the bargain worth it.

After which it all happened so fast, Elizabeth de Lacy becoming a Malinder bride rather than a Bride of Christ before she could even catch her breath. Lips touched in a cool and symbolic kiss. And the gold ring, deeply engraved, slid smoothly—very smoothly—over her knuckle and on to her finger.

They feasted in the Great Hall.

Elizabeth shared the bridal cup and the plate with her lord to enthusiastic cheers as their guests began to empty their own cups of ale and wine, liberally supplied, frequently filled. In a futile attempt to turn her mind from the hours to come, she sought out her family in the mass of guests.

There was Sir John, dark and saturnine with just a hint of arrogance and condescension. Beside him his wife of a second marriage, Lady Ellen, quiet and introspective. She could see Lewis, a little farther away, festively garbed but looking particularly solemn tonight, neither content nor at ease, which for him was unusual. And David, high spirited, enjoying the spectacle with bright eyes. At that moment she caught the direction of Sir John's eyes as they focused sharply on Richard. Appraising, calculating, his lips pressed close, something there she could not quite decipher, but knowing it was not pleasant. Beside him sat Master Capel. Now that was a surprise, that he should have accompanied her uncle to the marriage feast. The man leaned to murmur in Sir John's ear, causing Sir John to smile. Elizabeth lifted her shoulders against the softness of the velvet. Sir John always had some scheme in his mind.

The banquet was coming to an end. A fluttering of anticipation and of distress blossomed in her belly, moths' wings, as she remembered all too clearly Anne Malinder's spiteful words, intended to hurt.

What will Richard say when he sees you?

Anne had laughed, pretending dismay at her remarks. Elizabeth felt nausea rise in her throat at the thought of the public bedding. How much of her scars had he already seen? Enough to repulse him? She did not even have the luxury of retreating behind a silken fall of hair when the revellers invaded the bedchamber. When her chemise and veil were removed. What, indeed, would Richard say? What cruel, humiliating comments would the guests exchange over their ale?

'What is it?' Richard's voice was low, between them alone.

Apparently he had been watching her. When she turned her head she saw an awareness in his eyes, and was moved that he should be concerned for her. 'Nothing, my lord. Other than being watched for every move I make, by your family and mine.'

'Does it matter? You are Lady of Ledenshall and may do as you please.' Then as she frowned down into her silver goblet,

'Look at me.' He smiled as she did so, his austere features softening, sending a little flush of heat across her skin, dispelling the suspicion from her dark eyes. 'Let us then give our interested guests something to nudge and speculate over.'

Elizabeth found herself smiling in return. 'What do you suggest?'

Before she was aware, he leaned smoothly, bent his head and kissed her full on her mouth. Not the cool brief symbol of the marriage ceremony, but something far warmer, full of promise. Her lips remained parted as he retreated. Heat pooled in her belly and bright colour surged into her face.

'That will make them talk,' she managed.

'So it will!' And, to her astonishment and delight, Richard kissed her again.

With the memory of his wife's mouth warm on his, Richard deliberately found the opportunity to circulate amongst the guests. All his senses were on the alert despite the numerous toasts. It was clear to him that Elizabeth was not the only de Lacy to be showing signs of tension.

'Lewis.' He hooked an empty stool next to the young man and sat.

'My lord…'

'Richard!' He smiled. 'Your brother already makes free with my name.'

'My brother has no respect!' Lewis also managed a smile, if bleak.

'You're very sombre for such an occasion. Problems?'

There was a pause, brief as a heartbeat as Lewis obviously made a decision. 'No. Except that… I would say…' Richard found himself fixed by Lewis's troubled stare.

'You can tell me, you know. I can be very discreet—for a Lancastrian.' He tried to infuse some humour into the situation, to draw the poison from whatever ailed Elizabeth's brother, but failed.

'Nothing.' Lewis's face remained set in severe lines and he broke the eye contact. 'I have no excuse and shouldn't inflict my bad mood on my sister's celebration. I'm glad for you. And for Elizabeth.'

Which left Richard with no choice but to let his concern drop. But without doubt Lewis had something on his mind.

'I hope your marriage is blessed.' Ellen de Lacy's hands gripped Elizabeth's as she wished her well, far more fiercely than the occasion warranted. 'That you bear a son. As I have failed to do.'

'I am so sorry.' Elizabeth knew the yawning grief in Ellen's life and heart but it had never been spoken of so openly between them as now. A most private lady, and apparently dominated by her often insensitive husband, Ellen kept her thoughts to herself. 'And you must miss Maude.'

'I do. We all do. I loved her as if she were my own daughter. But Sir John hoped for a son of his own.'

'I am sure he does not blame you, Ellen.' Elizabeth found that she was not sure at all, but did not know what to say to comfort the grief in the lady's eyes. There was much tragedy here. Lady Ellen had carried two male children, but neither to full term. Both had been dead before they ever took a breath.

'It is not important.' The reply was cool, carefully controlled.

'Are you not happy?' Elizabeth risked.

Ellen squeezed her hand. 'There's no need for your concern, Elizabeth. Enjoy your bridal day.'

But Elizabeth knew that Ellen had not answered her final indelicate question, and thought she detected a bleak unhappiness before the lady turned away. It was all strangely unsettling.

Chapter Six

Elizabeth's gown was removed and folded away. The chemise she retained, and replaced the intricate veiling with a soft linen covering, secured by a simple filet. She would not take them off yet. Jane would have continued to fuss, but Elizabeth had had enough and finally ordered her out, then sat on the edge of her bed and waited, hands clasped. She had been offered much advice as a virgin, most of which she had heard before, most of which she thought she should ignore, and was given a cup of spiced wine to calm her nerves, but she put it aside without drinking. She would rather face Richard Malinder with her wits about her.

It did not take long. Richard and his rowdy escort climbed the stairs and approached along the corridor. It would have been impossible not to hear the shouts and laughter, the ribald jokes at his expense. She braced herself, pushed herself to her feet and retreated to stand with her back to the low fire, partly shadowed by the bed hanging. It was one thing to face the ordeal with de Lacy courage, it was quite another to invite attention and speculation. The door opened, the noise flooded in. Elizabeth tensed, swallowing against the knot of sheer panic in her throat, forcing herself to stand straight with eyes level.

Richard did not enter. He remained in the doorway, turned his back to her and blocked the door to those who would follow. 'You go no farther this night, my friends.' His voice was low, full of humour, but not to be ignored. It was also perfectly sober.

'Embarrassed, are you, Richard?'

'Experienced, I think. I've suffered this once before.' Richard stayed foursquare in the doorway, his hand on the latch, an effective bar. 'I received all the advice I needed on that occasion. From some of you here, as I remember. It did me no good the first time.'

'Perhaps not—but you've been putting it into practice ever since!' Laughter, loud and appreciative, filled the room.

'As you say. So I don't need you tonight. Goodnight, gentlemen. Ale is still to be had in the Great Hall—you can drink my health and that of my bride until you no longer have the strength to raise your arms.' And Richard closed the door in their faces, leaned back against it as the shouts and hoots of the revellers faded.

'Thank God. You forget how noisy feasts are. I'll be deaf for a se'enight.'

Elizabeth could not believe her good fortune. Had he done that for her? His consideration took her aback, and his perfectly commonplace comment went a little way to soothing her fears.

'That was masterly. And very kind.'

'That was self-preservation.'

When Richard began to unbuckle his sword belt, Elizabeth found herself automatically approaching to take the sword from him, and the gold chain, which she placed on top of a coffer. If he noted her return of confidence when given something to occupy her mind and fingers, he made no comment, but handed her the gold-and-ruby brooch that had secured

the neck of his tunic. She laid it aside and then helped him
unlace and removed the furred garment, folding it away as
he slid off the heavy rings. When he stood in shirt and hose,
she waited. His gaze was speculative. A shiver traced its path
down her spine.

Then he grinned. 'Now…somewhere…' He looked round
the room, before walking to the corner beside the door. 'I had
this brought up earlier.' He lifted a large wrapped package.
'I had to return to Hereford for this—almost missed my own
marriage for its sake.' He slanted a wry smile at her. 'I hope
you like it, lady—and will not take me to task again.'

Elizabeth had the grace to blush and catch her bottom lip
in her teeth, remembering her brusque acknowledgement
of his return, all based on her fears that he had spent the
intervening days in the arms and luscious curves of Mistress
Joanna. Recalling the confrontation between them when she
had greeted him so gracelessly, she felt a shiver of anticipation, like a fingernail tracing down the length of her spine.
He had won that encounter, had he not? And she had had
a foretaste of his formidable will. He was not a man to be
challenged without due cause, and yet he had brought her a
gift.

'What is it?' She took the parcel from him.

'You'll not know unless you open it.'

Elizabeth repressed another shiver, this time of delight at
any present, and that he should have thought about her. She
ripped the ties from the coarse linen covering so that out, on
to the bed, tumbled a cloak. A little sound of pleasure escaped
from her throat as she lifted it. Blue velvet, dark as night, fine
as any garment made for the royal court, lined with the finest
sables, a deep hood to protect from the coldest weather.

'You need it.' He sat on the edge of the bed with a little
smile as she crooned over the gift, stroking her hands over the
luxurious weight of it, marvelling at its softness and quality,
before swinging it around her shoulders. It draped in sump-

tuous folds to her feet, swirling with a glamorous life of its own as she strode the width of the chamber and back.

'Definitely Penthesilea,' he remarked as Elizabeth swept once more across the room.

'Hmm?' She halted, to look back over her shoulder.

'Queen of the Amazons, if I remember my education.'

'So she was,' Elizabeth replied, casually revealing her own knowledge of classical texts and the Siege of Troy. 'But she died in battle. And fought bare breasted.'

'So she did,' Richard replied calmly.

Elizabeth continued her perambulations, to come finally to a stop before him. 'It is…beautiful.' She raised her eyes, luminous with pleasure. Then lifted the fur to her cheek. 'I suppose I have to forgive you your late return.'

'Indeed you do. And also—I have this. You'll need this too.' He held out a small package, the size of his palm, wrapped in leather.

'Another present?' Her eyes narrowed in confusion. 'Have you done something other that I should know of and be willing to forgive you for?'

At which he laughed, a robust sound that filled the chamber and tinted her cheeks with colour. 'No, I swear it. But, yes, another present. You are my wife and it is my pleasure to give you them.'

It was a brooch to fasten the cloak. But not like any brooch she had ever seen with its entwined circles of gilding. A medley of miniature lions and red boars with tusks and tongues of gold leapt and snarled in her hand, the gold-and-red enamel gleaming in the candlelight as she moved her palm. Vividly alive and colourful, the little animals made her smile.

'How did you know?'

'I have my sources.'

'It was my mother's emblazon. Matilda Vaughan of Tretower.'

'I know.'

'You had it made for me.' Astonished pleasure swamped her.

'I commissioned it from a metalworker in Hereford. And I think it most appropriate for you. For so a fierce lady.'

'Am I so?' Her glance flew to his face, certain that he must be laughing at her expense, but he was not.

He chose not to reply, but stretched to pour her wine. 'Sit with me.' Elizabeth held the cloak to her, unwilling to be parted from its sensuous folds for a moment, and placed it on the bed as she sat. He poured wine for himself before regarding her seriously. 'I suggest, my wife, that we make our own vows. To loyalty and honesty. To allow no one to come between us. No matter who. No matter what.'

Elizabeth nodded, absorbing his words. 'I will do that.'

'Then let us drink to our future together.'

They raised their cups and drank the spiced hippocras, until, with a dramatic shudder, Richard set the wine aside. 'Too heavy on the spices for my taste. Now I must indeed take you to bed or risk comment on my virility.'

He stood in one easy movement and pulled back the linen from the bed. Then froze, the linen still grasped in his fist.

'What is it?' Elizabeth took a deep breath. She thought she knew.

'Come and look.' The coarse cream linen was covered with a deluge of dried leaves, discoloured flower petals and twiggy pieces of flower stalk. 'What are they?'

Elizabeth raised her hands to her mouth, unsure whether to laugh or curse her serving woman. Jane was leaving nothing to chance. 'I won't tell.' The words were muffled.

Richard's eyes gleamed. 'Is it my virility or your fertility to be enhanced here?'

Elizabeth sighed. He was not angry after all. 'Both, I imagine.' She poked at the pot pourri, recognising Jane's favoured means of aiding conception in mistletoe and hazel leaves, lavender to arouse sexual desire. Even, she thought, some ground acorn, and a preponderance of dried yarrow flowers and rose petals to ensure a long and happy union. 'It's Jane Bringsty's doing. I should tell you that she means well.'

'Does she? I see no sign of well meaning in the woman. As for this… But no harm done.' He swept the debris from the bed to the floor with firm gestures. 'More like to produce a rash from the sharp edges than a heightening of physical powers. Perhaps I shouldn't ask what was in the hippocras.' All Elizabeth could do was watch him with some degree of awe until Richard straightened and turned to face his wife. 'Come then, lady. Let us try the sheets.' He drew her towards him, his hands softly around her wrists. 'Permit me to unveil you.'

And did so.

And looked. Elizabeth would have closed her eyes, but forced herself to acknowledge his reaction to her. Despair held her motionless. Richard made no comment, his face impassive. He unfastened the neck of her chemise and pushed it to fall to the floor, leaving her to stand defenceless before him, whilst Elizabeth again denied the urge to close her eyes against any pity she might see, or distaste. She would invite neither, but face him. She swallowed and waited, nor would she look away from him as his eyes moved slowly, tracking down her body and back to her face. He hissed in a breath through his teeth, as if helpless to prevent it.

'Turn around, Elizabeth.'

She did, now closing her eyes against a threat of tears when he could not see. Heard him inhale firmly through his nose.

'Look at me.' He waited until she had gone full circle and faced him again before speaking. His voice was low, firm. She could detect neither pity nor revulsion there, for which she was grateful beyond her imaginings. 'Ah—Elizabeth. I did not realise.'

'What did you not realise?' She ran her tongue over her dry lips.

'That is was so… That it was so bad.'

Elizabeth once more found the need to blink away tears, but would not allow them to fall. 'I thought you saw me. That you knew the worst. That first night…'

'Only a glimpse in the shadows. I thought there were marks of a whip. But I had no idea of this… Llanwardine?' He looked at the short silk of her hair. Lifted a hand as if he would have touched it—but let it fall.

'Yes.'

'And this?' His gaze lowered to the silvery scars marking her ribs.

She shivered at the calm inspection, his eyes flat, face determinedly impassive, and thought for a moment, before deciding on the truth in the face of his calm acceptance. 'In some part.' And she thought by the mere tightening of his lips that he understood the lack of explanation.

'I would hope that it was not to persuade you to marry me.'

'No. Owain Thomas was the one I could not stomach. But—more recently—I was not a conformable novice.'

'Neither did you eat, I think.'

She knew that he saw the press of her collarbone against her skin, her slight breasts, narrow hips. Tried to make light of it. 'Your cook has a campaign to fatten me.' And was unable to prevent a shiver, still standing unclothed with the cool air spiking her skin, Richard frowning at her.

His response was immediate. 'Forgive me. That was thoughtless.'

It was the simplest matter for him to lift her new cloak and wrap it around her, soft and warm in the sable folds. It enabled Elizabeth to mask her relief. She would accept his compassion tonight. She might not want pity from this man, but it was far better than disgust. She could do nothing but admire his sensitivity and consideration. To her relief she found her composure restored, the trembling in her limbs eased.

Until Richard raised his hand, impelled by some basic impulse, to smooth it over her cap of hair. Without thought, she flinched, eyes wide.

And he immediately drew back his hand as if singed in a flame. 'Don't flinch from me. I would not hurt you. How could you think that?' His tone was harsh and his eyes flashed with naked emotions that were beyond her interpreting. For a moment Elizabeth thought she saw anger there. Or perhaps it was even despair, although why it should be she did not know. It forced her into an apology.

'I did not mean to. It is just that… It surprised me. I dreamed of you doing that. I liked it. In my dream my hair was as it used to be, long and thick—not like this. I am ashamed of this,' she explained.

Richard visibly relaxed with a long exhalation as if in relief. What had he thought she meant? Elizabeth did not know, but something had disturbed him. Something she had said or done. But whatever it was, the moment seemed to have passed. The hard lines bracketing his mouth had smoothed out.

'There's no need for shame. The blame is not yours. It's lovely, Elizabeth, the softest of sable pelts.' Richard leaned forwards to press his lips to her temple. 'Soon your hair will be long again and very beautiful. And when it is,' he continued, 'I will touch you again as in your dreams.'

Elizabeth smiled, an incredible flicker of anticipation for the future in her heart. He had forgiven her sharp tongue. There again was the depth of sheer kindness, of understanding she could never have hoped for.

'Will you put out the candle?' she asked. And he did.

The darkness would prove a soft benediction for them both.

For Elizabeth it cloaked her in blessed anonymity when he

touched her again with shocking intimacy. Anything to hide her scant knowledge, her lack of confidence in her ability to please, her sharp anxieties. Too self-conscious, too aware of her lack of attractions, it soothed her immediate tremors. In the dark it did not matter. If there was a disgust or a mere distant tolerance on his face she would not see it. She must only endure.

But then, *endurance* was not the word that forced its way into Elizabeth's mind. Rather, startled pleasure. She found her fears melting as she warmed under the firm stroke of his hands and the delicate play of his lips across her face. His smooth strength against her side, firm muscled, sliding flesh against flesh, astonished her, as did the cautious delight that she could find in it. If he could touch her, so could she touch him, and found in herself a strong desire to do so. And so she let her fingers press over the lean hard planes of his chest and shoulders, an intimate journey of their own. So very attractive. So very masculine. How could she not enjoy the sensation of banked power and purpose, even as her thoughts scrambled at the confusion of sensations that shivered through her at where it would all lead.

For Richard the lack of light made it easier to encourage and seduce. The shadows were soft and hid any lack of skill or knowledge on her part that might disturb an inexperienced bride. Yet there was no clumsiness in her responses, as she came to him readily enough, rather a lightness, an elegance. Nor was she ignorant. When her first trepidation had loosed its hold she turned confidently, her lips warm on his. Her skin was soft, smooth beneath his fingertips, her movements graceful and feminine as she lifted her arms to lock them around his neck, to curl her fingers into his hair. When, surprising him, she stretched against him, pressing firmly at breast and hip and thigh, a deep sigh in her throat warm against him, it stirred his desire until he was hard for her.

But he held back. Talked to her to ease her fears, knowing

already that she was a woman who needed the conviction of her mind above the seductions of the flesh. So he talked as he stroked and discovered.

Soft, foolish thoughts, Elizabeth acknowledged in passing, but so very appealing. Whispered words against her lips, against her hair, against the pulse that quickened its beat beneath the satin skin of her throat. Ridiculously flattering, as she knew, but they gave her a gloss of pleasure. Such consideration here for her naïvety. But also, she realised, an imperative demand as his mouth heated, his kisses became deeper, his tongue sliding between her lips to possess. Her skin shivered, but she did not dislike it. She could feel the urgency in the quick tense of his muscles, the need in his heavy erection against her thigh. Now a thrill ran through her, unexpected, a knot of heat in her belly, that it could be so, that he should want her so readily. Her secret fears that he would need to overcome distaste to take her coldly out of necessity dissipated in a bright flame as his mouth captured her breast.

Despite everything, Elizabeth de Lacy was entranced.

Slowly, deliberately slowly as his tongue caressed and excited, Richard let his fingers drift down over her breast, her flat belly, lower still. Felt her skin ripple in tiny shivers. With a gasp she stiffened, then once more stretched against him, breath warm against his neck, and as it must her thigh brushed against his erection. He shuddered on a hissed intake of breath, his control suddenly balanced on a knife edge. It would be so easy to push the matter on. But he drew back a little with his weight on his forearms and breathed heavily.

Elizabeth immediately became rigid in his arms, a stone statue of a victim of the Medusa's stare. 'What is it? Did I do something wrong? I did not know…' The words were dragged from her, harsh in the still room.

Here was panic. So the fears were not too far away. He silenced her with his mouth, still gentle despite the overwhelming need to bury himself in her and take what was his.

'No. Nothing wrong. You are all pleasure, lady,' Richard gasped.

For a long moment she remained tense in his arms, as if considering his reply. 'You have a way with words, Richard Malinder.' Then relaxed against him, her lips opening beneath his, all soft and silken heat. Did she know how alluring she was? Probably not. The desire to push her past edgy thought to drive her to pure sensation became imperative.

'It will hurt?' she asked. But not a question.

'Yes.' Honesty, tempered by a brush of lips, a slide of hands. 'But not beyond bearing if I have the skill to make it so.'

'As I am sure you do.' Her dark eyes caught a momentary glint of the distant light from the dying fire. He knew she was watching him, alert to his every move, still wary, still thinking. 'Then I will trust you.'

Such simple confidence in his talents was his undoing. His fingers sought and discovered that she was not unready as her thighs opened for him. He moved over her, into her, a slick wetness. Pushed against her until he was held deep.

There was discomfort and pain, but momentary and, as he had promised, not beyond bearing. Elizabeth stilled, held her breath, aware of nothing but the weight of his possession and the outline of his shoulders back-lit by the glow of fire. He filled her mind, her body, her whole vision. When, in her cold room at Bishop's Pyon where her uncle had taken her to task, also in the fastness of Llanwardine when marriage to Richard Malinder had never been mooted, she had vowed that she would allow no man such power over her. She had been wrong. She had given herself over to this man's demands in a haze of shattering need, with a complete lack of restraint. Even when he drove on to his own fulfilment, leaving her teased by delicious sensations that flooded her but yet remained tantalisingly out of reach. Slick with heat, her limbs pleasurably lax, Elizabeth turned her face against Richard's throat in shock at this new self-awareness.

'It is done, lady.' Some time later, sense restored, heartbeats evening, Richard lifted himself from her.

And Elizabeth turned away. Was that all he could say? Would he leave her now? Would he not wish her to curl against this warmth and rest within his arms as was her inclination? Suddenly Elizabeth was horribly shy, yet forced herself to ask because she needed to know.

'Was I…' she swallowed '…what you hoped for?' she finished in an agonised rush. *Was I an unspeakable disaster compared with the incomparable Gwladys?* She stared into the darkness, waiting.

'Elizabeth Malinder.' There was no condemnation here, only lazy humour in the use of her new name. 'Have you so little courage? I did not think you a coward.'

Was he laughing at her? 'I am no coward! I did not dislike it!' Elizabeth clutched the linen covers to her neck in sudden defence.

'Thank God! An honest woman!' Richard stretched out to push aside her hasty covering, and draw one long smooth caress from shoulder to wrist, finally capturing her hand and raising her palm to his mouth as he had once before. 'It will improve, lady. Now come here.'

He pulled her close again, holding firm when she would have struggled for her freedom. It was no contest. Elizabeth found herself pinned against that toned body she had so admired. And Richard felt all the tension drain from her, felt her smile against his chest.

'What is it?'

She hid her face. 'It's true. I did not dislike it.'

'Faint praise!' He laughed gently, her hair soft as matt velvet against his cheek. 'I'll try to do better. Later, lady.' Perhaps not too much later. His loins stirred as she sighed in utmost satisfaction, and surprised him by turning her head to press her lips in the lightest of kisses all the way along his jaw.

Warmth, a foolish little surge of triumph, sang through every inch of Elizabeth's body, with an exhilarating sense of achievement that had nothing to do with her own finesse of which she acknowledged she had none—and all to do with his. More satisfying even than scrying. Jane Bringsty had never warned her of that. And she drifted into unconsciousness.

Richard found himself far from sleep. His attention was thoroughly caught and his mind would not let his new knowledge go. Life had not been easy for her, as Lewis had intimated, and his hatred of John de Lacy deepened. Dispassionately, he considered his impressions of her. Yes, she was slender—thin, he supposed—but not unattractive. Her skin was firm yet soft. Not at first glance a figure to suggest that child bearing would be a simple matter for her, but she would bloom with the life he could give her. His thoughts snapped back to the present as she sighed in sleep, her hand splayed against his chest.

So this was Elizabeth de Lacy. A complicated weave of inhibiting fears, fearsome honesty and driving emotions. He would wager his best stallion that her responses had not been influenced by duty or the careful teaching of her serving woman in the role of her mother. There was a fire here, or perhaps more apposite, a deep well of untapped passions. He could discover them. But then an uneasy premonition touched him as he rubbed his cheek against her hair, not a difficult foretelling to interpret, in the circumstances. It would not be an easy task to woo and win the lady—if that is what he truly wanted. He had looked for no more than an understanding, an affection at best in this union, and yet… The thought caught him unawares but did not displease.

It might be an exhilarating experience, perhaps for both of them.

* * *

'My lord! My lord Malinder!'

At some time in the dark hours between midnight and the late winter dawn there was an urgent but discreet knocking on the bedchamber door, and a ferocious whisper, enough to rouse the occupants, but not the whole household. Richard came awake, aware at first of nothing but the warmth of Elizabeth turned into him, cradled in his arms.

'My lord! You must come!' As the hammering and the summons grew more demanding, he sat up with a groan, lit a candle and swung his legs out of bed.

'What is it?' Elizabeth, awake but sleepy.

'I don't know. Some emergency that cannot wait.' He yawned, shivered from the cold and scrubbed his hands over his face. 'Probably one of the guests fallen into the well after a skinful of ale.' Resigned, he began to pull on hose and tunic. 'Go back to sleep, Elizabeth. I'll not be long.' He stayed to press a kiss to her hair and tuck the coverlet round her shoulders, grabbed his sword and a cloak against the night's cold. The door closed and all was silent.

Elizabeth rolled over into the heat of his body's imprint and went back to sleep.

In the courtyard, in a shadowed corner between the keep and the chapel, Richard crouched beside a body, face down where the shadow was darkest. Master Kilpin, Simon Beggard, Richard's Commander of the garrison of Ledenshall, and one of the guards stood uneasily beside him. Simon held up a shuttered lantern, conversation was in muted tones. Better not to alert everyone yet.

'Who found him?'

'I did, my lord,' the guard replied. 'It's my watch. There's rats here—so I came down to see…and when I saw, I roused Commander Beggard.'

Richard touched the body, already cold. There was no

question but that he was dead. The lantern, flickering in the fitful wind, was sufficient to show the spread of the dark stain between the shoulder blades. One of the guests, velvet and damask, now bloody and soiled. Wedding clothes.

'Hold the lantern up. Now, Master Kilpin, help me turn him over.'

They moved the body so that the light might fall on his face. Richard hissed out a breath at the confirmation of his worst fears. He had known the dark hair, the slight build, the damask finery, as soon as he had seen it.

'Bad, my lord,' Simon Beggard stated.

'Couldn't be worse.' Richard rose to his feet, his face unreadable. Recognising the remains of the man at their feet, the little audience knew why.

'What do we do, my lord?'

'What, indeed!' Richard continued to stare with mounting dismay. He would do what needed to be done and worry about repercussions later. 'Let's move him into the chapel. It's nearest and suitable for the purpose, I suppose. God's presence in the face of violent and useless death.' His terse instructions could not hide the anger that flooded his body at this worthless—and possibly disastrous—spilling of blood.

Between them they carried the body in and laid it on the wooden bench along the back wall. Richard took off his cloak and spread it over the still figure. The lantern shone down on a face empty in death, eyes wide perhaps with surprise, lips lax, skin grey with a waxen tinge. A sudden draught fluttered the edge of the material and the ends of the dark hair.

'Robbery, my lord?' Simon Beggard whispered, but his voice echoed unnervingly in the roof space that arched into blackness over their heads.

'It's possible. His jewels are gone.' Richard remembered them. His fingers had been stripped of costly rings. Perhaps a chain. And his sword was taken. 'God help us. This is a bad night's work.'

Then he began to issue orders. 'Master Kilpin, you had better find Sir John. Try not to wake the whole castle. The fewer people here, the better. Tomorrow will be enough and more for that. Simon, fetch Sir Robert, if you will. And then ask the guards if they saw anyone out and about after midnight. Anything at all, no matter how trivial.'

They exited smartly, leaving the guard to stand sentry beside the body.

'Keep this door locked until my return.' Richard stood for a moment at the top of the shallow steps where his vows had been taken earlier in the day. 'I need to go and tell my wife.'

Elizabeth awoke fully from a light doze, her mind still suffused with contentment as Richard entered the room. He came over to the bed with a lantern.

'What's happened?'

He sat on the edge of the bed. Set down the lantern and curled his hand around hers. 'It's bad, Elizabeth.'

She pushed up onto one elbow. 'Did someone indeed fall into the well?' Then the amusement drained away as she saw, despite the shadows, the brutal lines of his face.

'I need you to get up.'

'Tell me.'

There was no point in prolonging it with soft words. 'Your brother. Lewis. He's dead.'

There was a moment of intense silence. Elizabeth felt the words freeze into a solid mass in her chest, so that she could not breathe. Could not speak. Could not think beyond that brutal announcement. Then a low strangled sound deep in her throat. Her hand tightened on his, nails digging in as blood drained from her face in the lantern's yellow glow. Her eyes were hot and dry, beyond tears, but dark with anguish. Then she was pushing him away as she struggled to leave the bed.

'Will you take me to him?'

'Yes.'

He helped her pull on her chemise, put on her shoes. Wrapped her new, festive cloak around her and pulled up the hood to hide her from any encroachment on her privacy. If only he could obliterate her pain quite so simply. Then he took her cold hand in his and led her to her brother.

Elizabeth knelt beside Lewis's body and turned back the cloak. Someone had closed his eyes, folded his hands on his chest so that he looked at peace. Disbelieving, she touched her fingertips gently to Lewis's face, his lips. Then to his hands.

'Lewis. Ah, Lewis.' Her voice broke on the name he could no longer hear. She smoothed her hands over his shoulders, his chest, as if searching for the fatal injury. 'How did he die?'

'A knife,' Richard answered. 'In the back.' He stood protectively, one hand on her shoulder. She could feel his presence and was grateful for it even as her whole world was caught up in the lifeless body of her brother.

'I can't believe that he will never wake again. Never speak to me again. He brought me here from Llanwardine.' She ran her fingers through his matted hair, smoothing it along his temples. 'I loved him. And he was one of the few people who loved me. But now he is dead.'

Richard lifted her, enfolded her so that she could press her face against his shoulder. And she clung to him. Through her grief she felt the strength of his arms giving her comfort. As did his words, even though her heart was rent in two.

'Whoever is guilty, Elizabeth, he shall pay for this.'

'Indeed he will.'

A harsh voice from the open doorway. Elizabeth found herself released and pushed gently behind him as Richard took up a position between herself and her uncle, almost she thought as if to shield her from what might be said.

Sir John de Lacy was cold sober. As was the commander of his garrison at Talgarth, Sir Gilbert de Burcher, a thickset soldier who stood at his shoulder. Elizabeth felt the fierce tension in her uncle as his eyes snapped from Lewis to herself, to Robert, who had followed Sir John into the room. And then to Richard, who stood in the centre of the chapel, in Sir John's direct line of sight, beside the dead body of his heir.

'Who has the blood of my nephew on his hands?'

'We have no evidence. We have the knife.' Richard raised his hand to show the poignard on his outstretched palm, the blade rank with dried blood to the hilt. 'It was left beside the body. But as for its owner…' He shook his head. 'It's plain and serviceable, such as might belong to any man.'

'An arrogant gesture, some might say, to leave it there.' A new voice. Softly, dangerously said, full of implication. Elizabeth was aware of the tall presence of Nicholas Capel, who had emerged out of the darkness. She felt the slide of his eyes over her and shivered involuntarily.

Sir John marched forwards to stand at his nephew's side. 'I demand retribution.' His lips were bone-white, his face uncompromisingly judgemental.

'Against whom?' Richard asked. 'No one was seen in the courtyard after the celebrations ended. My commander is still questioning the guards, but we have no evidence against any man.'

'Whom do *you* suggest, Malinder? I wager that it would not be a *de Lacy* to commit such a crime against my heir.'

Elizabeth stiffened at the blatant accusation. What was this? Would her uncle accuse a Malinder of the foul crime?

'So you imply it was a Malinder.' Richard's eyes blazed as he echoed her thoughts.

'Sir John is overwrought. He makes no such implication,' Capel intervened smoothly.

'Enough!' Sir John snapped at his adviser. 'I think everyone will come to the obvious conclusion. We came as guests into your home, in search of a lasting alliance with our erst-while enemies in the March.' Sir John's words were viciously direct. 'We came in good faith and I entrusted my own niece into your hands. And now my heir is dead. Even you, Malinder, must accept where the burden of evidence would seem to weigh most heavily.'

Beside her, Richard's stillness became a threat in itself. Beneath the superbly controlled surface Elizabeth could almost feel the temper roil and bubble. Through her grief at Lewis's death, she found herself praying that his control would hold. When Elizabeth saw Richard's hand close in overt warning on the hilt of his sword, she was driven to step close and grasp his sleeve. Anything to prevent a conflagration that might ignite to turn the marriage celebration into a gory massacre. Briefly his eyes flickered to hers, and through the heat of temper, read the message there. To her relief he kept his voice light.

'There's no evidence as yet to smear anyone with guilt. I would suggest that you take care whom you accuse, Sir John. Without a shred of evidence, it would be unwise to whip up enmity against me and mine.'

'I'll take care as long as I am under your roof, without pro-tection.' Sir John's lips twisted in a sneer. 'So much for our promising marriage alliance, for the hopes of friendship.' He addressed Elizabeth, still at Richard's side, her hand warn-ingly on his arm. 'You are joined to this man now by the bounds of law and by the vows you made before God, but be sure you know whom you can trust in this household, Elizabeth. My advice is to trust no one.'

'I hear your advice, sir.'

It was all she could say. Horror, sharp-edged and lethal, engulfed her. Richard accused of killing her brother in cold blood. She could not think of that yet. Instead, divorcing her-self from the naked aggression in the room, Elizabeth walked forwards, pulled the cloak softly, neatly over Lewis's body to the chin and bent to kiss his brow, touching his lips with her fingers for one final time. Then, before emotion could completely overwhelm her, she walked out of the chapel without another word or a backward glance.

Later, left alone in the chapel in the aftermath, Robert looked at his cousin, his red brows raised towards his hairline.

'I can't believe this has just happened. It almost persuades a man never to marry.'

'I'm almost tempted to agree, Rob.' Richard stood and looked down at the body of the young man who had been willing to offer friendship. Who not a handful of hours ago had seemed troubled, but unable to share his concerns. *He was one of the few people who loved me.* Which heartbreaking little statement from Elizabeth had made Richard long to sweep her up and take her away from this tragic loss, to stroke and comfort her. Instead all he could do was stand beside her and let her grieve as she wished. And as he recalled Elizabeth's anguish, he felt a wave of compassion for her wash over him, to be quickly overlaid by a cold dread.

'What are you thinking?' Robert asked.

'That before this day is out, my name will be linked with a particularly brutal and unwarranted crime. My home, my marriage ceremony, my motive—all dragged in the mud of bloody murder.' He turned his head to fix his cousin with a cold, flat regard, the blazing anger when he had faced Sir John now turned to ice. 'Sir John will not leave Ledenshall without making public the ultimate connection between myself and this crime. And one that I am in no position to refute since, even though I am innocent, his words will contain enough truth of the long-standing rift between Malinder and de Lacy to attract interest and speculation.' He paused, his mind running over the events of the past hour, returning, lingering on one.

'You think he will accuse you openly? But what motive could you have?'

'Think about it, Rob. Think about my position within the de Lacy family dynamics because of my marriage.' Richard shook his head and strode out of the chapel without further reply to face his wife. To try to salvage some hope, some measure of understanding with Elizabeth, from the cold ashes of his marriage.

She had resurrected the fire and now sat in its warmth, waiting, as she had waited for him earlier that night before death had struck to tear and divide. To shatter her heart in grief. *Dead. Murdered. My brother is dead.* Her mind simply could not accept what her eyes had seen. Her cloak was still round her shoulders. She had not lit the candles so the room was dark and intimately shadowed, but there was no rest or comfort in the air. The warmth of the fire did not touch her blood.

'Well?' She turned her head sharply at his entrance. All her earlier bright hope for the future, her astonished pleasure in her husband's arms, obliterated to be replaced by raw desolation. And a degree of hurt that her mind could not yet grasp. Sir John's accusation clawed at her mind, but had not yet fully struck home.

'I have left Lewis in the care of the priest. Arrangements have been made to take him to Talgarth tomorrow. It is Sir John's decision to make, I think.' Richard unbuckled his sword belt and laid it aside before pouring water from the ewer and washing his hands.

'Do you know any more?' She thought he looked weary to the bone.

'Nothing. No one heard or saw anything.' He walked to where she sat as he dried his hands on the coarse linen. She felt he was watching her, tuned to her reaction to the night's events. 'No one remembers Lewis leaving the Hall at any

time. We know his jewels are missing and his sword. I have
set Simon Beggard to go through the servants' quarters, but
I doubt we'll find anything. Whoever took them must have
known that I would order such a search. Then, short of searching every guest…' He stifled a groan at the prospect. It could
not be done.

He had brought a flask of Bordeaux with him, so poured it
and drank, tossing back the contents. And, as control momentarily snapped, flung the pewter at the wall, watching in disgust as the dregs of wine stained the tapestries and the dented
cup bounced to lie on the floor. Elizabeth did not even flinch.
She was beyond feeling.

'Forgive me. That was unpardonable.' She watched as he
reined in his rage, came to sit opposite her and forced his
voice to become dispassionate. 'You heard Sir John's words.
The culprit has to be a Malinder because for it to be a de Lacy
is unthinkable. What do you think, Elizabeth?' It seemed
to matter to him what she was thinking, when she did not
know herself. 'We promised mutual respect and trust—so
few hours ago—but this death… It has placed a vast obstacle
in our path and we have no prior knowledge of each other to
negotiate it.'

'We promised to let no one come between us,' she recalled,
the vow echoing in her mind as if from another life.

'So we did. And now Lewis, in his death, has done just
that. And Sir John's accusations would rend us apart.'

Elizabeth sensed the overwhelming bitterness beneath the
anger. There was a decision here for her to make. An impossible decision. 'You did not do it.' Her eyes were steady and
unflinching on his as her voice made of it a question.

'No. I had an excellent alibi, did I not, in your bed? But
one of mine could have wielded the dagger at my instiga-
tion—even if it was not my own hand. You do not know me.
How can I blame you if you lay the guilt on my shoulders?'

The harshness in his tone, the self-mockery, hammered its

way through the grief that dulled every reaction in her body.
It forced her to remember his tenderness, his ultimate consideration. He was no enemy of hers, of that she was almost
certain. Elizabeth weighed what her head told her, and also
her heart. No, she did not know him, but she wanted, more
than life itself, to trust him. And yet her uncle's words could
not be dislodged.

*You are joined to this man now by the bounds of law and
by the vows you made before God, but be sure you know
whom you can trust in this household, Elizabeth. My advice
is to trust no one.*

'You would not have stabbed Lewis in the back,' she
stated.

'No. I would not,' he conceded, rising to pace the room.
'But if I had paid a willing assassin, he might not have been
so concerned with the niceties.' And she knew he was paint-
ing the worst scenario for her before Sir John did. Richard
stopped, mid-pace, his back firmly towards her, head thrown
back. 'Do you believe me capable of arranging the killing of
my wife's brother on our wedding night? At the same time
as I was holding her in my arms and kissing her?'

'Richard.' Suppressed tears roughened her voice, but she
swallowed and pressed on. Knew what she must ask. And
instinct told her that he would not lie. 'We promised we
would be honest with each other. To listen and trust our own
instincts. Not allowing others to manipulate us. I know you
enough to know that you will keep your word. So you will
tell me the truth.'

'Yes, I will.' The agonised plea in her voice halted his restless pacing. Richard came to kneel before her, stormy eyes
searching her face. Offered his hands, palm to palm, so that
she might enclose her cold hands around his as if he would
make a binding oath of allegiance and fealty to a sovereign
lord. Stern and reverent, he bowed his head. 'Before God, I
would not bring about the death of one of yours in cold blood.

I did not kill Lewis. I did not authorise anyone to do so. I am not responsible for his death. You are my wife. I will protect and honour you until the day of my death.'

Elizabeth focused on his dark head, the disordered waves of hair. She longed to reach out and touch, in gratitude and acceptance of his oath. *I did not kill Lewis.* But not yet, even though she wanted to hear those words. Even though she wanted to believe him. Then Richard looked up, their eyes caught, held despite the tension between them. Whatever she read there—uncertainty, banked fury—caused her to turn her hands within his, to clasp his.

'Yes. That is what I wanted you to say.' She had not realised the depth of her fears. Or her need to accept the sworn word of Richard Malinder and trust him. But between them were vast stretches of blood and violence between their families. And now in the lifeless body of Lewis. Tears began to slide down her cheeks as she saw the enormity of the rift between them.

'Can you trust me, accept my word?'

'I want to. I will try to.'

'I know it is difficult for you. Your brother is dead under my roof and your relationship with me is—well, it's like a fortification without foundations. How can I expect you to give your heart and soul into my hands after so brief a knowledge?'

His brutally frank words hit home. As did the shocking reality of Lewis's death. Elizabeth's breathing shuddered with sobs that quickly became beyond her ability to control. Her whole frame shook as she covered her face with her hands and allowed the grief, held at bay for so long, to overwhelm her.

'Ah, Elizabeth.' He pulled her to the floor beside him, before the fire, held her, brought her firmly against him so that she wept against his shoulder. And she wept for Lewis, for herself. For the impossible rifts caused on this day between two powerful families, between herself and Richard. Whilst he cradled her without words, able to give nothing but the strength of his arms, the warmth and security of his body.

She could ask for nothing more, even as Sir John's accusation still stood between them.

At last when the sobs began to abate, Richard lifted her to carry her to the bed. Held her until she fell into an exhausted asleep. He remained awake as the sky grew bright, thinking over the events, the peace of the March effectively destroyed if Sir John decided to pursue a personal vengeance against him. Another bloody wound in the struggle for power between York and Lancaster. With Elizabeth at the very centre of it, pulled between her family of birth and her allegiance through marriage. His heart ached for her. Turning his head to press his lips against the soft skin at her temple, he made another vow, determined to pursue it until the day of his death.

'I swear before God that I will discover the murderer, Elizabeth. And bring him to justice at your feet. Then you will give me your trust.'

And God give them strength and wisdom to weather the vicious arrows that Sir John de Lacy would loose before he shook the dust of Ledenshall from his feet when the day dawned. Anger and hopeless pain on her behalf welled in him, bitter as the lees of hops in old ale.

Chapter Seven

Elizabeth took in the scene as if through the barrier of a veil.

As if to mock the events of the previous night, the sky grew clear, a cloudless pale blue, sharp and clean with the aftermath of frost. The sun bright with winter clarity, the shining beauty of it in terrible contrast to the stir of emotions—grief and impotent fury—that ripped apart the scene in the courtyard at Ledenshall.

Most of the de Lacys and Malinders had already left at daybreak, wedding finery packed away, uncomfortable and aware of the nerve-tingling apprehension created by the violence. All to remain in the courtyard were Sir John and Lady Ellen, already mounted, without any of the usual polite leavetakings. Nicholas Capel waited with Sir Gilbert de Burcher and their escort at a little distance beside the wagon that would bear Lewis's body home. And standing near the de Lacy party, yet slightly apart, was David, dressed for travel and holding the bridle of his horse. In the short hours since the bridal feast his face had become drawn, pale.

'Mount up, boy. We can't wait longer for you.'

Sir John's clipped tones drew Elizabeth's attention. Rigidly composed, restored to her wimple and veil, the cloak falling in straight lines from shoulder to heel, she bore herself with dignity, the forceful presence of her husband on her right. There was no means for her to guess Richard's emotions. Seeing the iron-hard muscles in neck and jaw, she knew he had them under control, to finish this business as rapidly and painlessly as possible. And within the realms of good manners. But now her uncle's words struck her with a totally unexpected development.

'David?' Her eyes flew to her brother, registering for the first time his clothing, his horse. 'David? Would you leave now?' She could barely hold the building panic. To lose David as well as Lewis at this moment was beyond what she could bear.

'He comes with me.' Sir John stared at his nephew, not at Elizabeth, challenging him to refuse his sister's plea. There had clearly been words already spoken between them on the matter.

'No.' She shook her head, kept her voice low, even when she felt the urge to shriek with the pain centred in her heart. 'Let him stay. Let David stay.'

'He comes with me.'

David ignored the harsh command. He thrust the bridle into the hand of a waiting groom and walked instead to Elizabeth's side, to hug her, clumsy with grief, but knowing instinctively what was necessary. 'Elizabeth,' he murmured huskily, 'I would stay—I would rather stay then go to Talgarth—but he gives me no choice. He holds my lack of years over my head. And my position, now that Lewis…' He swallowed before he could continue. 'Now that I am the de Lacy heir.'

'But why?' Despair rose to lodge in her throat, a hard knot, at being abandoned here to mourn alone with a family who were still strangers to her. Continuing to grasp David's forearms, she turned to her uncle. 'Why can he not stay?'

The dark features, the austere, lined face, contained not

one hint of sympathy. Sir John's lips tightened around the words. 'David is my heir. I'll not have him remain here.'

'It would please me, Uncle.' She would not beg. She must not beg. 'If only for a little time.'

'Do I have to say it aloud, Niece?' Sir John used his heels to edge his horse closer to his Malinder hosts, looked down on them, raised his voice. 'Has your woman with her accursed magic been unable to see into the hearts of those who surround you? Those who would wish our family ill? I should never have proposed this match. The events here this night have confirmed every suspicion that I have ever harboured against the Black Malinders.'

'What need have I of magic?' Elizabeth met his eyes defiantly, leaping to protect Jane Bringsty as much as the Malinders. 'You do my lord Malinder an injustice. I have been made welcome here—'

Sir John cut her off. 'I have no heir of my own body.' He ignored the quick intake of breath from Lady Ellen behind him, at the cruel and all too public thrust at her failure to carry a child to term. 'Lewis is killed. After David, who would inherit all the de Lacy lands in the March? You do not need me to tell you that, girl.' His eyes snapped, lips tightened. '*You* would, of course. And who would stand to gain most from *that* inheritance?'

Richard! The realisation struck her a blow beneath her heart.

'Do I need to spell it out further? I will not leave David unprotected in this place.' Sir John all but spat the words.

'It is as Sir John says.' In the interchange, Capel had quietly manoeuvred his horse closer. His tone was calming, placatory, for which Elizabeth could not fault him, but she noted that his eyes darted, bright, uncomfortably assessing. 'It is better in the circumstances if the young lord comes with us.'

Elizabeth looked from David to her husband of twelve hours. David uneasy, embarrassed at the interchange in which he had unwittingly become the centre of attention. Richard stony-faced, silent, yet his eyes steady and level on the man who was deliberately destroying his character and his reputation as a man of honour. Was it possible that her husband, in the coldest of blood on the night of their marriage, had wilfully plotted Lewis's death to strengthen his own claim on the de Lacy estates? All Elizabeth could bring to mind was the oath Richard had sworn to her the previous night. The clear honesty, the utter integrity that she had read in his eyes as he had knelt before her. She would give anything not to believe in his guilt, but the weight of uncertainty was there between them, as surely as the body of Lewis. His blood would stain their newly fledged relationship until the truth was revealed. Beside her she felt Richard stiffen, anger vibrate from him, but his command was impeccable. Had he expected this? It seemed he had. His voice was coated with ice.

'David is in no danger here and never will be. Lewis did not meet his death at my hands or at my wish. I have no claim on the de Lacy estates.'

Sir John lifted his hand to thrust aside Richard's words and, without another word, jerked his reins, pulling his horse back and away, signalling for the driver of the wagon to start, the escort to fall in behind. The leave-taking with all its poison and malice was over. Lady Ellen strained to look back for a final moment, to send some unspoken message to Elizabeth, eyes stark with remorse.

'David!' Sir John snarled.

But he would not be hurried. He reached up to kiss Elizabeth's cheek. 'This is not of my choice.' He grasped her hands and she held on tight. 'I can't believe Sir John. And neither should you. It will make mischief—and you must not allow it.'

'Your words touch my heart.' Thinking of him only as a young boy, his quick assessment amazed her. Perhaps he had grown up since Lewis's death. He kissed her fingers in formal salutation, then turned to Richard as he gathered up his reins and prepared to mount. 'I enjoyed riding with you, Richard.'

As they clasped hands in formal farewell, Richard forced his mouth to relax in a genuine smile. 'You'll always be welcome here, for your own sake as well as that of your sister.'

'I know. I will come if I can. *When* I can. It may be difficult… Take care of her.'

'It is my intention.'

He swung into the saddle. 'I know you did not kill Lewis.'

Elizabeth gripped her brother's hand once more until the horse's movement forced her away. Then, because the de Lacy party with its escort had already made its way to the main gate, she was given no choice but to allow him to go.

Elizabeth climbed to the battlements alone, to watch the sad little procession. All her family leaving, the silver on blue of the de Lacy heraldic emblems glittering in the sun's rays through the trees. So much bad blood, so many irreconcilable differences. She saw David look back once and then they were swallowed up in the trees on the edge of the village, until the silver lion could no longer be detected, leaving her to worry over the demands on her stretched loyalties. How could she fix her opinions with no chart to guide her in a new relationship, no links of tradition with her new family? But of one thing she would try to hold to. Her heart and her instincts hammered it home when her mind threatened to give weight to her uncle's spite and malice. She spoke the words silently in her mind, praying that she could truly believe. Richard Malinder was not responsible for Lewis's murder. Nor had David thought so.

She turned to descend to her new life, fighting the despair and distrust. Wondering just what she would say to Richard Malinder when she reached the courtyard where he was doubtless waiting for her.

* * *

To Elizabeth's sharp annoyance, Richard hardly took the time to note her approach. He was already deep in conversation with Robert Malinder.

'What would you do now, Rob, if you were Sir John?'

'Encourage someone to put poison in your ale. Or use a length of cold steel against you on a dark night.' Robert flushed brightly as he saw, belatedly, the appalling similarity with recent events, and registered Elizabeth's presence at Richard's elbow. 'Forgive me, lady. That was thoughtless and cruel.'

She shook her head. It was all she could manage.

'Sensitivity was never Rob's strong point.' Richard surprised her by taking her hand to pull it through his arm and hold it there, his fingers warm and linked with her cold ones. A casual gesture of ownership, of unity, she thought. It comforted her a little, allowed the tight bands of distress and uncertainty around her heart to loosen. 'Other than plotting my demise in revenge for his nephew's life,' Richard continued, fingers even firmer on hers when she might have pulled away, 'how do you now see his activities in the March?'

'Well!' Robert rubbed a hand over his face as they strolled a little way into a patch of sunlight, allowing Richard to manoeuvre Elizabeth into perching on the steps leading to the battlement walk. He still kept possession of her hand. 'I would go out of my way to cause you as much trouble as possible. Attack one of your castles, perhaps.' His russet brows twitched into a heavy line.

'Exactly. So I need to put out an immediate show of force.' Richard's angled glance down to his bride was not unsympathetic. 'No one would expect me to be about in the March so soon after my marriage. It would be best to make a show with an iron fist before Sir John can return to Talgarth and get himself organised to take to the field.'

Robert nodded, seeing the plan of action. 'Do you want company?'

'If you will come.' Elizabeth felt Richard's fingers clench around hers like a vice as the promise of action began to pump through his bloodstream. 'Two hours. I'll leave Simon Beggard and a garrison of men here. Can you be ready, Rob?'

'Of course.' Robert was already on the move.

So was Richard. Releasing Elizabeth's hand with no more than a preoccupied smile, he abandoned her on the steps and strode off in the direction of the soldiers' quarters, leaving Elizabeth to follow him with irritation in her eyes. If she had believed that her status as a new Malinder bride should have some claim on her husband's time and attention, she had been entirely wrong. She might as well have been a stone in the parapet in the previous discussion. Except for the lingering strength and warmth of his hand around hers, of course.

Two hours later, Richard saw her standing on the steps to the Great Hall, cloak wrapped closely, veil fluttering in the sharp wind. Guilt scratched at his skin, a new and uncomfortable experience, but he had to admit also to an element of uneasy relief at their parting. There would be no opportunity to pick at the painful wound of Lewis's death for some time—until the dust had settled for both of them. Then he would discover what her thoughts were. Yet to leave her now seemed impossibly insensitive, with not one comforting word to remain in her mind other than his empty denials of Sir John's impassioned accusations. But it could not be helped. To have the de Lacys undermining his authority in the March, attacking his property, could not be allowed. Given any encouragement, the whole damned area would rise in rebellion. And with the Welsh propensity to become involved in any conflict...

Yet guilt still swam queasily in his belly and the urge to stay was strong. There she stood, tall and straight, the pride and dignity of her breeding wrapping around her as did the folds of the glorious cloak. He had no doubt that she would hold his authority at Ledenshall in his absence. In spite of all the events of the past twenty-four hours—or perhaps because of them—he trusted her to keep faith. But to abandon her at this moment would not be good strategy. Pale and strained from lack of sleep, there were prints of grief beneath her eyes and in the tight corners of her lips. Richard stifled a groan as his thoughts ran round in circles from which there was no escape.

'Elizabeth.' He trod the steps to her, his eyes on hers, willing her to understand and accept. 'This would not have been my plan.'

'No. I don't suppose it would.'

'A quick sortie through the March. I'll return as soon as circumstances allow.'

'Yes.'

'You are chatelaine in my absence and carry the final authority. Don't open the gates to anyone but myself, on my return. I would even say not even for your uncle in my absence, but I think he will not come here after last night's events.' He took her hands. 'Unless it is to take you back to Talgarth, out of my influence if he believes me complicit in Lewis's death.' The statement implied a question—she saw it immediately and was quick to answer.

'Sir John will not come. And I would not go with him. Is that what you wish to hear?'

'Yes. Yes—I needed to know.' And Richard realised what had troubled him during the hours of preparation.

'I am your wife and my duty is here.' There was no joy in her avowal, but he must accept that. With time, perhaps it could be put right.

A gleam of sunlight speared through a break in the clouds, to highlight the gold and enamel of the brooch on her shoulder. It pleased him that she had chosen to wear it. The fierce little animals gleamed with fire and light. Unable to resist, he touched it with gentle fingers.

'It shines as brightly as your spirit, lady. I can only be thankful to have a bride of such strength and purpose.' Richard bowed his head and kissed her hand. Then, in spite of the waiting retinue, he pressed his mouth to hers. A firm, hard kiss. Leaving her with the taste of him, the touch of him. He saw the blood surge to her cheeks and her eyes darken.

'Farewell. Have courage, Penthesilea!'

Without another word he gathered up his reins and swung into the saddle, motioning Robert and the soldiers to precede him through the gate. Except that she left her entrenched position and ran down the steps at the last.

'Richard.' He stopped, looked back. When she had reached his side, she raised her hand to touch his where they grasped the reins. 'God keep you.'

'Pray that He does, lady.'

Later that night, before she took herself to her empty bed, Elizabeth sat alone in her chamber. She had dismissed Jane Bringsty, but kept the cat by her, a decision that had Mistress Bringsty narrowing a glance, but offering no comment. Now Elizabeth sat and thought as the silence of the room settled around her, the shadows closed in. One brother murdered, the other ordered away. Her uncle prepared to make public accusations of greed and death—vowing revenge for blood spilt. She knew well the dangers, the looming presence of death from a careless moment, a stray arrow. A deliberate attack.

Her heart was sore. She found herself rubbing the heel of her hand along her breast-bone as if the rhythmic pressure could ease the pain. How could she possibly be expected to sit and read, set stitches or play chess when her loyalties and emotions were being so torn apart? She knew what she should do, but it must be done quietly, secretly.

'Why should I not make an amulet?' she asked of the

somnolent cat. 'It will harm no one. And if it keeps Richard safe…'

The cat leapt on to the bed with her ears pricked, her tail twitching as if aware of her mistress's dilemma. Elizabeth took it for approval, lit a candle and sat before it. On the table to hand was the result of a timely sweep through the herb garden in all its winter devastation. 'Mullein, for courage—not that he needs it. I think Richard does not lack for personal courage. Comfrey for safety on a journey. Vervain and woodruff.' She picked them up, ran her fingers over their aromatic leaves. 'For victory and to escape from the plotting of one's enemies.'

She put them together into as tidy a bundle as she could manage, then moved to the bed to hunt amongst the covers and pillows. Yes—as she had hoped. A black hair, easily recognisable as too long to be her own. She added it to the twiggy bundle and tied it all securely, one knot, with threads of red silk discovered in an old work box. And then three more knots, murmuring with each knot, *'I bind thee to protect him.'*

'It's all I can do,' she murmured. 'He cannot wear it, but I can lay the protective charm in his name. If my uncle would ride against him… It must not be. Who killed Lewis? Tell me it was not Richard Malinder.' But the cat made no sound, merely stared with unblinking eyes that caught the light as they followed the movements of Elizabeth's hands. So Elizabeth on a little sigh completed the charm, stroking the cat from ears to tail in long soft movements before lifting the charm to hang it high on the bed canopy where none would see it, or would simply dismiss it as a notion against the ravages of the moth.

When the cat began to purr deep in her throat, Elizabeth came to sit again beside her. 'I have done all I can. Pray God that he returns safe. All this, and I have barely been married for a single day. I know not my feelings for him, but I am not ill disposed towards him.'

The animal leapt from the bed and stretched.

Chapter Eight

Elizabeth stood with Jane Bringsty in the sheltered corner between the new living accommodations and the original outer wall of the castle. Even in the drear cold of this March day, it was clear that it had once been a garden with symmetrical beds, narrow pathways, cobbled edges still intact.

'Someone here had more than a passing interest—this was once well laid out and tended. Look at this.' The new Lady of Ledenshall inspected an espaliered fruit tree growing against the most sheltered wall. 'I think it is a peach. Now all is wilderness.' Everything was choked with weeds and couch grass.

'Lady Gwladys had no interest here,' Jane announced.

Gwladys! Elizabeth felt the familiar little tug of jealousy at her heart—*Gwladys*, the incomparable—but shrugged. 'So Gwladys had no interest in plants.'

'Gossip says that Lady Gwladys had few interests. They say that…' Jane folded her lips tight.

'What else does gossip say?' Elizabeth asked curiously.

'Not much. She was comely enough.' Jane sniffed her displeasure. 'They're a close-lipped lot here at Ledenshall. If you wish to know more about Lady Gwladys, you must ask Lord Malinder.'

'Then perhaps I will.' Elizabeth set off to pace the indistinct paths, skirting the puddles, conscious of a familiar tremor of disquiet in her belly.

Mistress Anne tripped elegantly into the enclosed space to join them, halting at the edge of the beds, her skirts lifted in delicate hands, lovely mouth pursed in distaste. The dark fur collar that snuggled around her neck softened her features, illuminated her hair. She was without doubt, Elizabeth acknowledged to herself, a remarkably beautiful girl.

'Here you are. I had no idea until I heard voices. What could you find to do out here?' She looked down her nose at the puddles, the mud, widened her eyes. 'What are you doing?'

'Thinking of planting a garden.' Elizabeth turned to retrace her steps. There would be no pleasure here with Anne.

Anne fell into step with her. 'You must hope for Richard's return.'

'Yes. Of course.'

'My dear Elizabeth…' Anne tilted her head with a winsome expression '…you must not allow your hands to become rough and ingrained with soil.' Anne stretched out her own elegant fingers. 'Richard likes a woman to have smooth hands. So feminine. So he has told me.'

'Then I must take care, must I not? Perhaps I should sit within doors all day?'

'It could not but help,' Anne agreed in all seriousness. 'But your hands were ruined at Llanwardine, as I recall.'

'Yes.' Elizabeth refused to make any attempt to hide them in her skirts despite her first instinct.

'Perhaps Richard will return this week. He'll enjoy some female company after days spent in travel down the March— all dirt and lice and male company.' Anne wrinkled her nose at the prospect, then slid a wide-eyed glance to Elizabeth. 'Do you sing, Elizabeth?'

'No.'

'Perhaps you play the lute?'

'No. I do not.' Elizabeth seethed silently. She could play the lute, and more than passably adequate, but she would not set herself up in competition.

'I do both, of course. My mother considered them essential skills for a lady who wished to make her home comfortable and welcoming for her lord. It will please me to sing and play for Richard.'

'Will you not wish to go home when Robert has returned?' Elizabeth asked as Anne quickened her pace at a sudden and heavy shower of rain.

'Eventually.' Anne cast a bright glance over her shoulder as she headed for shelter. 'I thought you might enjoy my company for a little time yet. Family connections are so important, are they not?'

'Although they can sometimes be stretched beyond bearing.' The quiet words at Elizabeth's shoulder burst from Jane's lips as if her frustrations could not be contained. 'I am more tempted than ever to dose that woman's cup—before this day is out. Vomiting and the stomach cramps would give her something other to think about than her likes and dislikes. A little humiliation would be good for her soul.'

Elizabeth felt a reprehensible urge to agree, but Jane needed no encouragement when in this mood. 'You must not do it, Jane. Do you hear me?'

'Of course I hear you,' Jane hissed. 'You're too principled for your own good, my lady. It's my duty—as it has been since the day of your birth—to see to your happiness.'

'But not to poison my lord's cousin.'

'It's not the woman who is your lord's cousin who concerns me. It's the woman who would be his *lover*.'

'Jane…she would not—*he* would not!'

'That is exactly what Mistress Anne would want. Is that what you will allow? Under your own roof? She would be in his bed if he but lifted an eyebrow.'

'And you think my lord would treat me with such disrespect?'

'No! I did not say that. But look, my lady, I think Mistress Anne would wilfully misread any gesture on your lord's part. Men are ever fools when in the coils of a manipulative woman.'

'She flirts only.'

Jane snorted. 'Flirts! She's more malicious than that.'

Which Elizabeth on a sigh knew to be true. 'Don't. I forbid it.'

Jane opened her mouth, clearly to blister her ears with another warning, but decided against it. 'Have a care,' was all she said before marching off to her own quarters, leaving Elizabeth surrounded by decaying foliage, hoping that she had made her wishes clearly understood in the matter, but without any real conviction.

That night, in her own chamber, Jane Bringsty ignored her mistress's wishes with an entire absence of guilt. No one must be allowed to undermine the happiness of Elizabeth de Lacy. No one! She and the cat watched the antics of the rat in the cage. It sniffed the contents of the little dish, the bread soaked in some dark blue substance, then nibbled until the dish was empty. Still the audience watched without compassion, until the rat began to twist and leap in its death throes. Until it fell on its side and failed to stir again.

'Dead!' Mistress Bringsty muttered in disgust, picking up the cage to carry it to the midden to dispose of the body. 'I must be more careful, more precise in the amount. Belladonna can be a chancy poison. Can't afford to kill the girl, whatever the temptation. Even though she's like a bitch in heat.' She eyed the cat with a smirk. 'That would put the cat amongst the pigeons.'

The cat brushed against her skirts as if in agreement.

'We'll watch Mistress Anne Malinder,' Mistress Bringsty murmured. 'And if she sinks her claws into the Lord of Ledenshall, we shall know what to do about it, won't we?'

When Richard returned, tired but briefly satisfied with his efforts in the March, Elizabeth was not automatically there to greet him, being engaged in struggling with a mass of impacted roots and rampant weeds in her garden. She heard the warning shout of the sentry, the metallic rattle and grinding screech of the portcullis. By the time she had beaten her garments into some sort of order, the small armed force was already dismounting with much noise, confusion and loud conversation.

There he was at the centre of activity as he swung down from his weary stallion. Richard was—as were they all—coated with the dirt and sweat of the campaign, armour, boots and cloaks impartially smeared with dust and mud. He looked totally disreputable, not much better than a border raider—but if that were so, why did her pulse pick up its beat, her heart give a single thud of awareness? Elizabeth was immediately conscious of her own appearance, unfortunately little better than his, an old gown with mud around the hem, and inexplicably on much of the skirt. Even the fine edge of her veil seemed to have collected old dried seed heads and fingerprints of dust. As for her hands—as Anne had warned, they were beyond redemption without a good scrub to remove ingrained soil. What a hopeless impression she would make on this man whose opinion seemed to matter to her. She hissed in exasperation, wiped her palms ineffectually down her skirts, and prepared to approach.

Anne Malinder was there before her.

Of course she was, Elizabeth acknowledged in silent

disgust. She would have been waiting for him. Wrapped around in her flattering cloak, which did not quite cover the lovely gown or disguise its deep neckline. A light veil drew attention to her oval face, the carefully plucked brows, those deeply sparkling eyes, fixed even now with warmth and invitation on Elizabeth's husband. Elizabeth could do nothing but momentarily close her eyes to the obvious comparison with her own appearance. And recall Jane Bringsty's blatant accusations.

When she opened them it was to watch the little scene—surely carefully planned by the lady at the centre of it—as if it were an episode in some dramatic tale of high chivalry of King Arthur's Court. The knight returning from a difficult quest, weary and weatherbeaten, stern and solemn, to answer his lady's bidding. The lady, polished and gracious, placing one white hand on her champion's arm, looking up into his face with such practised ease. The knight inclining his head to hear the words drop from those enticing lips. How often had Elizabeth seen those exact gestures used by the Malinder girl? She stalked forwards to join the gilded tableau that had no place for her in it, feeling neither polished nor gracious. She was more like Morgan Le Fay, she acknowledged with a sharp edge of black humour, an ill-wishing spirit arriving on the scene. She arrived perfectly in time to hear Anne murmur in the softest of voices.

'I have missed you, Richard. I could hope that you have missed me—a little.'

And to see Richard smile down into his cousin's upturned face. 'Anne…of course I have—' What other he would have replied they were not to discover because Elizabeth's sudden presence brought the welcome to a halt.

'I was just telling Richard how much *we* have missed him, dear Elizabeth. That we are so grateful for his safe return.' Anne's smile was brilliant. The obvious change of pronoun rattled in Elizabeth's head. The down-flutter of thick lashes on to smooth cheeks clawed at her gut. Deliberately she forced an equally complacent smile. The words, beyond a mere greeting, were far more difficult.

'Welcome home, my lord. It is as your cousin says.'

'Elizabeth.'

He smiled at her, the eye contact deliberately strong. With one hand as filthy as her own, he drew a gentle caress down the length of her arm from shoulder to wrist. *As if he truly cared*, she thought. *As if to ask—are you well? Are you dealing with your grief?* She felt the bright blood rise to her cheeks, when he leaned to press a fleeting kiss to the edge of the veil at her temple.

'You appear to have been busy in my absence,' he remarked, his smile becoming wry as he took in her appearance.

'Yes, I have.'

Elizabeth took a breath in despair. Was he aware of Anne's perfect little hand still possessively on his sleeve? He looked weary, she thought, bone-deep, noting the grim lines beside eyes and mouth, perhaps too weary to pick up any nuances in the girl's greeting. Nor did he resist when Mistress Anne tugged again on his sleeve and encouraged him inside the keep. Elizabeth could hear her words fade into the distance. 'Come, Richard. You must be tired and thirsty… I have instructed the cook to prepare some of your favourite mutton pasties.'

Has she really! Mutton pasties, indeed! And why did I not know that Richard enjoyed mutton pasties?

Spirits sinking to the depths of her mired shoes, as she turned to follow, Elizabeth came face to face with Jane Bringsty standing just a little above her on the top of the staircase. What was written on her face could not be mistaken. Her eyes were fierce and hot, not well disposed to any one of the party—not even her mistress, who refused, so the glare announced, to open her eyes to what was going on under her very nose!

Implacably Elizabeth held Jane's glare and shook her head. Whether the silent instruction was clear or not, Jane immediately turned her back with surprising fluency for so solid a figure and vanished, leaving Elizabeth to follow at her leisure, in no way comforted, silently calling down curses on everyone concerned.

And nursing a sore heart.

Within an hour, the weary soldiers had gathered in the Great Hall to relive in vivid detail the success of the expedition to ensure that all Malinder strongholds were secure. Vast platters of meat were brought in. Ale flowed liberally. The volume of sound rose with the amount of food and drink consumed, as the exploits of the soldiers waxed in bravery and daring. It was an atmosphere of minor celebration that Richard did nothing to curb, so the feast brought the campaign to an end on a high note until all that was left were the bones and scraps for the dogs to gnaw, the High Table set with cups of hippocras and platters of sweetmeats.

Very soon, however, Mistress Anne began to shuffle on her stool in clear discomfort. The blood leached from her face, leaving a greenish tinge to her complexion, not complimentary to her russet hair. Her fingers clutched around the chased stem of her pewter cup. She pressed her hand to her stomach uncertainly.

'Perhaps I've eaten too much.' She caught her bottom lip with her teeth with evident force. 'Too many sweetmeats, I expect.' Her skin had become alarmingly pale with a sheen of sweat on her top lip.

'The hippocras is too spiced, perhaps—it may have that effect. I'll speak with the cook about a lighter hand with the nutmeg.' Elizabeth looked sharply at her, a wave of suspicion racing along her spine as the girl's symptoms took her attention, the slick of sweat, the darkened pupils.

A muffled groan was the only reply as Anne folded her lips

close. She rose to her feet, awkwardly, hands pushing down hard on the table before her. 'I must go... The wine! I think that...' Anne's hand was now pressed to her lips. 'I feel most unwell...my head aches so...' And Anne turned, staggered somewhat and fled the room, holding her hands to her mouth as she escaped.

Elizabeth sat as if turned to stone. This was no chance chill, no reaction to the spices in the wine. She knew exactly what this was and was consumed with fear, a fear that was enhanced when, by fate or ill luck—or perhaps by design— Jane Bringsty entered the room from the direction of the kitchens to approach the high table. The expression on her face as she passed the fleeing Anne was bland, beautifully controlled, but unmistakably, to Elizabeth's experienced eyes, smug.

Had not Jane Bringsty poured the wine for them all?

Elizabeth could not take her eyes from Jane's face, struck with a terrible conviction. Jane's brows rose infinitesimally as she caught her mistress's regard, and with supreme satisfaction she held the eye contact. There might even have been a little smile hovering in the tight corners of her lips. And Elizabeth knew! Her fingers clamped on the edge of the table. What could she possibly do or say? If Jane, her serving woman, was guilty, then so was she. Her lips felt stiff, her mind unable to grasp the full horror of what Jane had done. The tension stretched, Elizabeth to Jane Bringsty, with a tangible metallic reality in the atmosphere comfortably redolent of cooked meat and wood smoke. Elizabeth found herself barely able to breathe as her mind raced with sheer terror.

What if Anne Malinder were to die?

Abruptly Elizabeth rose to her feet.

'If you will excuse me, my lord. There are things that need my attention here. I will leave you to your ale. Jane—I need your help.'

She did not even look at Richard—dared not, for fear of

what she would see, or what he would surely interpret from her own rigid demeanour—as she stepped down from the dais. Her belly churned, her face almost as white as Anne's. Without waiting to see if Jane followed, she strode towards an empty anteroom where they could achieve some degree of privacy. Once there, Elizabeth spun round and wasted no time on polite enquiry.

'What was it?'

'Nothing too potent. She'll not die from it.' Jane lifted her chin. There was no remorse. 'I know what I am about.'

'Jane…I *forbade* you…'

'I know you did, my lady—but she deserves every second of her present discomfort. She's little better than a common whore.' Jane's expression became contorted with bitter malice. 'I warned you. Since you disregarded me, I decided to ruffle the fine feathers of Mistress Anne Malinder.'

'Jane! Do you not realise what you have done?'

'It was easy enough to achieve,' Jane Bringsty replied, deliberately misunderstanding, hands folded comfortably at her waist, only triumph in the flat gleam of her eyes. 'You wouldn't do it, so I did.'

Frustrated beyond bearing at her failure to undermine Jane's belief in her own rightness, Elizabeth could only stare. Jane would never be contrite and Elizabeth knew she must damn her servant for her cruelty. Yet she knew why Jane had taken such a step, could not blame her entirely for her reading of Anne's character.

'Belladonna?' Elizabeth asked.

'Yes. As you should know. I taught you well enough.'

'I suppose I should thank God it's no worse. Aconitum could kill her.'

'She'll recover soon enough. Perhaps she'll return to Moccas. If you'll take my advice, my lady…'

But Jane's advice died on her lips, her eyes widening. And Elizabeth realised, with a prickling along her hairline, that they were no longer alone. Slowly she turned, the worst of her fears confirmed. *Richard*. Richard with barely controlled temper in the hard planes and angles of his face, sheer disbelief in his eyes as he had moved with soundless and strangely unnerving grace to stand beside them. His stare locked on Elizabeth's, held, as he chose to address her, not her servant.

'Tell me about this little incident. Am I wrong in my interpretation of what I have just heard and seen between you and your woman? Surely I am mistaken.' Soft, menacing.

Elizabeth, her heart beating thickly in her throat, sought for an explanation that would melt the cold fury in him. He could hardly have mistaken the playing out of the little scene, could he? The quick meeting of eyes that suggested conspiracy. Jane's terrible complacency, the intimation of *knowledge*. And now he awaited her explanation, condemnation looming beneath the soft questioning. Whilst it leapt into her mind that he should not be so quick to blame her, unfortunately the evidence was clear. Still, she would try to protect Jane.

'I do not take your meaning, my lord.' Her first reaction was to step back from the judgement in his face, but she stood her ground. Her mind sought feverishly for words that might defuse the sting of accusation. Could find none.

'Yes, you do. You take my meaning very well. You are no fool.' He seized her wrist, holding her close, unaware that his grasp was imprinting her flesh, although she felt she deserved no less. 'What do you know of this, Elizabeth? Tell me that I am mistaken.'

Elizabeth swallowed, wildly searching for an explanation. It went against the grain to lie, but to speak the truth would bring his wrath down on Jane's head.

'No, Elizabeth. I'm not mistaken, am I?' His voice dropped to a silky purr which was no less threatening, as he pulled her with him, a number of paces away from Jane's side. 'Are *you* responsible for Anne's reaction to something she ate or drank?'

'Why should I be responsible?' Would he take issue with her so harshly, without true evidence? Dark blue eyes held dark grey, a challenge issued—and accepted.

His voice was hard with accusation. 'There's something here. You have a reputation, madam wife, that preceded your arrival in my home. That you are not unacquainted with the black arts.' He waited only the length of a beat of her heart, fingers holding firm when she would have pulled away. 'Have you poisoned her?' His voice was hard-edged in outrage.

There was no denying it. Elizabeth drew on all her courage. Without hesitation, she leapt into the crevasse that had widened between them and made her admission. 'No. Not poison. She will not die. A mere discomfort from which she'll soon recover.' What could she say? Merely to deny all knowledge would, in the circumstances, be patently ridiculous.

'In her wine?'

Elizabeth did not even risk a sideways glance at Jane, standing motionless, listening to the exchange. 'Yes. In the hippocras.'

'You would poison my cousin?' The flare of anger that flooded Richard's face with contempt and disdain for her, as all his suspicions were incontrovertibly proved to be correct, all but singed her. He gave a harsh laugh. 'Why in God's name would you cause Anne to suffer? I suppose I should be thankful the potion was not dropped into *my* cup. Has Sir John advised you to take revenge on anyone who bears the name of Malinder, in repayment for Lewis's death? A few drops—of what?—in my ale and the de Lacy revenge would be complete.'

He did not trust her. Lewis's death loomed between them still, as did the old rifts between Malinder and de Lacy. Elizabeth saw the truth and feared it, but was now committed to protecting Jane and her own honour. 'It was belladonna.

And, no, my lord.' She drew all her de Lacy dignity around her. She was as cold as his temper was hot. How dare he be so ready to condemn her without evidence? 'If I had truly wished to kill you and avenge my brother, Richard, I would not have used belladonna. I would have used aconitum. It is far more difficult to amend. Your death would have been almost assured, and without remedy.' Now she showed her teeth in a bitter smile. 'Or, if your death had truly been my intent, even more effective would be a sword between your shoulder blades when you slept in my bed.' She remembered Robert's carelessly flippant words that she had overheard. De Lacy methods of retribution.

Richard appeared stunned by her apparent admission of culpability. 'So you were indeed guilty.'

Sensing Jane's approach, Elizabeth immediately put out a hand to touch her servant's wrist. For support or in warning. But she did not turn from the Lord of Ledenshall. Before Jane could speak, Elizabeth made her own confession. 'The responsibility is all mine, as you suspect. Attribute it to female jealousy, if you will. Because Anne Malinder has all the attributes that I lack.' She turned her head, her voice firm, fierce almost. 'Go now, Jane. I don't need you here. You know the remedy that will give Mistress Anne some relief. We don't want her to suffer overmuch. Her family would not wish it. Go now!' she repeated with all the authority she could muster when Jane would open her mouth to argue. 'There's nothing for you to do here. You will say nothing more about this affair.'

The outcome hovered on a knife edge. Elizabeth willed her servant to obey, uncertain, until with a brusque nod of the head Jane did as she was bid. Leaving the bridal pair to face each other in a vast space of vitriol and poison, far worse than any produced by the belladonna. Elizabeth at last wrenched her wrist from Richard's grasp, but they remained facing each other.

'I cannot believe what I have just heard from your own lips.'

'Yet you were quick to accuse me, were you not? Without evidence. Without firm knowledge that your cousin had been poisoned.'

'God's blood, Elizabeth! It was difficult not to see the guilt between the two of you. You and your damned serving woman. Her complicity—and yours—was written all over her face.'

'It was only difficult if you had no trust for me, and were determined to find proof.'

She watched him for a moment, refusing to be impressed by the magnificence of his anger, which lent vibrancy to his features, power to his splendid eyes. She took a breath against the lick of flame in her gut at the sheer magnetism of Richard Malinder before hugging her sense of injustice to her. How *dare* he judge and condemn her? As the injustice swam through her blood, she allowed another weighty issue to escape the guard of her teeth. She would not be the only one to shoulder blame here. She might regret her words, but despair drove her on.

'Did your journey through the March take you to Hereford?'

'Yes. What if it did?' She was rewarded with a narrowed look. 'What has that to do with your poisoning my cousin?'

'Since we are discussing the issue of *trust*, I suppose you found the time in Hereford to visit your mistress. And that the visit was not spent purely in conversation and discussion of the price of cloth in Hereford market.'

'What?' If he had appeared stunned at her previous admission, he was even more startled now. For a moment he was speechless, only able to glare at her, his wife who would dare to question his actions and his integrity.

'Did you expect no one to tell me?' she continued, refusing to be silenced by his fury. All the bitterness of her knowledge, her humiliation that he must find physical satisfaction elsewhere, flooded out. 'Of course they did, even before our marriage. It seems to be a matter of open gossip here. I had hardly been at Ledenshall a day before I was informed of your liaison with a woman in Hereford. *Joanna*, is it not? And yet you say *you* have no trust for *me*. You have not kept your marriage vows intact for long, have you—a matter of days? I would say that is the strongest evidence for mistrust.'

Richard frowned, a heavy black bar. 'It's not your concern who or where I might visit in Hereford,' he snapped.

'No?' All Elizabeth could think was that he had not denied it. So it was true after all. 'I am your wife. I think it is my concern.'

Nor did he deny it now. 'This is nonsense, madam. Nothing to do with the case at hand. You have admitted the deed. How dare you use poison against one of my family?' Richard strode to the window and back, prowling with restless power barely curbed. To come and stand before her again. 'Have I married a witch? A poisoner?'

'Have I married a murderer and adulterer?' Elizabeth to her horror found the words spoken before she could check them. How terribly destructive they were in their power. They were on her tongue, in the air between them, in pure retaliation before she could give it thought. 'The death of Lewis is still unproven. Anne may be uncomfortable for a few hours, but I have not plotted her death. My brother *is* dead!'

Which left nothing more to be said by either combatant. Elizabeth drew in a breath at the vileness of the accusation she had made.

'Richard… I did not…'

'You have said enough.'

Elizabeth resisted the urge to watch him as he flung out of the door. She would not let her grief show in her eyes, the devastation that he now thought of her as a woman who would use so despicable a weapon as poison to achieve her own ends.

What hope was there of trust, when what poor foundations there were had been so cruelly undermined? Destroyed by Jane Bringsty, who had thought to act in her mistress's best interest. Elizabeth laughed, a harsh sound without mirth at the disaster that faced her. If she did not laugh, she feared she would weep.

She made her way to the kitchen, to find Jane already employed there to produce a willow bark infusion to heal Anne Malinder. It would be easy enough, far easier than to heal her rift with Richard. Which path her relationship with her husband would follow now, she had no idea.

Chapter Nine

Anne Malinder took to her bed, too smitten, too overcome with weakening bouts of vomiting and purging to question the source of the problem that attacked her belly and her gut with such virulence. As Jane Bringsty had predicted, the belladonna was easily remedied and flushed from her system. After three days all that would remain to remind the lady of her ill luck was a severe ache between her eyes and a tender stomach that revolted against any thought of food. She was able to rise from her bed, sit beside the fire in her chamber and sip a cup of wine. There would be no lasting ill effects. It was the only good news at Ledenshall.

Richard Malinder prowled his castle in a cloud of bad temper. He kept his distance from everyone, burying himself in estate rolls and rent demands. It was rare, the inhabitants of the castle concluded in keen speculation, to see their lord so sharp and short in his responses. Richard kept his thoughts to himself. At the root of it all was one problem. Elizabeth. What had possessed him to be persuaded by John de Lacy to wed her? Within days of the ceremony she had cast his life into turmoil. What could he say to her when she had admitted to a wilful attack on the well-being of his cousin, perhaps on her life? And she, who had administered the lethal draught, had the temerity to accuse him anew of her brother's murder! After all that had passed between them, when he had thought they had come to some semblance of understanding, when riding home he had looked forwards to being with her again, she had astounded him by exhibiting the purest level of hatred against all Malinders. How could he have been so gullible? His hold over his control was tested to the limit as he slammed a pile of rent rolls down on the table in a cloud of dust. How could he have believed that this marriage had any hope of success?

Self-righteous anger burned through him.

But Richard Malinder had a conscience that did not make for an easy enjoyment of that anger, a conscience that forced him to face the truth of her other accusation. He had assumed her guilty before she had even confessed. And if he had indeed misread the situation… He bared his lips again in a snarl at the possible injustice here. But then, she had confessed, had she not? He remembered Robert's caustic words about poison and cold steel, as had she, uttered half in jest. Elizabeth had been standing there when they were made.

And yet he could not believe that she would use poison.

But she had admitted it, hadn't she?

And to accuse him of having a mistress in Hereford. To deflect attention from her own sins, of course. Richard's sense of injustice promptly flared into life again.

Heart-wrenchingly unhappy, Elizabeth took to her bed-chamber where she was driven to desperate measures to ease at least one of her wounds. It was not sensible, but her misery had driven her beyond sense. Surely it could not make the bottomless abyss that separated Richard from her any wider? It could, it did.

* * *

Discovering that he had misplaced a pair of gauntleted gloves, and since he could recall having them with him in Elizabeth's bedchamber, Richard went in search. He could have sent his squire—contemplated it—but that would have been cowardice. If he and his wife had nothing to say to each other, then so be it. On a brief knock, knowing she might well be there, he entered, to discover his wife seated before the hearth, in candlelight, a startled and distinctly uneasy expression when she looked up.

'What are you doing?'

Before her on the floor was a bowl of liquid, the candles. With a swift, practised gesture, she drew her hand across the surface, doused the flames.

'Nothing.'

'Don't lie, Elizabeth. What is this?' He towered over her, apprehension growing and with it a renewal of the anger that his growing respect—liking, even—for her should be once again compromised. Black arts practised at Ledenshall? He would never sanction it.

'I was scrying.' Elizabeth stood, brushing the ash from her skirts, and looked him full in the eye.

'Scrying?' He knew what that was, felt a lurch of his heart. His voice dropped to a harsh murmur as if they might be overheard, but did not disguise his anger, although at the practice itself or for Elizabeth's safety he could not have said. 'You would use such practices in my home? Do I want my wife apprehended and burned in the fire as a witch?'

Elizabeth tilted her chin. 'Since no one other than we two knows what I do here, then I doubt *that* will happen.'

Richard ignored the challenge. 'What are you doing? Discovering more successful means to rid yourself of my cousin?' The sneer was heavy.

So he would damn her again and again, without proof. 'I don't need scrying for that.' Elizabeth hesitated for only a second before stirring the small flames into a conflagration. 'I am trying to see the face of Lewis's murderer.'

Which brought Richard up short. 'Ah! So that's it. Cheap revenge, Elizabeth! So tell me, did you see my face in your scrying bowl?'

'No.' Her reply was candidly direct. 'I did not. I see nothing but darkness.'

'But you don't trust me. You can't accept my word that I am innocent. I doubt you ever will.' Now the sneer was overlaid with terrible bitterness.

Elizabeth could not afford to soften. He did not trust her either. 'I have no experience in my life to lead me to put my trust in any man. I don't know you, Richard Malinder, beyond the shortest of acquaintances and your expressions of innocence. They may be shallow and empty for all I know of you.'

A desperately bleak admission that Richard refused to acknowledge. He focused instead on the present. 'How can you be so indiscreet?' He flung out his hand in frustration at her waywardness. 'I at least expect discretion from you.' He grasped the bed hanging at his side, tugging it impatiently into shape, to find a cloth-wrapped package fall from the folds to land at his feet. 'What's this?'

Elizabeth shook her head.

Scooping it up, Richard unwrapped it with impatient fingers. Two wax figures, tightly bound, obscene in their crude sexuality, lay in his hand. Suddenly he was very still. He heard Elizabeth draw in a hiss of a breath.

'Elizabeth!' Richard looked from the images to his wife, incredulous. 'Answer me. This is even worse. What is this?'

And Elizabeth could not hide her horror. 'Witchcraft!' she whispered.

'Witchcraft! Well, you'll know all about that. And if these—these objects—are what they seem to be...' He bared his teeth in a snarl. 'Do you think me incapable of getting a child on you without the aid of this obscenity?' His eyes, usually so cool and controlled, blazed.

'No… It's not my doing.'

'Are my skills as a man so limited, then? I don't recall your complaining that I was unable to perform, that I was incapable of taking your virginity.'

Elizabeth still could not tear her eyes from the slick wax of the two creatures, the traces of dark hair, the limbs forced into stark proximity. 'I did not make them.'

'Then your serving woman did. I recall the herbs in our bed on our wedding night. Send for her.' He made as if to throw the figures into the fire.

Elizabeth sprang forwards. 'No…!' She grasped his arm, fingers digging deep.

'Why not?' But he halted.

'Don't, I beg of you. These are…difficult magic. Fire could harm you if they burn, if they melt…'

And Richard saw such anguish in her face it stopped him, forced him to drop his hand. 'Send for your serving woman.'

Dour and uncommunicative, Mistress Bringsty came to stand just within the door, heavy with self-righteousness. Her scowl took in the whole room until it lighted on the wax images. Elizabeth saw her stiffen, all expression on her face wiped away.

'Did you do this?' Richard demanded immediately. 'Is this your work?'

'No, my lord, it is not.'

'Can I believe you?' He looked from one to the other of the two women. 'Can I believe either of you?'

'These are harmful images, imposing the will of another. Jane would not hurt me,' Elizabeth answered for her.

'But she might hurt me! Who knows what the pair of you are plotting?'

'No, my lord,' Jane replied simply. 'I would not harm *you*. Only those who would bring harm or pain to my mistress. Lady Elizabeth cares for you more than you know. More than she knows. Why should I harm you?'

'I suppose I should be grateful!' Shaken to the core at what was going on in his home, Richard found himself unable to think of a further response. 'Get rid of these. I presume you know how.' Pushing them into Jane's hands, he stalked out, any thought of the gloves quite vanished.

'Whose are these? Who put them here?' Now Elizabeth allowed herself to express the fear that Richard's accusations had kept in check.

'I don't know. Nor how they got here.' Elizabeth could feel Jane's tension, a palpable thing in the room, which did nothing to ease her own. 'Someone far too interested in you and your lord's marriage.' Jane managed a bleak smile. 'Don't worry, my lady. I'll destroy this abomination, with no lasting effects. I'll not allow anyone to harm you.' At the door Jane turned to look back. 'You should have let me tell him the truth, lady.'

'Should I? Well, he certainly won't trust me now, will he?'

The sheer width and depth of the abyss between the Lord and Lady of Ledenshall was painted in the gloomiest of colours when two days later Richard walked into the small parlour where Elizabeth broke her fast. Acting on impulse and her careful training as chatelaine, and perhaps with an intent to mend the breach, Elizabeth rose to her feet, poured and carried a cup of ale to her husband when he came to the table.

His expression was glacial as he looked at the cup, at his wife.

'Thank you. But, no.' He deliberately walked around her

to pour his own ale, leaving her standing with the cup in her hands. Her cheeks were suddenly white as the ash in the fireplace, her eyes dark with distress.

'Richard.' Elizabeth's voice was clear, commanding. She might have been standing on the battlements to face a besieging army as she demanded Richard's attention. Tall and straight, the elegant stemmed cup held in both hands.

Richard turned his head, brows raised in polite and freezing enquiry.

Quite deliberately Elizabeth lifted the goblet to her lips. Drank one mouthful, and then another, never once taking her eyes from his face. Then once more.

'That should be sufficient to bring me a painful death, I think.' She placed the cup carefully on the table at her side. 'If I am still alive and well, I shall be present at the mid-day meal as usual. You will have to decide, Richard, if you are willing to sup with me.' She swept past him, head high, all arrogant pride. 'As you see, as yet I have no ill effects from the ale.'

'Elizabeth…' Richard stretched out a hand.

Elizabeth ignored it. She closed the door behind her with the quietest click.

Hell and the devil! What had possessed him to that piece of provocation, other than sheer bad temper after another restless night? He knew he had been wrong to reject Elizabeth's olive branch. Knew immediately he had acted that it was graceless and unwarranted, cruel, even, but he had been driven by a band of hurt around his heart that he could not dislodge. Herbs and dried flowers between the sheets were one thing—old wives' stuff, harmless enough. But scrying, wax figures—it made his blood run cold. Did she really hold such a low opinion of his sexual powers? She had shivered beneath him willingly enough. Pure masculine anger bubbled to turn his blood from ice to raging fire. She had made no complaint in his bed, none at all. As he recalled, she had responded with astonishing readiness, had warmed and arched under his hands. What had prompted her to resort to so blatant a piece of witchcraft to lure him into her bed? His potency had never been in question.

As for the black arts, how could he pretend either ignorance or acceptance of such diabolical practices in the hands of his wife and her woman? Turning a blind eye was not a possibility. Yet now he had hurt her—again! Guilt and contempt for his lack of control whipped his unsettled emotions into turmoil, overlaid by a slick of admiration for his wife. As a challenge, her draining the cup of ale had been a powerful blow with a heavy gauntlet and Richard knew it.

What was it that her serving woman had said, surprising enough to grasp his attention, the words even now lingering in his mind?

Lady Elizabeth cares for you more than you know. More than she knows.

What should he do now?

Elizabeth wept helplessly as she had not wept since the death of her mother and she a small child. How could he be so cruel? How could he believe so ill of her? The damage was beyond repair, as evidenced by her empty bed at night—and every night since Richard had returned. Her heart was as empty and desolate as her bed.

Jane Bringsty folded her in her generous arms, murmuring words of comfort until Elizabeth could cry no more.

'Hush. He matters so much to you, sweetheart,' Jane crooned, unusually soft.

'Yes.' A bald admission.

'He could be the dark man of the scrying,' Jane warned, her cheek against Elizabeth's hair. 'He could be your enemy.'

'No. He is not, unless by my own making. It seems that I have made him so. How could I have acted as I did, Jane?'

'He hurt you, dear one. And you struck back.'

'I did not think. He hates me now.'

'Never.'

Misery returned. 'Am I so unappealing, Jane, that I need you to deploy the black arts to claim his regard, as he accused? Am I so lacking in glamour that I must use poison to remove a rival? I know I cannot hold a candle to the attractions of Anne Malinder.' Unwittingly revealing the cause of her sadness.

'I'm sorry I have brought you pain, lady.'

Elizabeth pushed herself upright, wiping away the tears. 'I know you did it for me. But the divide between myself and Richard is, I think, impossible to bridge.'

'Was there ever any chance before?' Jane asked caustically. 'He was quick to judge, quick to condemn. Where was the respect in that?'

And that was the crux of the matter, weighing on Elizabeth's heart, her soul.

Richard forced himself to do a lot of hard thinking, with unpalatable results. When the flames of his righteous anger had died to a mere flicker, common sense began to hold sway. It was not in Elizabeth's nature to use poison. The sharp blade of a knife, perhaps, but not poison. So where did the guilt lie? Was it not obvious? A short stout figure holding a pair of wax figures, and having the knowledge to take care of them, to dispose of them…

Mistress Jane Bringsty.

She had the skills, of that he was certain. What her motive might be—how could he be expected to know what motivated such a woman? The key question now was, did Elizabeth know what her serving woman was about, had she given her permission? But did Mistress Bringsty need her mistress's permission to apply her black arts? Richard's new sense of moderation wavered at the thought that they might be in collusion, and then settled under another brisk dose of common sense. Even after a short acquaintance, he knew beyond doubt that Mistress Bringsty was perfectly capable of acting on her own initiative, and to the devil with the consequences. Elizabeth, he supposed, finally, had acted from some sort of misplaced honour to protect her servant. Whereas he had been intolerant and judgmental. He had been neither kind nor understanding…

So much for their original pact to deal openly with each other, to deny the opportunity for outside pressures to divide them. How rapidly they had fallen into a morass of distrust and wounding accusations. And since the first harsh words had been his own, the burden was on his shoulders to make his peace with her. A vague unease churned in his gut. It was worse than going on campaign against a chancy enemy.

God protect him against difficult and opinionated women.

Richard found Elizabeth in her chamber. He knocked, allowed her the time to bid him enter, or go away, closed the door quietly at his back. It was a time for careful strategy if this contest of wills was to be laid to rest and peace restored.

She was sitting in the window seat, half-curled on to the wide cushioned ledge with an open book on her lap, the cat curled and asleep at her feet. He could see from the doorway that it was a little Book of Hours, gilded and painted in bright jewel tones, its binding tooled in rich leather. He got the distinct impression that her attention was not on the devotional pages. She raised her head as he came in, but did not speak, did not move. The light was behind her, touching the edges of her veil with soft shadows. He could not see her face, her reaction to him, so fell back, as he must, on instinct and an innate integrity to deal with her as she deserved. Perhaps it would also ease the knot of guilt in his own gut. He walked slowly forwards to stand before her, but halted before she could think that he would intimidate, deliberately keeping his voice even, unthreatening.

'The book. It is very fine.'

'Yes. It was a gift to me from the Prioress at Llanwardine when I left.' Elizabeth smoothed her fingers over the black script, taken aback since she had expected more bitter recriminations. 'She said that I had no calling to the life of a religious, but perhaps the words, the beauty of it, would bring me solace.'

'And do they? Bring you solace?'

'No.' Her voice was little more than a whisper. 'They bring me no ease.'

He took a step nearer. 'We promised to talk to each other, Elizabeth. To be honest as far as it was possible.'

'Yes. How impossibly long ago that seems.'

'Why did you not tell me the truth? Why did you not tell me it was your woman's doing?'

Sharp surprise jabbed at her. She closed the book, put it aside and stood so that their eyes were more nearly on a level. 'How did you know?'

'When I finished being furious with you, I knew you could not have done it. So there was only one other possible, obvious source. Why did you not tell me?'

And Elizabeth answered with devastating candour, 'Because Jane is mine, which makes me responsible. And because you believed me guilty before you even knew there had been a crime. You can't deny it.'

No, he could not. So he made the apology. 'I was at fault. I misread the signs between you. I was entirely wrong. I have no excuse.'

Silence stretched between them. Elizabeth stood with her hands at her sides, at a loss. *Now what do I say? What does he want of me?* Until Richard inclined his head with solemn formality. 'My judgement was amiss. Will you forgive me, my wife?'

'Yes.' Her heart shivered uncomfortably at his words, but still she could not admit to the flicker of relief. 'But Jane still did it. And your cousin suffered.'

He drew in a deep breath. 'But why? What could possibly have been her motive?' When Elizabeth would have looked away from the embarrassment of it, he placed his hands on her shoulders, forcing her to face him. 'You must tell me.'

Elizabeth sighed. 'It is just that—' Well, she would tell him, whatever the outcome between them. 'Anne sets herself in your way to catch your attention, to my detriment—which I admit is not difficult. Jane is jealous for me, and sought to teach her a lesson.'

Richard was surprised into a bark of laughter, amazement evident. 'But she is my cousin. A mere child, even if she is a nuisance with her airs and consequence. She enjoys fine clothes and the attention of those around her. As the only girl in her family, she was always indulged and petted. I have known her for ever. A child, surely.'

'Then you have not looked recently, Richard,' Elizabeth responded with a decided edge, yet she was conscious of the warmth of reassurance from this blind admission, the casual rejection of Anne's charms. 'She is a child no longer, as she frequently informs us!'

His brows arched. 'I thought your complaint was that perhaps I had looked *too* closely!'

'I would not so accuse you.' For in truth she had never seen him encourage the girl. 'That does not mean that Anne does not have an eye for you. She flirts—you cannot be unaware.'

'No. I see it. But it's a silly girl's foolishness.'

'I could not be half as skilled.' Elizabeth looked down at her fingers, twined them together to still them. 'I understand she is very like Gwladys in colouring. She is very beautiful.'

'Yes, she is,' Richard admitted, accepting the consequence

of his own thoughtless acceptance of a girl he had known from childhood. 'And, yes, Anne has the look of Gwladys, more so as she has grown. They were related, of course. Did you suspect me of trifling with her, within weeks of our marriage?' He was unsure whether to be flattered that Elizabeth cared enough, or annoyed that she would misjudge him. Until the deep sapphire eyes that took and held his left him in no doubt of the depths of pain caused by Anne's sly behaviour and his own carelessness. He should have known. He should have seen what was happening. He smiled at Elizabeth, a little sadly at the hurt he had caused, then lifted a hand to draw his fingers down her cheek. A most tender gesture that, if he had known it, melted the final ice crystals of Elizabeth's resistance. 'I am innocent of all charges, Elizabeth, except for an appalling naïvety in allowing the situation to go unchecked. Anne is no danger to you. Will you believe me?'

She tilted her head to watch him, then nodded. 'Yes. I am sorry for the things I said.'

'And I. I did not murder your brother.'

'No. You made an oath that you did not.'

'But it still hovers there between us, a dark entity of mistrust, doesn't it?' he acknowledged. 'Elizabeth?'

It struck her that he was frowning at her, even a little unsure, as if searching for the right word. 'What is it?'

'Was it Anne who told you I had a mistress in Hereford?'

'Yes. Joanna.'

'I did once. I have had no dealings with Joanna since long before you came to me. I ended the understanding between us.' Faint colour slashed his cheekbones. 'You are my wife. I would not hurt you or humiliate you by keeping a mistress. I promised to honour you. My vows, despite your accusation, are intact.'

'Oh. I thought that…'

'Well, now you do not need to think. I have told you the truth.'

'Yes.' Words were difficult for her, but a strange, sweet relief pulsed through her. 'I hated it,' she admitted despite her usual reticence. 'I could understand your need…but, I hated it.'

'I regret our estrangement,' he said, his smile a little sad. 'When I came home I found myself looking forwards to seeing you. And then found myself dragged into an unexpected drama. It's not what I would have wanted.' He lifted her hands to enclose them warmly, palm to palm, within the shelter of his, a reverse of his gesture on their first night together. Infinitely reassuring. Then stiffened a little as her sleeves fell back from her wrists. He saw the fading bruises.

'I did that.' His eyes widened, bleak with regret.

'Yes.' But there was no condemnation in her reply. Instead she turned her hands so that her fingers might interlock with his. 'You were so angry.'

'Forgive me,' he murmured, horrified that he should have marked her without thought, and vowed silently that he would never do so again. 'I would never deliberately hurt you. Even though it seems I have done so.' He sighed, bent his head to press his mouth against the tell-tale shadows.

'I do not fear you.'

'There are no excuses.'

'No. Not for either of us.'

Richard searched her face as once more he lifted a hand to draw his knuckles down her cheek. 'Perhaps I can make amends.'

'Perhaps you can,' Elizabeth found herself replying in like vein, the flutters that had set up in her belly increasing with anticipation. Perhaps it was possible for the hurts to be mended between them after all.

'The cat is asleep, I see.' Smiling, he glanced down to their feet, a warm glint in his eye.

'Yes.'

'Then I'll risk it.' He pressed his mouth against the tip

of each finger in turn before splaying her hands against his chest. 'If you are a clever woman, you will notice that my heart beats hard. I have a need of you, lady, if it's safe for me to come to your bed.'

'I'll welcome you there.'

In spite of her words, Elizabeth did not find it easy. Too much lay between them, too many angry words on both sides for her to open her arms and her mind to him in seamless intimacy. She shivered a little, muscles tense, aware all over again of her inadequacies in her relationship with this man. But Richard unlaced her gown with deft competence, velvet rubbing and catching against velvet, allowing it to fall when she might have clutched it to her, made love to her slowly, tenderly, inexorably when he felt her resistance. Used limitless patience to conquer her wariness, to overwhelm the hurt he knew she must have felt. To heal her anxieties over the bitter seeds of infidelity sown by Anne Malinder.

Until the residue of the clash of wills between them gradually softened, dissipated, dissolved under his slow caresses with hands and mouth. Soft touches, gentle pressures. A healing of the wounds they had both inflicted so that Elizabeth found she could sigh against him, melt into him. And confidence returned to her as the strains vanished under the heated glow of her skin.

'I am so sorry,' Richard murmured, his words muffled against her breast. 'Sorry at my lack of trust. Sorry at my hard words.'

'And I regret my temper,' Elizabeth's breath hitched as his tongue aroused a nipple. 'My lack of faith in your integrity.'

There were no more words. Elizabeth's mouth traced a path along Richard's shoulder to where she could feel the heavy beat of his blood in the little hollow at the base of his throat. There she paused to savour the life-force that drove him as she allowed her hands to drift and mould the muscles of his back and hip.

Richard's patience grew thin under her assault until it snapped.

'Do we need the power of wax figures?' His eyes were forceful, holding hers.

'No.' Elizabeth did not look away. 'You need no power but your own.'

Sliding into her, Richard's possession was forceful, thorough, outrageously satisfying, until Elizabeth found herself smiling, when she had thought she would never smile again.

Then physical desire flamed to blot out all harsh memories, all differences between them.

Chapter Ten

With clear weather from the west, the garrison at Ledenshall took to training in earnest and with some relief. It might be hard graft, but the physical demands relieved the monotony of the winter months. The Malinder men-at-arms stretched and worked their muscles as they honed their skills with sword and dagger, pike and halberd, in hand-to-hand combat. Every room in the castle, Elizabeth decided at some time within the first week of this activity, rang with the clash of metal against metal, the bellowed orders of the sergeant-at-arms. The plates of armour, susceptible to damp and tarnish, were unwrapped, cleaned, polished, repaired. Bows restrung, arrows refeathered.

Inevitably it became dull work. A bright morning saw a series of straw bales dragged into the flat combat area outside the barbican and the setting up of an archery practice in the form of a contest, with, to inspire interest and a depth of concentration, some serious betting on the outcome. It would, as the Lord of Ledenshall knew, add spice to the proceedings.

It had the desired effect of a holiday festivity. The sun shone, lifting pale winter spirits. Benches were provided for those who would be an audience, Master Kilpin offered to record the bets and a keg of ale miraculously appeared. The servants who could escape their tasks ventured out. Elizabeth dutifully took her seat. Mistress Bringsty stood behind with arms folded. Even Anne drifted down from her chamber, despite the keenness of the wind, well muffled in winter furs, knowing they would enhance her beauty.

The contest began. They used the longbow, much loved for its accuracy, speed of delivery of the long flight arrows, its power when delivering the final blow. Six arrows each to be notched, sighted and loosed at the distant, but distinct, splash of colour. Shoulder and arm muscles flexed and stretched to pull the impressive yew bows with their notched horn tips and bowstrings of plaited hemp. Robert Malinder proved to be more than good and preened with typical, but charming, lack of modesty and an extravagant bow. His appreciative audience applauded after much informed betting on his achievements. His expertise was well known.

But Elizabeth wanted to see Richard, drawn to compete towards the end. A little thrill of anticipation shivered over her skin. It mattered to her, ridiculously so, that he should win, should prove himself in victory. How foolish she was! But that did not stop her waiting and hoping.

Only to be disappointed. Elizabeth quickly realised that Richard would never win, nor was it expected. Even the man himself admitted it with a negligent shrug as he flung himself down on the bench beside her to watch and cheer on his garrison. Archery was not his sport, never had been. His lack of the ultimate skill was accepted with tolerant good humour. After all, none could doubt the excellence of the Lord of Ledenshall with a sword and his ability with a lance astride a horse in the formal jousts. Ah, now there was a knight who could hold his own in any company.

In the end it did not matter. Elizabeth watched him as he took his stance, sideways to his selected target, as he ignored Robert's enquiry as to which target he intended to hit and should they all take cover. Watched as the planes of muscle flowed and rippled under his tunic, smooth as water, as he pulled back the bow to full stretch, thighs braced, and sighted the yard-long arrow, as his dark hair was lifted by the light wind. Saw the utter concentration on his face, in his narrowed gaze, as he aimed and loosed the arrow. Saw and heard also his self-deprecating good humour, his handsome features vivid with laughter, as he failed to hit the centre.

Elizabeth saw and heard, allowed her eyes to linger on the long, lean lines of him and sighed. Her blood ran hot, her cheeks flushed. She thought, with a little puff of breath, that she was even more foolish than she had realised.

The contest came to its end. Master Kilpin stepped forwards to oversee the payment of the bets and Richard looked round the assembled crowd. 'Does anyone else here wish to test his skill? Perhaps we have a champion not yet discovered.'

On her bench, Elizabeth fidgeted as her fingers itched to hold a bow again, to feel the taut strength of the bowstring as she notched her arrow. It had been so long.

'My mother would forbid me,' Anne murmured softly, disparagingly, as if she sensed her intention. 'So presumptuous! I wager Richard would not approve.'

Which settled it. Elizabeth stood. '*I* will. I will take part,' she stated, raising her voice. 'If someone would be willing to risk a coin or two in a small wager on me hitting the target.' She looked around her, caught the interested glances, the sly nudges.

'Well, now… This I had not expected.' Richard held out his hand and beckoned her forwards. 'I presume, in the face of such a challenge from my wife, that I must be the source of the wager.'

Elizabeth walked forwards to the line, delighted with his response, tucked her veil back into the neck of her gown out of the way, already having shrugged out of her cloak. Richard selected for her one of the smaller bows. Picked out six well-fledged arrows, sleek with their grey-goose feathers, and stood at her side. His lips curved, his eyes gleamed, caught up by the unexpectedness of the moment. Elizabeth took the bow, yet made no effort to face the target.

'What is your wager, my lord?' A solemn enquiry.

'What is your intent, my lady?' Equally solemn.

'To hit the target every time. Otherwise I would not put myself on display here.' Now her lips twitched.

'Do I detect the sin of pride here? Then I'll wager a gold noble that you cannot do it, my lady.' He turned his head, raised his voice. 'Master Kilpin. Do you hear?'

'I do. For shame, my lord! The lady deserves your support.'

'And so much for faith in my talents. Only one, my lord?'

Richard looked at her for a long moment, at the suddenly flirtatious curve of her lips, of the down-sweep of dark lashes. So many hidden facets to this woman whom he had married simply because she would bring a strong alliance in the March, hoping for an easy, tolerant relationship for political ends. Hoping that at best they would not dislike each other. Yet here she challenged him and he did not dislike it at all. What he felt for her was… Well, he wasn't sure. But it was far different from easy tolerance. Then she glanced up at him, over the deadly weapon she held with such assurance, and his heart thudded, a strong bound in his chest, enough to take his breath.

All he could see, all he could think of, in that moment, was the indigo depth of her gaze that drew him in, then seemed to swallow him whole until escape was beyond him. He drowned in the rich blue sensation of sweetness. The warmth of the sun on his shoulders, the ripple of conversation around him faded. Her lips were parted as if beckoning him to take and taste. And did he not know how softly seductive they could be? They were all but a breath away, whilst her body was close enough for him to savour the sharp herbal scents she used in bathing, to feel the warmth of her skin as if the layers of linen and silk did not exist. Desire punched at his gut with astonishing speed. The muscles of belly and loins tightened uncomfortably, shocking him into an awareness of his very public surroundings.

'Richard…?' Elizabeth prompted.

Taking himself to task with a grimace, he bowed with formal acceptance. 'Pride goes before a fall, Elizabeth.' His breath was warm against her face as he whispered in her ear, setting up a trail of shivers along her spine. 'Very well!' he announced for the benefit of the crowd. 'Two gold nobles that you do not strike the target.'

Indulgent laughter rippled around them. Confident, assured, Elizabeth took her stance, lifted one of the arrows, notched it, pulled the bowstring to her ear as she had indeed been taught. Focused on the target. And let the slender missile fly.

It hit the straw bale. Of course it did. She had not a doubt of it.

A silence settled on the little crowd.

She could feel Richard's eyes on her. With an outward serenity she took another arrow, dealt with it in exactly the same manner. Then another, and another. Calm, controlled, perhaps the slightest toss of her head when she came to the final arrow, until all six were buried in the straw. And two of them within the red mark. A roar of appreciation rose around her. Elizabeth turned to Richard, flushed, bright eyed, successful. Victorious.

'You lost, my lord. You owe me two gold nobles.'

'So I do. And I will pay my debts.' He took the bow from her, sliding an arm around her waist as he did so. 'It seems that I need not fear for the defence of my home in my absence.' Then he leant close and surprised her by kissing first her cheek, then her astonished lips most publicly, which made her flush even more. She had won his notice, his admiration. His very public approval. 'So who taught you so masculine a sport to such effect?'

'It was Lewis,' she replied simply. Elizabeth refused to drop her gaze when she saw the bright humour suddenly quenched, saddened that her brother's name should cast them into a quagmire again, but refusing to allow the raw misery as memories flooded into the happy event. 'Lewis taught me,' she repeated. 'He delighted in angering Sir John. Lewis was very good. Better, I think, than Robert.'

'And so are you, very good. I think Lewis would have been proud of his pupil today. And of her courage.'

Richard could not, Elizabeth thought, have spoken better. He took her hand, palm against palm, allowing the warmth to soothe her sudden grief.

'Richard!' Anne Malinder, insistent despite her pale and beautiful fragility, was suddenly beside them, her elegant long-fingered hand on Richard's arm to draw his attention away from Elizabeth. 'I was impressed with your skill. I thought you were magnificent.'

Breathless, Elizabeth waited. Would he see what Anne was doing? Would he still be oblivious to her talent for flirtation?

Richard laughed. 'Then you must be blind, Anne. Here is your champion of the day. Not I, but my wife.'

A little line marred Anne's smooth forehead, her eyes widened. 'But is it seemly for the Lady of Ledenshall to promote herself in such a manner?'

'Undoubtedly it is. My wife was the magnificent one in this contest.'

His smile was for Elizabeth alone and she breathed out slowly in a moment of intense and blinding clarity. Somewhere between his wagering gold against her skill, and this blatant compliment, she had… Well, what? What was it that she had done? Had she fallen in love with Richard Malinder?

Elizabeth had no experience of love, but it was as if the arrows had struck her heart, wounding her for ever. Elizabeth might step back from an open avowal of love, but the realisation of strong emotion quivered through her, swamped her, filling her mind and her heart. But in a sudden moment of despair, it also kept her lips sealed. For how could she burden Richard with an emotion he did not want from her?

'Then perhaps you will teach me, dear Richard?' Anne persisted, dark lashes sweeping down to hide the emerald gleam of pure jealousy.

'No, cousin. Your brother would do a far better job of that than I.' Stepping back so that Anne had perforce to remove her hand, Richard raised Elizabeth's fingers to his mouth, a deliberate act of ownership, answering all her insecurities. 'Let us go in and celebrate your victory in a cup of wine.'

And, turning their backs on Anne Malinder, they walked together.

Perhaps it was the foolish achievement. Perhaps the warm acclamation. Or even the pride in her husband's face. For whatever reason Elizabeth opened her arms and her bed to her lord with a rare confidence and a light spirit. When he offered to demonstrate the accuracy of his own aim in fields other than archery, she encouraged him without reticence. Under the slyly skilful investigations of his hands and his mouth she discovered a whole tapestry of sensation of which she had no experience, and a lack of control that was unthinkable. Immediately, she struggled to free herself.

'No! You must stop…'

'Not in this life. You might even enjoy it.' Richard's tongue continued to slide along the edge of her collar bone to the swell of her breasts where he lapped at the swelling peak of a nipple. As for his fingertips—they knew no limitations as they dipped and tasted the dark wet heat between her thighs.

'I might…' If she had but known what *it* was. Elizabeth

held her breath as his teeth grazed along the soft skin of her belly. Her fingernails scored into his shoulders as she clung on.

'Unknown territory,' Richard murmured, his breath heating her skin, setting off little ripples. 'Look on it as an adventure. Afraid, Elizabeth?'

'No. Never…'

And Elizabeth found herself driven to grasp Richard's long-suffering shoulders even more fiercely as the shivers built in her belly, hot and sweet, to explode with bright light, like the tinted illustration of a shooting-star in one of Jane Bringsty's more questionable documents, all fire and sparkle.

'Oh!'

'A true understatement,' Richard remarked on a ghost of a laugh, still holding her safe, close guarded, as the tremors died away. Then with breathtaking speed he moved so that his body pinned her to the bed and she could not wriggle and escape. Not that she had the energy to do so until she recovered from the glory of it.

'You look very smug.' Elizabeth informed him, still shivering with the splendour of her discovery. His lips curved, his eyes gleaming in the soft darkness.

'So I do.' He pressed his smiling mouth to the shallow valley between her breasts. 'And now, my Amazon, you can use your womanly wiles to torture me beyond bearing.'

Elizabeth did so, with most satisfying results, overcome with her new-found confidence. Whilst Richard, roused and painfully ready, surrounded by her, driven to shattering completion by her, could only marvel at the depth of desire this complex woman distilled in him.

Chapter Eleven

'Richard. I miss David.'

Richard had just returned home after accompanying Robert and Anne along the March on part of their journey back to Moccas. He had been away almost two weeks. Elizabeth refused to admit either to him or to herself how much she had missed him. The days of Richard's absence had hung heavily. Hardly waiting for him to dismount from his horse, she had followed him to his bedchamber.

Richard seemed not to have heard her, so she tried again. 'I wish David was here.'

'I know.' Richard eased his thick leather jerkin from his shoulders, unbuckled his sword with a sigh of relief. 'And I see no remedy for it as long as David is under your uncle's authority. Perhaps when he's older he'll make a bid for freedom.'

Elizabeth pursed her lips. Increasingly estranged from her family, there had been no letters, no communication of any nature. Not that she had expected any, but she missed David and, when Richard was absent in the March and she was alone at night, she wept and dreamed of Lewis.

'Perhaps. But I wish I knew...'

'You wish you knew whose hand was on the blade, or whose gold bought the deed. You wish you knew whether it was mine.'

Uncomfortable, embarrassed, Elizabeth frowned down at her clenched fingers, astonished at how intuitively Richard could follow her train of thought.

'And I can do nothing to help you,' he continued as he stretched his hand to turn her face to his. 'Except perhaps this…'

Surprising her, he leaned forwards, his hand sliding around the nape of her neck to draw her close, then rested his lips against hers. A light caress of mouth against mouth, until the soft pressure hesitated, withdrew until a breath separated them, then returned, warmed, deepened. The kiss lasted longer than either expected. Nor did Richard release her when he lifted his lips, but continued to cradle her face in his palms. His eyes searched her face as he clearly followed a thought.

It had surprised him, and still did. A lot of things had surprised him recently. Like how much he had missed his wife over the previous days. How he had found his thoughts returning again and again to what she might be doing, his overwhelming concern being whether she was safe in his absence, whether she was content. Did she perhaps miss him? He dared not think along those lines, yet was forced to admit that he missed her. No, he had not expected this, and was uncomfortable with it. He frowned at her upturned face, held softly between his palms. The distrust was still there, however much he might try to deny it, and not much he could do about it, as he had just acknowledged. But the kiss had stirred his blood, his loins. He would like nothing better than to push her back on to the bed, strip her of that heavy woollen gown, no matter how elegant it might be, and rediscover the slender length of firm pale skin beneath. Nothing better than to stretch over her, flesh sliding against flesh, and bury himself in her to assuage the imperative demand that must be as obvious to her as to him. He could do all of that immediately…

He was brought back to the present, reminded that he was frowning at her, when Elizabeth touched her fingers to his face, in an attempt to reassure him. 'I don't mean to blame you, you know.'

'No. I don't suppose you do, but the wound doesn't heal, does it?' She winced at the bleakness, but Richard shook his head to clear his mind of sheer rampant desire and deal with Elizabeth's anxieties. He found it was becoming a need in him to do so. 'Well, my troubled wife, it's as quiet in the March as it will ever be. I could take you to Talgarth, I suppose, to visit your brother.'

'You could.' She discovered that she was holding her breath, not just from the kiss, but willing him to make the decision, to take the risk.

'I'll not willingly put your life in any jeopardy,' Richard said, weighing up the dangers. 'But Sir John can, I presume, be trusted to deal with us in a civilised manner on his territory. He would not choose to soil his own lair. And you are of his own blood after all. Lady Ellen would be more than pleased to welcome you.' He smiled at her, suddenly, devastatingly, warming her blood. 'I'll send a messenger to tell him we'll come. Then he can have no excuse that he was taken by surprise,' he added, drily cynical. 'I'd not wish to be repulsed as an invading force.'

'It's David's birthday within two weeks.'

'Well, then. What better time for a loving sister to visit her brother?'

Elizabeth returned his smile, and on impulse leaned forwards to press a fleeting brush of her lips to the corner of his mouth. An impromptu gesture that surprised her as much as it surprised him.

'We seem to be very much in agreement suddenly, my wife!'

'Do we not.'

'If you can arrange for some hot water, perhaps you would care to help me scrub the dust and debris of the roads from my suffering skin? Then I might be in a fit state to kiss you properly. As well as other gestures of my esteem...' His glance speculative, he brushed the pad of his thumb along the line of her jaw. 'And you can welcome me home in a manner completely suitable for a wife to show her appreciation of her lord.'

Swiftly Richard drew her close, hard against him, regardless of the dust and sweat, and captured her mouth with his. His hand smoothed slowly down her side, along the length of her from breast to hip. Came to a stop. He lifted his head. His hand moved again, to stroke over the fullness of hip, the dip of waist, back to the undeniable swell of breast.

She looked up quizzically, but with a glint of mischief.

'Curves, are they? Now when did you get these?'

Pleasure rippled through her, from her own satisfaction and Richard's awareness. Her reply was for Elizabeth positively arch. 'When you were not looking, it seems.'

'Perhaps I should look more closely.' Richard again framed her face with his hands, now aware of the flattering fullness that overlay her cheekbones, drawing attention to her magnificent eyes, the delicate arch of dark brows. The renewed demand in his loins, the force of his erection, thundered in his head. And this time his mouth held a heated promise that tingled through her blood, into her bones. 'Can we manage the hot water soon?' he whispered against the curve of her throat.

'It can be arranged, my lord,' she gasped, now as aware as he. 'Immediately.'

Elizabeth turned away to hide the sudden rush of heat to her face, the pleasure that sang in her heart. Yes, she had missed him, whatever her doubts and uncertainties, and she would welcome him home.

* * *

'So, what would you wager, lady? Will they open the gates? Or will Sir John drive us off in a hail of arrows?' Richard shifted in his saddle as his substantial armed escort drew rein on a slight rise, allowing them to look down on the principal source of power of the de Lacy family. Before them rose the brooding grey walls, the raised drawbridge and lowered portcullis of Talgarth.

Elizabeth did not know. Solid in her chest was a knot of foreboding and she understood Richard's reluctance. 'Perhaps we shouldn't have come.'

'It was not my choice, if you recall,' he responded sardonically.

Elizabeth glanced across at the compressed lips, the heavily engraved line between his brows. 'I'm sorry. But you did agree.'

There was no softening in him, instead the brutal truth. 'I had to bring you to prove to you I have David's interests at heart, did I not, after you and your family would accuse me of murdering Lewis!'

Which made Elizabeth bite her tongue. Such residual bitterness still between them when Richard let down his guard. The accusations of Sir John, and her own ambivalent acceptance of his oath to her that he was innocent, still rankled. The edgy silence between them stretched uneasily.

'There's a magpie on the branch to our left.' Behind them Jane Bringsty muttered with a hunch of her shoulders, apropos of nothing at all. 'It's looking at us. It's not a good omen.'

No one replied to that. Elizabeth cast a glance at the iridescent magnificence of the bird. No, it was not a good omen, but they had come this far. She shortened her reins and kicked her mount on to Talgarth.

The Malinders were to spend only two days at Talgarth. They were not turned away at the gates of the massive barbican, but it was made clear that they were accepted within the walls under sufferance. As their horses and escort were led away to their accommodations, the Malinders were bowed into the Great Hall with all the chilly hauteur that Sir John would have accorded an enemy whose presence he must tolerate. There on the dais stood Sir John himself with cold eyes, Lady Ellen smiling bravely at his side, risking her lord's disfavour with any show of warmth. Behind them Master Capel, black and brooding as one of the crows that gave their harsh cries over the battlements. Or perhaps more likely a bird of prey, Elizabeth decided, as she felt the power of the hooded eyes rest on them. And then there was David, who responded immediately as his heart prompted. Despite the warning lift of Sir John's hand, he leapt from the dais to hug his sister with obvious pleasure.

'Elizabeth! And Richard. I have so much to tell you. It is an age since…well, since I saw you last.' Elizabeth felt relief flood her body at his obvious well-being. But the relief was short-lived. For the bright welcome in his face was suddenly quenched, as a candle-flame under a snuffer, his lips folded in a straight line, giving his face an edgy maturity. There was trouble here, if she were not mistaken. But she could hardly broach that until they were alone.

'I think you have grown,' she merely stated instead. 'You are almost as tall as I.'

David would have replied, but was called to order by Sir John, who brusquely acknowledged the presence of the visitors in his home. Richard replied with equal composure and a curt inclination of his head. Ellen expressed her quiet pleasure. Master Capel preserved his habitual silence. Then the Malinders were shepherded away to the guest chambers.

'Do you know the sign against the evil eye?' Richard murmured to Elizabeth as they climbed the stair behind Sir John's uncommunicative steward.

Elizabeth, brows climbing at such an unexpected request,

glanced around to Jane, who followed close behind. Jane looked away. 'Yes,' she admitted.

'Then I suggest you use it. For all our sakes.'

'Master Capel?' Elizabeth too had picked up the strange implacability behind the calm stare that had flickered over the guests. It had been almost impossible to overlook it. The fervour, almost antagonism, the eyes that would search out every secret, every weakness. Elizabeth shivered at the memory.

Richard waited until the steward had gone, the door closed. 'Master Capel indeed. I wonder what his role might be in this household? What can possess Sir John to keep such a man at his side?'

'They say he is a necromancer,' Jane Bringsty interjected with flat certainty.

Elizabeth sighed. 'So I think. I don't like to think of David being here.'

'No. Nor I.' Richard cast an eye around the rooms assigned to them. 'Capel makes me think of bats and toads.' He grimaced at his fanciful thoughts as he strode to look out of the window to the mist-shrouded hills of Brecon that hemmed them in. 'I shall be glad to be gone from this place. It encourages me to sleep with my sword beneath my pillow.'

They had brought David a gift. A dark grey falcon with heavily barred wings and tail, complete with decorative jesses and bells and tasselled hood. A handsome bird from Richard's own mews, a bird that would fly true and give David much enjoyment. But the lad was neither to see nor to appreciate the gift. Not an hour after their arrival it was announced that the young lord had fallen foul of a fever that would keep him to his bed. When Elizabeth, in sudden panic, insisted on seeing him, she was allowed to do so, to discover her brother propped against banked pillows, only semi-conscious, hot and uncomfortable, his face flushed and his skin dusted with a light rash. He tossed and turned under her hand on his forehead, neither recognising her nor responding to her voice. Master Capel stood in close attendance beside the bed, hands folded over his black robes.

'What's wrong with him?' Elizabeth demanded, anxiety not quite replacing her dislike of the man.

'Nothing untoward, my lady.'

'The pestilence?' She could hardly swallow as she spoke the dread word. 'I don't think it is, but—'

'No. It's not the pestilence. There's nothing to fear, my lady.' Master Capel's voice was deep and surprisingly gentle. Much as she imagined the velvety tones of the snake to be when it tempted Eve to bite into the apple. 'One of those sudden fevers to which young men often fall prey when they outgrow their strength. He'll recover soon enough with rest and sleep.'

'What are you doing for him?' She closed her hand over one of David's restless, unquiet ones. 'I have some knowledge of fevers. I could—'

'There's no need, my lady. I have my own methods.' He advanced to lift her to her feet from the stool beside the bed, one hand firmly beneath her arm so that she found that she had no choice. 'I advise you to leave now. Your brother should be left in peace. And if the fever *should* prove to be contagious, I would not wish your ladyship to suffer for your kind visit here.'

'You think I am in danger?'

'No.' His eyes fixed on her face, full of inner knowledge, full of kind understanding. She could almost believe him to be sincere. 'But your well-being is of our utmost concern. You must carry an heir for Ledenshall. A son who will one day claim the Malinder lands.'

'Well…' She hesitated at this unexpected turn in the conversation. 'Of course, it is my hope.'

'Your uncle has a concern for you that his brusque manner might sometimes disguise.'

* * *

'And,' as Elizabeth informed Richard later, 'I was then swept out of the room as if I were a servant who was in the way. And what's more, I am forbidden to return there, for the sake of my own health.'

'Is David in danger?' Richard watched as his wife prowled their chamber, as tense as a hunting vixen.

'He says not.' She lifted her shoulders in frustration. 'I do not know. But the fever attacked very suddenly, and Master Capel holds the keys to David's room. How can I not worry?'

Richard's frown deepened. 'I think we should leave. Whatever the problem, we're doing no good here. I would rather have you back within the security of the walls of Ledenshall.'

'And leave David?' Elizabeth's hands clenched into the material of her skirts. 'Master Capel swears David is in no danger, but I may not enter for my own good!'

And seeing the fear, the glimmer of tears on Elizabeth's cheeks, Richard's concern for her overrode his anger at their treatment at Sir John's hands. 'Lady Ellen will not allow him to come to harm,' he urged, praying that it was so and that Elizabeth would allow herself to be persuaded. 'I want to take you away from here. Tomorrow at first light. Do you agree?' Elizabeth's safety was fast becoming a matter to engage his whole mind. The urgency of it rode him with sharp spurs. He drew her into his arms, surprised by the need to hold her close.

And Elizabeth, allowing herself to be soothed by those strong arms, took a deep breath and leaned into his care, her forehead resting against his chest.

'I suppose we must,' she sighed.

Richard tightened his hold. 'Then let us go home.'

The Malinders were mounted and ready to leave. Sir John, making no attempt to dissuade them, left the polite farewells to his wife, who with a wan smile approached Elizabeth as she sat her horse.

'I'll take all care of him,' Lady Ellen assured. 'To me he is the son I never carried. I'll let no harm come to him.'

Elizabeth grasped her hand warmly. 'I am grateful beyond words.'

'I have something for you.' It was little more than a whisper so that Elizabeth had to bend low to hear the words.

Ellen took Elizabeth's hand again as if to press it in fare-well. Into the centre of her palm she carefully pressed a small hard object, closing Elizabeth's fingers tightly over it with her own. 'From David,' she murmured. 'I got past the guard. He was lucid. He said to give it to you.' Then Ellen took a step back and smiled brightly up into Elizabeth's face. 'I have this for you.' She handed over a bulky package, raising her voice to normal pitch. 'I know you are skilled in the use of herbs. My herb garden has grown so well this spring. The comfrey is overrunning the whole patch, and so is the lovage. Perhaps you can make use of them.'

'I will, Lady Ellen.' But despite the normality of her reply, Elizabeth's fingers were clutched tightly around the object in her palm and her heart thundered in her chest. Surely all around her could hear it, feel the vibration.

Ellen's voice was a whisper again, eyes wide. 'I'm afraid.'

Richard urged his horse closer. 'Can we help?'

'Ellen.' Sir John's voice rang out. 'Let them go. It's a long enough journey without your detaining them.'

'Yes, my lord. Of course.' Ellen lifted her face, unwilling to let them go without a final word. 'Goodbye and God keep you. No, you cannot help me, Richard. Go home and keep Elizabeth safe. I'll look after David, never fear.'

And then they were riding out from under the massive portcullis, their faces turned towards the gentler hills of the middle March, Elizabeth accompanied throughout the whole journey by sharp fears. She knew exactly what Ellen had given her, what was now tucked securely within the bodice of her gown.

As soon as they were dismounted at Ledenshall, Elizabeth did not linger. Without a word, she picked up her skirts and ran up the steps and into the Hall, then to her chamber, where Richard came to find her sitting in a chair before a fire, loosely wrapped around in a heavy velvet robe, her veil discarded. He thought he had not seen such anguish on her face since the night of Lewis's murder. A single sheet of parchment lay unfolded on a coffer at her side and two items of jewellery beside it. She was staring at them, face drained of colour, eyes wide with lingering horror. The rich emerald colour of her robe merely enhanced her bloodless cheeks and lips.

'Elizabeth.' He closed the door softly. It must be worse than he thought. 'What is it? You must tell me.'

She shook her head as if to shake her thoughts into some sensible pattern. 'I don't know. I'm not sure.' He could see her grip the arms of the chair. 'No—that's not true. I think I am very sure. I just don't want to believe it.'

He pulled up a stool to sit opposite her, leaned his forearms on his thighs, but did not pick up the items until she was ready. Did not speak until her thoughts were sufficiently ordered that she could raise her eyes to his face. When she did, his heart was wrung by the wretchedness he saw there.

'Oh, Richard…' She picked up the silver circle set with a crude amethyst, held it out on her open palm. 'I know this ring. David gave it to Ellen to give to me.'

'And?' he prompted as her explanation dried.

'It belongs—it belonged to Lewis.'

Richard's brows snapped together as he lifted the simple crude circle of silver from his wife's hand. 'Are you sure?'

'Oh, yes. I could not be mistaken. I gave it to him, you see. When I was very young and very foolish—I wanted to give him a gift. His horse—it broke its leg and was killed. He was so young and so sad, and tried to be so brave, but I knew that he wept for it. I had nothing else to give of any value. It had belonged to our mother and probably her mother before her. The engraving is very worn, as you can see, and the stone is not well cut. It was a silly gesture, but I wanted him to have it.' She swiped at a tear that overspilled. 'It was far too small for him to wear even then—so he put it on a cord around his neck and promised me he would wear it for ever. And for all I know, he always wore it beneath his tunic.'

'Perhaps he gave it to David?' Richard sought for reasons, any reason other than the obvious, however unlikely.

'No. I think he would not. It was my gift to him. I don't think he would give it away.'

Neither did Richard. 'What about that?' he asked after a brief silence, angling his chin to the other jewel.

'Ah. The brooch.' The muscles in her jaw clenched. 'This was in Ellen's packet of comfrey and lovage, well disguised if anyone should see fit to pry.' She pushed the jewel towards him with the parchment. Three short scrawled lines only.

I found this in your uncle's possession. I know there is more.

You will recognise it.

I can only guess at its implication.

It was a brooch, a fine piece of value, fashioned of gold with rubies in a cabochon setting. Richard lifted it from the table, held it in his hand, admiring the weight and workmanship even as his gut clenched with the knowledge it brought. If his fears were true, what depths of misery this would bring for Elizabeth. Surely ownership of this gem would point an accusing finger at the man responsible for Lewis's death. The rubies reflected the candlelight, an inner blood-red fire in their heart.

'When did you last see that?' Elizabeth asked when he said nothing.

'I'm not sure.' Richard hesitated, unwilling to put his fears into words. 'The workmanship is magnificent. A splendid piece, of Italian manufacture, I think.'

'Yes. And of considerable worth. As I know. So I also know it was hardly ever worn. It was a gift to Lewis from our father, a de Lacy jewel.'

'I see.' He looked up, eyes suddenly narrowed as his fears were confirmed.

'When I last set eyes on it,' Elizabeth continued, 'it was pinned to the brim of Lewis's hat to secure a flamboyant feather—on the day of our wedding.' As if the full meaning of the words, of the situation they painted, struck her for the first time, Elizabeth covered her face with her hands. 'I dare not think of the reasons for these to fall into the hands of David and Ellen.' Then she thrust back her chair, sprang to her feet to pace the chamber from one end to the other in an outpouring of furious energy, kicking the heavy skirts of her robe from her path. 'I know what I suspect. It can be the only answer. He killed Lewis. Sir John killed him—or had him killed. Surely that can be the only reason for these pieces of jewellery to be discovered at Talgarth. And the brooch in Sir John's own possession. I cannot doubt Ellen's word. What other reason can there be?' Her thoughts continued to flow out in an uncontrolled flood of words. 'Now he has David under his hand. And I am powerless to do anything about it.' She raised her hands in helpless fury, swinging round to fist them on the back of the chair that she had just vacated.

'You still have no proof beyond the circumstantial,' Richard answered with the voice of a man who would uphold the law of the land, despite the anger that had begun to churn in his gut at the logical brutality of his wife's thought processes. Trying for her sake to remain impartial, rational. Balanced. If she was not capable of cold reasoning, then he must be, for her sake.

'It's the only explanation. How else could they be there?'

Elizabeth began to pace again. 'Why would Ellen pass them so secretively to me?'

'Yes.' He sighed. 'I have to accept that.'

'Will you help me?'

At the far end of the room she swung round to face him again. The insubstantial light of the candles masked the worst of her anguish, but her voice trembled. It was a cry for help that he found impossible to ignore. Yet his instinct was still to weigh the evidence and consider. Cautious now, Richard continued to lean on his elbows, folded his hands, rested his chin there.

'To do what, exactly?'

'To rescue David. To make Sir John pay for his despicable crime. What else?' Elizabeth flung our her arms in impatience.

Richard breathed out slowly as he realised the weight of what she was asking, and how she would react if she read his reply, his advice, as an outright refusal. Hurt she must already be. He had no wish to add to her pain 'Elizabeth—listen to me. I think David is in no danger at Talgarth. I think he has a role in Sir John's plans, whatever they might be. Sir John will use your brother, perhaps attempt to mould him to his own desires as heir to the de Lacy lands—but he will not *kill* him.'

'I do not want him there, a virtual prisoner, to be *moulded*, as you put it, by a murderer. Do you really think David's sudden illness, which kept him delirious and confined to bed, was purely coincidence? I do not. I cannot but fear for his life.'

'No, I don't believe it was a coincidence. I think it was to keep him from too close a conversation with *you*. Most likely the fever was a product of Master Capel's skills. But now that you are gone, I think David will come to no lasting harm. His is the only de Lacy blood—apart from yours—to inherit the Talgarth lands after Sir John's death.'

'But if it's all a matter of inheritance—if that means so much to my uncle,' Elizabeth fretted, 'why would he kill Lewis?'

'I don't know.'

'My uncle killed my brother.' She repeated the words once more, as if she could not take in the true meaning of them. Then pinned Richard with a stare. 'He must be brought to justice.'

'I agree. But what can I do?' He rose to his feet to close the distance between them. 'We have here a case against Sir John that will not stand in a court of law. No witnesses to call who will speak the truth, no evidence to point incontrovertibly to his guilt. His retainers will not speak against him if they value their pockets—or even their lives. All we have are two pieces of jewellery discovered in the wrong place.' He was as frustrated and hedged about as she, but his control was better than hers. 'I am no ancient god who can wreak deadly vengeance with a well-aimed bolt of lightning, without consequence or responsibility to a higher power.' Elizabeth continued to pace, stepping around him when he would have barred her path, until he stretched out an arm to stop her. 'I cannot rescue David, short of a full-blown siege of Talgarth. Think of what you suggest, Elizabeth.'

But she was beyond reason, her eyes wild. He could feel the tension in her arm where his hand rested. 'My brother's blood cries out for vengeance, my lord.' Her deliberate descent into the formal was bitter indeed. 'And you stand there to tell me there is no proof!'

'I know, and it hurts you, but revenge must be under the banner of justice, by the law of the land, and that requires proof.'

'He murdered Lewis and callously heaped the blame on your head, before all your people. He deliberately sowed the seeds of doubt in my own heart. Can you overlook such undeserved dishonour? Do you tell me that he does not merit punishment?'

'No. But I think you are not listening to reason. You need to rest. You will make yourself ill if you cannot put it aside for tonight.'

'Reason! What role has reason in all this?' She almost snarled at him, eyes snapping in fury.

What could he say? He could no longer find the words. She was beyond soothing or comfort, but he would try again. 'Come to bed—and tomorrow we will think again.'

'You do not care! Are you not man enough to help me?'

With one sharp movement, a deliberate open-handed blow, she swept a candlestick and its candle, regardless of any danger from the leaping flame to the bed-hangings, to the floor.

Which pushed Richard into action. 'Stop this, Elizabeth.' He took her hands and pulled her closer, locking his fingers with hers to prevent her from snatching away. 'Yes. I do care. And I promise that I will do what I can.' And as he looked down into her face he saw the glitter of tears as anguish began to replace anger. His heart ached for her. He wanted nothing more than to bring her some ease from her torment.

'Do I have to get revenge myself?' she whispered, now clinging tightly.

'No.' He gave her a little shake, moved almost beyond words. 'Foolish girl! Have I not said? You are mine and so you are not alone in this.'

Their eyes caught and held, tight as a fist. Awareness one of the other, strange and unbidden, danced in the flickering light. Then desire arced between them, hot and ruthless as a flame. He drew her into his arms, held tight when she would have struggled against so unexpected a surge in her blood. He had planned to be gentle, to soothe the pain, stroke away the anger that rode her with kind words and soft hands, as he had when they were last at odds, but knew in that moment that such softness would not serve the purpose at all. Besides, he was overwhelmed, his senses all but overturned by a basic need. He wanted her, as simple as that. He desired her, so proud as she was, so driven to get justice for Lewis.

Richard allowed instinct to dictate, body to overrule mind, to band his arms firmly around her, before he bent his head to take her mouth with his. Not the gentle kiss of his original intent, but one of heady desire to part her lips and slide his tongue against hers, against the soft skin of her mouth. The fire so immediately kindled flashed, leapt between them. All-consuming, dominating. All the anguish and despair within Elizabeth bloomed impossibly into the heat of demand, spread to him and ignited them both, taking their breath, making them tremble.

It was not a seductive wooing. Desire and need, amazing them both, took control as Richard lifted and tumbled her to the bed. Her loosely laced gown presented no difficulty to his urgent fingers, nor his own more formal garments. Clothes were stripped away to allow flesh to slide invitingly, irresistibly against flesh. His thorough caress swept Elizabeth's new curves, curves that went unappreciated in the immediacy of the moment, from shoulder to waist to thigh, to return to cup her breast as his mouth assaulted hers, the press of his body demanding her response. Elizabeth shuddered, then arched against him, her fingernails scoring his back and shoulders as they stretched and rolled, heart to heart, thigh to thigh, the most perfect of fit. Sheets tangled around them, impeding, and were cast impatiently aside.

He entered her in a single powerful thrust.

'Elizabeth!' He groaned her name and stilled as she closed round him, burning with heat, soft as satin, intoxicating to his senses as the most wanton of pleasures. Even more when she lifted her hips against him to allow him greater access and watched his face with hooded eyes. As he watched her. They lay still for a moment, caught there, as their hearts thundered one against the other, their breath mingled.

'Elizabeth de Lacy,' he murmured, momentarily stunned, a flicker of uncertainty in the depths of his fierce eyes. 'What are you?' He feathered with utmost restraint a line of kisses along her jaw, along the elegant curve of her throat, before the need overruled and he began to move within her, against her, his rhythm flowing through her, encouraging her to follow, aware only of his magnificent dominance. Sensation building in her until she whimpered and shivered at its unknown power, far sweeter, far more intense than before. And her lax muscles tightened in his embrace as fear swept through her at her inability to resist him or control her body's response.

'I am afraid,' she cried out. But pleasure flooded through her to deny her words and lured her.

Richard gave her no choice, but pushed her on with clever mouth and practised fingers, with firm strokes that left her with no will of her own until she cried out with shock and delight. Only then, with hard-won control at an end, did he surrender to the woman who had considered herself to be his captive, stunned at his own helplessness in her arms.

Afterwards, some considerable time afterwards when she had collected her scattered thoughts from the debris of the emotional onslaught, Elizabeth lay in Richard's arms. Exhausted, momentarily. Sad, of course, but without the terrible weight of grief. At some time in the storm a measure of contentment had ambushed her, stolen through her limbs, to remain there a still and quiet river to stroke and soothe. As for the intense emotion that had driven her to respond to every demand he had made, she still resisted putting a name to it. Or to the explosion of lethal delight racing through her blood that had compelled her against all sense to make her own demands on him. She felt the flush of hot colour in her face at the memory of her wilful behaviour, grateful for the shadows, whilst a persistent voice whispered through her mind.

You have fallen in love with him. No matter how you deny it, the proof is there in your heated blood. You cannot step around the truth any longer. You love him.

And against such forthright words Elizabeth had no defence.

'Richard...' She turned her cheek against his chest, aware of the still rapid beat of his heart, his disordered breathing yet to settle. It pleased her beyond measure that he had been as compromised as she. 'I was unfair to you.'

'Yes. You were.' He pressed his lips against her hair. She could sense the smile. 'As I remember, you exhibited a very poor opinion of my abilities, both as Lord of Ledenshall and— even worse—as a man.'

She laughed, low and full of satisfaction. 'Not any more! I lack experience, but your abilities are—*miraculous*, I think.' She splayed her fingers over his chest, pleased when she felt the rumble of his answering laugh.

'So I should hope.'

Beneath the laughter, Richard was taken aback at his lack of control with Elizabeth. Her attraction for him had surprised him, as had the degree of respect he had come to give his wife. But the need to make her his, to possess her utterly, was overwhelming. Nor was it merely a physical connection. Something far deeper pulled him towards her. He found himself frowning into the curtained canopy of the bed as the problem teased his thoughts. Probably it was nothing more than compassion for the pain inflicted on her by a man, her own uncle, who should have supported and protected her. Perhaps there was a hint of admiration for her strong will when beset, even when it was turned against him. And respect, of course. Yes, that was it. There was no difficulty in giving her admiration and respect. And how could he have guessed that she would be so endearingly feminine beneath her sharp words and direct manner? So thoroughly desirable. So that was it, too. Lust was an easy answer.

The matter settled in his own mind, Richard stopped frowning and spoke quietly against her temple. 'Sir John de Lacy will pay for his crimes. Sooner or later. I will not allow him to go unchallenged for the grief he has brought to you. You are my wife and it is my duty and my desire to protect you. It is not permitted that anyone bring you harm.'

It was a solemn oath, recognised by both of them. As both were aware, even though the knowledge had until that moment been unspoken, any shadow of culpability for the events of that terrible night had effectively been removed from Richard's shoulders. Any barrier between them marked with Lewis's blood had been destroyed. There were still others, would be others in the future—Elizabeth was not so naïve that she could see only a smooth pathway for them—but at least that one despicable crime was laid to rest.

'I should never have doubted you.' It shamed her that she had.

'No. You should not. But as you once said, you did not know me. Our marriage was not destined to be an easy one. Perhaps we can now find a straighter path together.'

'Do you forgive me? For my lack of trust?'

'I could do that.' With agile power he suddenly rolled to reverse their positions, his weight pressing her into the soft mattress. 'But I think I need to know that you will not be so ready to doubt my abilities again.'

She saw the glint of his eyes, the curve of his glorious mouth, the spread of his shoulders as he obliterated the light, held her prisoner once again. 'What do you suggest? What can I do in recompense?' She felt his heart leap, his erection harden fully, heavily against her thigh. Her arms closed around his neck, pulling him closer still, his lips down to hers as her hips lifted, opened to him in invitation. There was no doubting the invitation.

'This…'

His mouth claimed hers once more with obvious intent, but now with time for tenderness. A slow cherishing. Elizabeth did not resist.

Richard did what he could. With an open purse, he bought information from travellers who would listen and gossip and report back. David had been seen riding with his uncle. He had been seen at his uncle's side in Hereford. He looked well and rode his horse with vital energy. Nothing to concern his anxious sister. It brought a measure of peace to Elizabeth's heart.

She and Jane made use of the scrying dish. It told them little, but there was no presage of death or disaster.

'It proves nothing.' Jane cleared away the evidence.

'But if you do not see it…'

'David is not harmed.' It was as reassuring as Jane was prepared to be.

Meanwhile the Lord and Lady of Ledenshall watched each other, neither able or willing to admit to the astonishing depth of awareness that had developed between them since that night of outrageous passion.

Chapter Twelve

With the passage of spring into early summer, travel on the rutted roads became easier, and so came the season of fairs and markets. The Malinders of Ledenshall, with two stout baggage wagons and a strong escort, found their way to Leominster to the May Day Fair with the prospect of stalls to browse over, the aromatic scents of spices to lure, music and entertainment, in Broad Street and the Corn Market, a mystery play and a maypole set up in the churchyard of the vast Priory Church, decorated with boughs of oak leaves and flowers and ribbons.

As Richard prepared to take himself off to do business at the Talbot, Elizabeth found herself subject to a sternly quizzical stare.

'What is it?' she asked.

Tight-lipped, face set in solemn lines despite the merriment around them, Richard, for a moment surprising her, stretched out his hand. She thought he would touch her cheek with his fingers, so public in a crowded street, but he merely tucked her veil more securely. Her breath caught on a little hum of pleasure at the warm intimacy of so simple a gesture.

'Do you fear for me? I shall be quite safe,' she reassured,

loosely encircling his wrist with her fingers. 'I expect you've ordered your men-at-arms to remain close.'

'I would never forgive myself if anything harmed you in any way.'

Delight bloomed, bright as the *rosa mundi* in her new garden at Ledenshall. Richard rarely voiced his personal feelings despite the possessiveness of his body. Would he ever say that he loved her? Would he ever feel such emotion towards her, the bride he had not wanted? Her love for him would have to be enough. She watched him, his broad shoulders, his lithe gait, as he disappeared into the crowd.

There proved to be little need for their guards, except perhaps to keep the thieves and pickpockets at bay, or deter the beggars who begged ceaselessly.

'Lady! On your mercy.' Elizabeth felt a tug on the sleeve of her gown.

They were standing in an inn yard to watch a group of travelling musicians, acrobats and dancers, with a welcome cup of ale against the growing warmth of the day. A lad, filthy, in ragged garments with long matted hair more worthy of one of the prize Ryeland sheep for sale in the High Street, his hat pulled low to his ears, had sidled to crouch beside her. Stooped with some disease, he held out his hands. Compassionate, waving away her escort who made to grip the boy by the arm and haul him away, Elizabeth pressed a penny into his hand, then returned her attention to the performance.

'Lady.' Again the tug at her gown, his voice little more than a low croak. She looked down at the battered crown of his hat. 'Go to the Priory. The south porch. Before mid-day.'

That was all, before her guard dispatched the lad to the edge of the crowd with a rough shove from a well-placed boot. Should she act on the plea of a filthy, flea-ridden beggar? Who wished to speak with her and could not do so in the public street? Well, of course, she could not but go to satisfy her own curiosity. No harm could come to her in so holy a place, busy with the comings and goings of the monks and the lay community on this market day. Elizabeth walked across the grass to the south porch.

It was empty, much as she had expected, but she could at least say a prayer for Lewis's soul. She entered the porch, lifted a hand to the iron latch and would have pushed open the great door when a shadow fell across the entrance behind her. A figure appeared, slipped into the soft shadows of the porch. She spun round, instantly alert for any danger, her hand clasped around the handle of the dagger she wore discreetly under her cloak.

Outlined with the sun behind him, it was the ragged boy of the inn yard.

'What do you want of me?' she demanded, keeping her voice strong despite the lurch of her heart as the boy approached. Would he attack her? Rob her? Was he an assassin sent by Sir John? She drew the dagger, its blade glimmering in the shadows.

The youth continued to shuffle closer.

'Where is she?' Richard demanded. His eyes swept over the crowd around them in the Butter Market.

'Gone to the Priory, my lord,' his man-at-arms replied.

Fear bloomed, racing through Richard's blood. He might play down his concern for David's safety at Talgarth to soothe Elizabeth's fears, but Elizabeth's safety was not a matter to be trifled with. A slither of alarm traced its nasty path down his spine.

'What do you want of me?' Elizabeth repeated.

'Sanctuary.' The lad's voice was not the pathetic croak of the inn yard. As a rich chuckle escaped, he pulled off the disreputable hat and the sheep skin that had concealed his dark hair. 'Sanctuary, dear sister. You don't need the dagger.'

'David! In Heaven's name, what are…?'

'Quietly!' He grasped her sleeve as he had tugged on it earlier, pulling her inside the Priory into the deep gloom, into the protection of a massive tomb of some past prior. 'Walls have ears. They certainly do at Talgarth.'

'What are you doing here?' Elizabeth closed her hand over his forearm, regardless of the lice and ingrained dirt, and held on. 'What's happened?'

'I had to get away. But I was watched…' He glanced over his shoulder towards the distant altar where sparrows fluttered amongst the carvings.

'How did you get here?'

'Never mind that. Suffice that I did. I know that you got the ring.'

'Yes, I did, but you must—'

The door to their right was pushed open. A footstep. David's sudden movement, the glint of a short blade in his hand, as at the same time he pushed Elizabeth farther back into the shelter of the tomb, both shocked and silenced her. Then her brother visibly relaxed with a little laugh, and she looked up at the echo of approaching footsteps.

'Richard!'

'Well, at least you are both armed, for which I suppose I should be grateful,' was his only dry comment. But his hand closed warmly on Elizabeth's where she still clasped the dagger, an intimate pressure, a comforting little gesture that made her sigh with relief. She allowed Richard to take the blade from her and slide it into his belt. 'Are you being followed?' was all he asked.

'Possibly…probably.' David's lips tightened, his eyes stormy, a challenge to the figure of authority now facing him. 'I'll not go back to Talgarth. I don't care what you say.'

Elizabeth read the proximity of panic in the stark statement. So did Richard, who did not argue. 'Stay here. Hide the dagger unless you wish to draw comment and wait by the gate. Give us thirty minutes. When the wagon passes we'll come to a halt—for some reason that I cannot yet foresee. Climb in and hide under the purchases. None of my men will stop you. There'll be some bolts of cloth to disguise you. Stay there—keep your head down—until we reach Ledenshall.'

'Yes.' David nodded, a flash of teeth as he grinned in the shadows, and sheathed the dagger. 'You don't know how grateful I am!'

'You can tell me later. Come on, Elizabeth. Let us set this little mummery of our own into motion.'

'So! Tell me what the de Lacy heir was doing skulking in Leominster Priory in beggar's rags.'

Back at Ledenshall in the private parlour, chairs and stools were pulled round a table. David, now stripped of his beggar's disguise, thoroughly scrubbed and clad in some borrowed garments from Richard, which were too large for him, but did the job, drained half the tankard in one gulp, wiped one hand over his mouth.

'That's better. But I think I still itch.'

'Tell us, David!' Elizabeth could barely restrain her impatience. She nudged him into reply.

'Where do I start?' It was a weary gesture now, she saw, as he tunnelled his fingers through his wet hair and there was grief in his eyes. Elizabeth stretched out her hands to offer comfort, but David shook his head, reached inside his tunic and drew out another jewel that instantly caught the light in a baleful glitter as he placed it on the table. It was a pendant, fashioned to hang on a gold chain to indicate a man's status, weighty with gold, the sapphires deep and lustrous.

'Lewis's?' Elizabeth picked it up, realising sadly that David was a child no more. These events had stripped him of his youth and innocence. She did not recognise the jewel, but her mind made the connection.

'Yes. A recent purchase.' The smile was twisted. 'Lewis

had ambitions as a courtier. I tormented him about it, made fun… I wish I had not.'

Elizabeth nodded in silent understanding. 'I suppose he was wearing it at the wedding?'

'Yes.'

'Sapphires are credited with magical powers,' she murmured as she turned the gems in her hand. 'They did not save Lewis's life, did they?' There was no possible answer. Elizabeth leaned forwards, reached out her hand to clasp her brother's wrist. 'Tell me about the ring, David,' she demanded.

'I though you would recognise it. I found it, of all places, in the possession of Gilbert de Burcher, our uncle's commander of the garrison.'

'De Burcher?' Richard, listening silently so far, sat up, pushed his tankard away untasted.

'Yes. De Burcher. It fell from his pouch when he laid it aside with his tunic during a wrestling bout. He didn't notice when I picked it up and pocketed it. Nor has de Burcher made anything of its loss. He must have realised it soon after I took it, but he made no fuss. Perhaps he dared not.'

'A gift from Sir John for services rendered?' Richard suggested.

'Yes. Or Gilbert simply kept it because it was of little intrinsic value compared with the rest of the gems. Perhaps he thought it would not be missed by his lord.' David's brow furrowed. 'Another thing—de Burcher's well supplied with coin at present. He gambles and has more at his disposal than one might think, even for one of his status at Talgarth.'

'And as I recall,' Richard dropped the thought into the mix, 'Sir Gilbert was here with Sir John for the wedding.'

'Would he follow Sir John's orders—to encompass murder?' Elizabeth asked.

Richard replied without hesitation, 'I've met the man. A fine soldier, but a hard one, not blessed with compassion. I think he would have no compunction.'

'No. He would not,' David agreed. 'It's my belief he would sell his soul to the highest bidder. He would follow Sir John's orders to hell and back if it was made worth his while.'

'And this pendant.' Elizabeth held it close in her palm as a tangible reminder of her brother. 'How did you come by it?'

'It was Ellen. She discovered it somewhere at Talgarth— she wouldn't tell me.'

'In Sir John's possession,' Elizabeth confirmed, 'or so she said in her letter when she sent the brooch. I presume they come from the same source.'

'Yes. She's very unhappy, although she hides it well. She helped me escape, deliberately to get me away from Talgarth. Whatever she suspects, she wanted me gone. I hid, with her connivance, in a wagon.' David rubbed his shoulder where it had suffered from the hard roads. 'I hoped I would see some of your people at the Fair. I didn't expect to see you.' He drank, then looked at Elizabeth with troubled eyes. 'I hope Ellen will not be blamed. Sir John can have a heavy hand. She can claim all innocence, of course, and put the blame on my absent head. Perhaps he'll disinherit me as an ungrateful brat.'

'Perhaps.' Elizabeth managed a tight smile at the attempt at humour. 'Would Ellen speak out against Sir John?'

David laughed, a harsh sound in the quiet room. 'Of course she would not! She'll not stand against him.'

'I think she might speak out about murder,' Elizabeth disagreed. 'I would!'

'I wouldn't wager my coat on it!'

'Nor I!' Richard agreed. 'I think you must accept, Elizabeth, that Ellen will be obedient to Sir John's demands. Not all wives are as forthright as you.'

Elizabeth flushed and shook her head. 'Why were you so ill when we came to Talgarth?' she demanded of her brother.

'I have thought about that,' David replied. 'Nothing lasting, but enough to give me a fever and blur my wits. I recovered amazingly quickly after your departure. Master Capel spoke of ill humours in my body, which his potions drove out.' He grimaced at the memory. 'I think I was not to be allowed to speak with you.'

'So we thought.' Richard traced patterns in the spilled ale on the table as he considered the boy's words.

'There's something else, Elizabeth. Master Capel wanted to know the day and time of your birth.'

She looked up, immediately alert. 'Did you tell him?'

David frowned, ill at ease. 'Yes. It took me by surprise and I could think of no reason not to. Although now I wish I had not. As for why he should wish to know… Who knows what Master Capel does in his locked rooms? Perhaps I'm letting my imagination run away with me.'

'I expect so.' Elizabeth's thoughts raced in circles, sensing Richard's sudden interest. She must not voice her fears. 'I doubt it was important. Perhaps he's compiling a de Lacy family history for Sir John's aggrandisement.' She turned to Richard, who still sat silently, considering. Had she done enough to deflect him? Of course he would not, as she did, see the implication of the information. 'What are we going to do now?'

'Do?' Richard tilted his chin as if he would read her mind.

'Against Sir John.'

'You can do nothing within the law.' He returned her gaze, his own uncompromising, brooking no argument. 'Sir John will deny all accusations and no one will stand against him who has direct witness of the crime.'

'Yes, but—'

'Elizabeth…' he sighed '…we've had this conversation before. There's no point in our going over old ground again. You know my mind on it. David's news has confirmed what we thought, but has not changed the situation at all. Before the law we are powerless.'

She turned her face away. It still stood between them.

Richard rose to his feet, placed his hands gently on her shoulders, so that warmth spread to the cold chill of her heart, although his face remained implacable enough. 'I'll leave you and David to work out all types of vicious punishments for your uncle. But I'll not be a party to them and I'll do all I can to prevent you taking any steps that will put yourselves in danger or cast the whole of the March into violent conflict.' His eyes transferred to David. 'I expect you to exert some sensible judgement here, David. Your sister, perhaps understandably, is given to extremes.'

He left the room, leaving Elizabeth torn between guilt at her own stubborn stance and frustration that she could see no way forwards.

'He's right, you know,' David stated. 'We can do nothing against Sir John.'

'You will condone Lewis's death?' Sharp, intolerant. And Elizabeth immediately regretted her baseless accusation.

David snorted inelegantly. 'Hardly. Do you need to ask?'

'No. But I think we should—'

'I'll not be party to murder—or whatever else you're thinking.'

'You're as uncooperative as Richard!' But she smiled at last.

'And I thought you would receive me here at Ledenshall with unalloyed pleasure. Now why did I think that?'

As Elizabeth moved to snuff out the candles before they parted for the night, David stopped her. 'One thing, Elizabeth.'

'What is that?' Still preoccupied with her task.

'When Master Capel asked the day of your birth, he also asked about Richard's. I didn't know, so couldn't say. I thought I should tell you.'

Elizabeth abandoned the candles, her fears suddenly leaping fully formed. 'Yes. You should.' But kept her thoughts veiled. No point in disturbing David further.

Elizabeth immediately delved into Jane Bringsty's wealth of knowledge.

'Jane. If you were to practise the secrets of astrology and seek to cast a horoscope...'

Despite the late hour, Mistress Bringsty was engaged in folding Elizabeth's shifts into a clothes press, but at this her whole body stilled, her hands flat on the soft linen. 'Do you wish me to do so, lady?'

'No. *If* you were to do so, would you need the day and time of my birth?'

'I would. To determine which planet you were born under.'

'And what would be your purpose in casting such a horoscope?'

'Well, now. I have rarely done so.' Elizabeth's brows rose at the admission that Jane had *ever* done so. 'And not at all in recent years. But I would do so to discover the state of your health. Of body and mind. The effect of the planets on your life and temperament. I would also use it—' She stopped, frowned.

'How?' Elizabeth found breathing suddenly difficult. Would Jane confirm her worst fears?

'To plot the day and time of your death.' The reply was distressingly blunt.

Elizabeth simply nodded. 'So I think.' And gave herself over to some unsettling thoughts. So Sir John's necromancer was dabbling in astrology, was he? But to what purpose? And why would he desire Richard's day of birth as well as her own? She did not like the direction her thoughts took, nor could she share her concerns. She would not tell Richard. There was enough between them to cause friction—bringing Sir John to justice—without this to muddy the waters further.

As for Sir John—he was guilty with blood on his hands. If Richard and David would not help her, then she must take his punishment on to her own shoulders. She had patience. She would wait and plan until the perfect moment arrived. No secretive poisonings or casting of dubious spells, as Jane would be quick to advise. Sir John must answer for his despicable sin in full public eye.

Except, her heart heavy, she knew she must have a care, must devise some means that would not bring shame on Richard. *I would never forgive myself if anything harmed you in any way,* Richard had said to her, simply a statement of a possessive husband to his wife, without, she accepted, the burden of love. Elizabeth carried that burden, willingly, joyfully, despite the pain it brought her. With all the weight of that emotion on her soul, she could echo Richard's words. Richard must not be implicated; she would never forgive herself if any action of hers brought condemnation down on him. He might not love her, but her love for him coloured every decision she made. Richard must not suffer for any action of hers.

Chapter Thirteen

Elizabeth sat in the solar, feet neatly on a footstool, making her intention clear. She wished her breath did not feel quite so constricted in her chest, that her heart did not thud so loudly in her ears. Surely Richard must hear it. It was June, Midsummer Eve, the traditional occasion for festivities and feasting, for trials of strength and skill in the March, the perfect opportunity for her revenge against Sir John, yet to achieve it she must lie to Richard.

She swallowed against a dry throat and looked up to where he waited for her. It was difficult to meet his eyes, but she forced herself to hold the keen gaze. 'I have decided. I will not go.'

'Why will you not go?'

'I feel unwell.' She bit her lip. 'My head—and my stomach feels uneasy.'

'You have the headache.' He failed utterly to disguise his incredulity. 'Enough to keep you from the Midsummer Fair?'

Elizabeth's determination all but wavered in the face of Richard's disbelief. 'Yes.'

Richard tilted her chin. 'Why do I not believe you?'

'I have no idea, my lord. It is not in my nature to dissemble. Don't you trust me?' It hurt that he might not, even as she accepted that she deserved his censure for what she was planning.

Richard looked askance, his blatant refusal to answer deepening the hurt further. 'Are you breeding?' he asked instead.

Elizabeth flushed to her temples. 'No,' she replied smartly. 'You'll be the first to know if I am.' But she could not deny the sweet flutter of anticipation.

'Then I can't persuade you to come with me?'

'No!' And she prayed he would not question her further. Lying to Richard made her heart ache as well as her head.

'As you wish.' She thought he had accepted at last. Then he swooped, fast as a hawk, leaned an arm against the high chair-back and kissed her full on the mouth. 'You seem well enough to me, lady.' He kissed her again, hard, demanding, his tongue owning the soft fullness of her lips, his hand clasping the nape of her neck to hold her captive. 'In fact, you seem far too delicious for an ailing wife. We could, of course, stay here together and celebrate the Midsummer Solstice entirely privately. It's high time you quickened. What better time than this?'

Lips parted, eyes wide, Elizabeth could think of no reply.

'Nothing to say? Why did I hope you might invite me to your bed? Take care, Elizabeth.' Another kiss to steal what breath she had. The speculative gleam in his eye as he left the room thoroughly unnerved her.

Elizabeth's face burned, her heart lurched, her breath hissed out between softened lips and her whole body felt tender. Had she detected the faintest shadow of disappointment in his face? Why did she have to dissemble and send him away? She breathed out slowly, accepting the need for it. Because Richard could not, must not, be involved in the momentous step she was about to take.

Alone, she bent her mind to her plan, focusing on the enticing tale of an ancestress, back in the distant days of the Conquest. Sybil de Lacy, a glorious heroine of Elizabeth's childhood, the subject of endless fascination, had taken a dagger to the murderer who had killed her lord because he desired her in marriage. Could she, Elizabeth, emulate Sybil? If she could not act within the law, then she would act outside it and take her revenge, by her own hand as Sybil had done. And that would take the burden from Richard and from David. As for the repercussions for herself, at that moment she neither knew nor cared. All she knew was that her brother's blood would be avenged. His soul that cried out to her would be laid to rest.

'Are they gone?' she asked Jane Bringsty.

'Yes.' Jane leaned forwards, watching, at the window. 'I still don't see why you would not—'

'Never mind that.' Elizabeth stood, her distracted air quite vanished. 'If you are of a mind to be useful, come with me.'

She took the steps at a brisk pace and vanished through the door of Richard's chamber where she began a hasty and selective search of the coffers and chests. The results were wrapped into a rough parcel with a cloak.

'Take this.' She handed over the parcel. 'Meet me in the stables within the half-hour. Arrange for two horses to be ready.'

'Leave well alone is what I say!' Jane clicked her tongue against her teeth. 'I don't know what you intend, but I see danger…'

Elizabeth rounded on her serving woman, all patience at an end. 'Leave well alone, indeed. Do nothing, my lord says. For once the pair of you are in agreement. But I will not allow my uncle to escape without retribution for spilling Lewis's blood! If Richard will do nothing, than I will.'

Then Elizabeth was already on her way to borrow a few necessary items from the soldiers' quarters. Within the quarter of the hour they were riding out in the direction of the Midsummer Fair.

The whole of the March had come together for the Midsummer Fair. Striking livery was evident on all sides, banners drifting in the warm air, both York and Lancaster well represented. But for this day, allegiance to York or Lancaster would be put aside. The sun shone and the ale flowed, conflict put aside in the cause of local unity and frivolous celebration.

Richard had anticipated the event with mild pleasure, as he did every year. Now he set the muscles in his jaw as frustration bit deep. He *ought* to be able to enjoy it. Instead, he found his thoughts returning to Elizabeth's strangely wayward behaviour and her sharp words. To his own regret that she had not turned to him and begged him to stay.

Don't you trust me? she had asked crossly.

Well, no, not always. Even now he was wondering what she was planning. When Elizabeth looked at her most innocent, he feared her the most. Not that she had appeared particularly innocent. As he knew better than anyone, she could be headstrong, foolhardy in her loyalty to those she loved. Difficult, wilful, capricious, and yet he admired her. Was intrigued by her, enjoyed the fire and heat in their physical union… His body leapt to uncomfortable readiness as he imagined her carrying his heir, before he deliberately turned his thoughts away from such pleasures and back to Elizabeth's unusual recalcitrance. Sharp intuition told him that something was afoot. Yet after the episode of the poison, surely he could trust her to keep her serving woman in check, and herself not to step beyond the line of what was acceptable behaviour for the Lady of Ledenshall? Perhaps there was a very simple explanation, he decided, even if it were not her usual *modus operandi*—that she would stay away to avoid any confrontation with her uncle, who had blood on his hands.

He found himself distracted by the approach of Mistress Anne Malinder, superbly and expensively gowned, magnificently victorious in the company of her newly betrothed husband, Hugh Mortimer of Wigmore, wealthy and well born. Richard did not linger. He could see the calculation in those sharp green eyes even at a distance. For the first time, Richard had to admit to a sense of relief that Elizabeth—and Jane Bringsty—were not present.

So with David at his side, purely male pursuits in mind, Richard made his way across the grassy space to accost Robert Malinder where he stood, cup of ale in hand, to watch the start of the archery competition.

'Richard!' Robert snared two passing cups of ale. 'And David. I heard you were back at Ledenshall. Does your uncle approve of your association with The Enemy or did you escape without his permission?' Tactless as ever, Robert grinned.

But David was not listening. He had stiffened, his eyes narrowed on the middle distance. He drew in a sharp breath. Then grabbed Richard's sleeve.

'Richard!'

Richard, indulgently, would have brushed the lad off. 'Go and find yourself another cup of ale and an archer to talk to, and give me some peace. It's not your turn at the butts for some time. You're like a flea on a warm dog!'

'But, Richard! Look. There!'

So he did, if only to keep the boy quiet, following David's direction. A figure, a tall, slim young man with a cloak draped over his arm, made his leisurely way around the edge of the crowd, his face averted from the spectacle. In a moment of terrible recognition, Richard's fingers tensed on the cup, blood running cold.

'God's blood!'

'I thought it was Lewis,' David murmured, 'but of course, it isn't. If you were to ask me, I would say that—'

'I know exactly what you would say,' Richard interrupted through his teeth.

'She used to do it when she was a girl—borrow Lewis's clothes, take a horse and ride out. Until our father beat it out of her. What is she about?'

'How would I know what my wife is about?' Richard retorted. They were already in pursuit with elbows and apologies, but the crowd was dense.

'Why was she carrying a bow and a sheaf of arrows?' Robert asked, following. 'Surely Elizabeth would not participate in so public a display as this?'

'No, she would not.' Richard's eyes locked on David's, horribly aware that the boy's thoughts mirrored his own. 'But she might just consider… And if she does, the Midsummer Fair will become a bloody battlefield.'

As the crowd thinned they ran in fear.

Elizabeth marvelled that her blood ran ice cold, her breathing still and calm. From the rise where she took up her position, she squinted against the sun to bring John de Lacy into sharp focus. How easy it would be to wing the goose-fledged arrow towards his arrogant heart so that Lewis's shade would rest in peace. There were no doubts in her mind. They had all been weighed and discarded. Sybil de Lacy would be proud of her. The slightest smile, stern and controlled, touched her face. With no further thought, Elizabeth selected an arrow.

Richard saw her immediately on the little hill. The cloak was laid at her feet with the sheaf of arrows. Except for one, which she was intent on notching to the bowstring. Her whole attention was focused on the distant figure of her uncle the murderer, clearly visible amidst the throng in his rich blue tunic, his draped and feathered hat. Richard found that he was holding his breath as she took up her position, lifted and pulled back the bow to her ear. Calm, composed, purposeful. Would she carry out her plan or lose her nerve at the last moment? No, he accepted. He could not rely on her rethinking her deadly scheme. Would she risk endangering others in the crowd? But her aim was excellent. In her eyes it would be a justifiable execution to avenge Lewis. Her face was pale, her lips set in a thin line, all sharp focus. Had she even considered the repercussions if she were to be successful? That she would be taken and brought before the weight of the law for murder, and with all the witnesses to so public an act, would undoubtedly be found guilty.

Richard felt cold sweat prickle along his spine. He doubted that she had given such trivial matters even a passing consideration.

All this swept through Richard's mind in a blink of an eye as he considered his next move. If he shouted to distract her, it would draw attention to them, something that he would avoid. Nor would it necessarily stop her. If he waited until he was close enough to wrest the damned bow from her hand, she could already have released the first arrow with dire results.

Oh, God!

But the faintest tinge of admiration brushed along his tightly wound nerves that she should consider such a plan and execute it so perfectly. Without David's eagle eye on the crowd, she would now be sighting along the arrow, aiming at John de Lacy's black heart with no one being the wiser.

The decision over what to do was taken out of his hands.

'Stop! Elizabeth…' David shouted at his side, his arms raised in furious gestures to gain her attention. 'Not that… Don't do it.'

Elizabeth stiffened, but did not lower the bow, merely turned her head. Richard looked on, appalled, as her eyes, bright with fulfilment, met his.

And then there was nothing for them to do but sprint ahead up the hill towards her. Elizabeth remained exactly where she was, bow still drawn to taut readiness. She sighted again and Richard knew with dread that they would not reach her in time. Answering his worst fears, he could only watch as she loosed the arrow to soar over the heads of the nearer crowd and vanished towards its living target. A sharp cry rang out above the general babble. An immediate confusion in the crowd, voices raised. And Elizabeth calmly fitted another arrow to her bow, drew it back, sighted, as if she had all the time in the world to unleash the arrow at an inanimate bale of straw as she had done at Ledenshall.

Impelled by a fear greater than any he had ever experienced in his life, Richard took the only option left to him.

Before she could release the arrow, Elizabeth found herself struck with force from the side, with an impact so great that she was flung to the ground, to be buried under a heavy weight. As a last-ditch effort, Richard had launched himself at her as if she were an opponent and they were engaged in mortal combat. Lacking finesse it might be, as he decided, as he lay above her, breathing laboured, but it had provided the solution. Elizabeth lay beneath him, winded, shocked from the unexpected attack, her face white, her eyes dark with thwarted passion. He felt her breath heave against his chest. Fury shimmered round her. It crossed his mind momentarily that she might be injured, but no time for that. Faces in the crowd were beginning to turn in their direction as a clamour of voices rose from the vicinity of Sir John, who might or might not still be alive.

'I can't breathe.' His wife glared up at him, hands braced against his chest. 'You're crushing me. How dare you interfere? You're hurting me! Let me up.'

'In God's name, Elizabeth! That's the least of our troubles!' He fought to temper the hot words that threatened to pour out and blister them both, pushing to his feet, pulling Elizabeth with him with a jerk of his hand around her wrist. It would be a disaster to be seen wrestling on the grass with his wife, a long bow and goose-fledged arrow on the ground beside them, if John de Lacy lay dead in the crowd with a similar arrow buried in his chest.

'You shouldn't have stopped me! Let me finish it.' Dishevelled and furious, she was beyond reasoning.

Richard kept his fingers tightly around her wrist and watched the surge of people, forcing his brain into icy calm. It would require more luck than skill to get them out of this without bloodshed.

'Sir John lives. But is injured—his arm or shoulder, I think,' Robert reported as he joined them. 'At least he's on his feet.'

'Right. Then there's hope for us.' Richard picked up the cloak and cast it round Elizabeth's shoulders. It fell to cover her from shoulder to ankle, to cover her unconventional appearance. He pulled the hat firmer on to her head. Then pushed her to stand behind Robert, as a young squire might wait behind his lord.

'Don't say a word. Don't move until I tell you. Try to be invisible.' He snarled the words, hoping that the venom might encourage his wife to obey him. 'If you value your life or your freedom, you'll do as I say. Or even if you value mine.' He ignored the quick reaction, the stiffening under his hands as she absorbed his words. There was no time for niceties. 'You are Robert's squire and will wait behind him in silent service. Keep your eyes down, your face in shadow, your mouth closed.'

Not waiting to see if she would comply, he spun around. A group of soldiers in de Lacy livery were covering the ground at a run, some with drawn swords. They had accurately judged the direction of the arrow. Praying their luck would hold,

Richard plucked up the longbow, the arrow, and thrust them both into David's hand.

'What…?'

'Play the role as if you life depended on it. Which it might very well do. A foolish boy, lacking discipline, judgement and ability with a bow. A lad who deserves a harsh beating for his stupidity this day.' Which was enough of a hint. David immediately fell into an arrogant posture and a suitably sullen expression. 'Let's pray your uncle is unwilling to push the matter beyond the obvious when he sees who's involved. If you ever had ambitions to be a mummer, now's the time.'

Richard brushed the dust from his own tunic, ran a hand through disordered hair and snatched at the veneer of confidence and authority that threatened to be overcome by the whole ridiculous situation. Praying that Elizabeth, his superbly unpredictable wife with a commendable passion for vengeance, however ill timed it might be, would remain silent, he turned with a stern expression to face de Lacy wrath.

'Malinder!' Sir John himself approached the little group on the hill, breathing heavily from his exertions. Blood stained the sleeve of his tunic and dripped from his fingers. 'What in God's name? Would you endanger another de Lacy life in so public a manner? When all the world and his wife is here to stand witness?' He raised a hand to signal his men-at-arms to move forwards and surround the culprit.

'Sir John… What can I say?' Richard also groped for any latent talent for acting. A heartfelt apology, a touch of wry humour, a dash of anger. 'Thank God you're not harmed.'

'No thanks to you.' Sir John's fist clenched on his sword hilt.

'Not guilty, my lord.' Lord Richard spread his hands in uneasy regret. 'Here's your culprit.' He grasped David none too gently by the arm and yanked him forwards to face his uncle.

'David!' Sir John's face reddened under a surge of blood as he found himself facing his sulky nephew. 'David?' His voice harsh with disbelief.

Sullen, full of misplaced confidence, David cocked his head, a youthful braggart. 'I was only practising. I would take my turn at the butts and not disgrace the de Lacy name against the Glamorgan archers.'

'You fired into the crowd?'

An insolent shrug.

'You fool! You put an arrow through me!'

'It was an accident. As I said, I was practising.' He cast a careless eye over his uncle's bloody garments. 'I think you're not badly hurt, sir.'

There was an intake of breath at such defiance and Sir John looked ready to explode. Richard stepped in with perfect timing. 'Practising? In a crowd of people? Aiming at a buzzard flying overhead, I suppose. Where did you expect the arrow to fall? You could have killed anyone.'

'I didn't think.' The sullen cloud thickened. David hunched a shoulder. 'I am a de Lacy. I am not answerable to you, Malinder, for my actions!'

'You appear not to be answerable to anyone.' Richard took on the mantle of strict guardian. He stared down his fine nose with superb and splendid disgust at the unrepentant young man and sliced at him with all the sharp precision of a boning knife. 'As you are living under my roof, at the request of your sister, whose wishes and happiness are my first priority, you'll accept my authority and my judgement. I'll brook no such disobedience or indiscipline.' Without warning he lifted his hand and dealt the lad a brisk cuff to the side of the head. It knocked David to the floor, more out of surprise than force, but with the desired effect. 'I've rarely seen such a display of thoughtless stupidity from one who would aspire to a knighthood. You should have been disciplined long ago. You could have had blood on your hands this day.'

'But I didn't.' David sat in the dust, managing a curl of his lip.

'No, you didn't. Fortune smiled on you, a situation you did not deserve. Sir John is only wounded. Get up.'

David did so, in undignified discomfiture, yet still as ungracious and unreasoning as before.

'Sir John could have you beaten to within an inch of your life. As it is, you've made us the object of speculation. We'll be the talk of every family the length and breadth of the March.' Richard spared him one final contemptuous glance, then turned to de Lacy. 'My apologies again, Sir John. Perhaps you wish to take him to task yourself.' Hoping he had done enough to allay all suspicions.

'Yes...well.' Sir John had remained a silent witness of the scene. Now he addressed himself curtly to Richard, but without the previous edge of aggression. 'There's no need, I think. He's young and will learn his lesson.' He eyed his nephew dispassionately enough.

Richard exhaled slowly, carefully, conscious as he had been throughout of Elizabeth's simmering fury behind him, barely contained. He could sense it in the air, taste it, as he could sense and taste the passion in her when he took her in his arms and kissed her into shivering compliance. How could John de Lacy not be aware of so much emotion around him? Yet Sir John had taken no account of the apparently insignificant figure, cloaked and eyes downcast, behind Robert Malinder's large figure. 'You need care, my lord.' Richard gestured. 'Your arm still bleeds.'

'A flesh wound,' Sir John answered curtly as he eyed David. 'It is high time you returned to Talgarth. Some self-discipline and good manners are required as well as training before you step into my shoes.' Then he inclined his head in final recognition of the Malinders and strode off back down the hill to where the archery contest had at last got under way, his retainers following.

David hung his head, scuffing his feet in the dust until his uncle had vanished into the crowd. 'Well? Did we do it?' he murmured, not yet looking up, but his grin wide.

'I think we did. You were magnificently disreputable throughout!' Richard managed a smile as he picked up the offending longbow and arrows again. 'You missed your call-ing. I owe you much and stand in your debt. Thankfully, you have a hard head!'

David laughed aloud, relieving the tension.

And that, Richard thought, as he disguised a sigh of relief, was that. Or at least until he took Elizabeth home and faced her wrath.

At Ledenshall, Elizabeth abandoned the cloak, suffocating in its folds, and the velvet hat, but she still wore Richard's tunic and hose. As the few short miles had passed on their silent and edgy return journey, she had begun to review her actions. Not that she regretted them. She could not! But the dangers attached to such public and provocative behaviour had been made very obvious. Without the intercession of her husband and brother, things might have gone very differently. Particularly for Richard, in spite of all her careful planning. Yet she was still not of a mind to repent.

'I can't think what to say to you.' Richard's voice held no condemnation, she realised, just a weary acceptance that served to increase her guilt.

'There's nothing that you can say. I know what you are all thinking.' She raised her chin. 'But if you had not stopped me, Lewis would have been avenged.'

'And you would have been hauled off in chains with the prospect of a rope around your neck. I think we shall not come off scot free, as it is. Too many people saw the situation. No one intervened or was willing to point the finger as Sir John was apparently fooled by our charade, but we shall hear talk. That the archer was not David de Lacy, but the Lady of Ledenshall in disguise.'

'Sybil de Lacy got her revenge with a knife to the heart of her enemy!'

'*You* are not Sybil de Lacy! And she, by God—whoever Sybil de Lacy might be—' Richard thundered his fist against the table in utter frustration '—should have known better! I suppose she became the talk of the March as well.'

It was true. She had been wrong. She had allowed raw emotion to rule her actions. The guilt intensified, but she would not retreat. 'Let them talk,' she announced. 'I have nothing more to say. I'll leave you to your destruction of my morals, my family and my character. To your squeamish morality. I'm not in a mood for repentance.' And, then on a final thought, 'No one has bothered to enquire about my state of health, after being dragged to the floor!'

'You deserved it.' Sympathy was entirely absent from her husband's reply.

If it was possible to flounce in tunic, hose and boots, Elizabeth did.

It could not be put off longer. Giving her temper time to cool, and his, Richard braced his shoulders and followed Elizabeth. She had exchanged her borrowed attire, as if suddenly finding it unseemly, an uncomfortable memory of the day, to cast it carelessly on the bed. Standing by the window of her chamber in a loose robe, she was now clearly waiting for him. Richard could read her resistance in every taut line of shoulder and spine, of raised chin.

Although she chose not to face him, Elizabeth spoke before he had even closed the door. 'Don't say it. I know I should not. I know I should have weighed the personal satisfaction against the consequences—and I did not.' Her voice hesitated on what might have been evidence of regret. 'But still I wish I had succeeded.'

Richard remained at a distance, his back against the door, his voice remarkably cool and at odds with the temper that still snapped at him. 'Then we should all have been in the mire. Did you actually consider the political repercussions of your assassination? With so many lords present with their retainers, with war on their lips and in their hearts, the death of de Lacy with an arrow through his heart could have been the flame to light the conflagration. Bishop's Pyon could have been recorded as the only Midsummer Fair ever to disintegrate into a total blood bath—with de Lacys and Malinders at the centre of it. My blood runs cold to think of it.'

Elizabeth kept her back to him. 'All I could think of was Lewis. I was wrong.'

Which confession was momentous in itself. Richard allowed his thoughts to drift a little. She looked alone and so sad. So his wife had borrowed Lewis's clothes, had she, when she had wished to run wild as a girl? Until Philip had persuaded her otherwise with the strength of his arm, as Richard could well believe. The anger that had simmered all afternoon retreated a little and he felt a need to lift some of the weight from her shoulders. She had been wrong—almost disastrously so—but he understood her motivation and the pain that drove her.

Quietly he came up behind her. Put his arms around her to draw her back against him as she stared out into the twilight. After an initial tensing of her muscles, she leaned back against him with a little sigh.

'I thought you would be so angry.' Her voice was tight from mortification.

'I am angry. But it seems that there is no more I can say that you do not already know. What point in my lashing you with words if you can do the job quite well yourself? Nor is there anything I can do other than rely on the return of your good sense—except lock you up or not take my eyes off you for a second.' He rested his chin against her hair, noticing inconsequentially as he did so that it was growing, thick and dark. It took no effort to turn to rub his cheek against it with an unwitting little murmur of pleasure. 'Do you realise that some at the Fair have already named you Malinder's Black Vixen?' he asked. He did not know whether to be amused or appalled at his wife's sudden notoriety.

'What?' Elizabeth angled her head to look up and back.

'Some, it would seem, saw the truth of the incident—and your dark tunic and hose... I heard the whispers as we came away.'

'Oh.' Elizabeth was silent, her mind turning over the day. 'I put David in danger, didn't I? When he took the blame.'

'You put us all in danger. Your uncle is probably at this very minute back at Talgarth, replaying the events in his head, rearranging all the details that don't quite fit the over-all impression. Why we should all have been standing on the hill, watching David loose an arrow at his uncle, I have no idea! Sir John will doubtless come to the conclusion that I put David up to it. A family conspiracy, if you will, a de Lacy to kill a de Lacy. Now there would be a fine thing.' Then he remembered. Tightened his arms around her as he felt her strain against his hold. 'Except that such an eventuality has already happened with Lewis. Forgive me, Elizabeth. I did not intend to be crass.'

She sighed against him, relaxing again.

'I am sorry.' It was the barest whisper, but heartfelt for all that.

'I know. I knew that you would be, as soon as you allowed your hard head to rule your heart.'

When she accepted this in silence he murmured against her ear, 'You must not do it again—or anything to harm Sir John or compromise our position. A spark is all that is needed to engulf the March in flames.'

'I just wanted to do something... To make him suffer as Lewis had suffered. And you would not...'

Richard chose not to resurrect all the old hurt, but remained silent for some time, his arms around her, wrapping her in warmth and comfort. Her head rested on his shoulder as he felt the tensions of the day ebb from her.

'You have to promise me, Elizabeth.'

'Very well.'

'Say it.'

'I promise that I will do nothing to endanger Sir John's life.'

'Even if you will do nothing to save it.'

A soft huff answered him, which might have been agreement. 'And I promise to do nothing to compromise your honour. Will that do it?'

'It's enough. What a problem you are to me!'

'Mmm. And I borrowed your clothes.'

He turned her round with careful hands, but did not release her. 'You are a brave woman, Penthesilea. A true Amazon, with or without your clothes. But next time leave the longbow at home.' Then on a sudden thought, his knuckles brushing along her cheekbone. 'Did I hurt you? It was the only thing I could think to do.'

Elizabeth sighed, turning her face into his palm that cupped her cheek so perfectly. It healed her heart that he should remember, and care. He might not love her, but this softness was more than she could ever have dreamed of and she was grateful.

'No. Nothing but a bruise or two. Perhaps I deserve that you had,' she replied with bitter acceptance.

'Never that.' And Richard kissed her, softly, lingeringly.

At Talgarth, Nicholas Capel breathed deep, donned his black robe and trained his concentration on to the matter at hand.

The cards before him were Italian in origin, their colours bright with power. The Fool. The Empress. The Hanged Man.

The Wheel of Fortune. Now, under his hands, they would work for Nicholas Capel. He scanned the chart at his right hand. Knowing the exact moment of Elizabeth's birth, there had been no difficulty in his drawing up of her horoscope. Now he would look more closely into her destiny. Into his mind he brought the image he had seen in his crystal. Richard Malinder and Elizabeth de Lacy standing face to face, hands entwined, a kiss a breath away. Sharp edged, their bodies melded, as their lips met, as he had bound the wax figures. Satisfied, Capel considered his question.

'Does she carry the Malinder heir?'

A brief pause. His breath barely disturbed the candle at his elbow.

'Will the child be a son?'

One by one he reversed the cards, revealing their message. His eyes widened, scanning from one to the other.

'Yes, and yes!'

He allowed his fingers to stroke delicately over the surface of each one as if to draw the power from them for himself. The time was right to act. If Elizabeth was fertile, if she already carried a male child as the cards foretold, then all was in place for Malinder to die. Capel blew out the candle. So would Malinder's life be snuffed out.

Nicholas Capel smiled.

Chapter Fourteen

Coins were exchanging hands between Richard and a cattle drover as Robert walked into the Great Hall at Ledenshall. 'Who was that?'

'A drover from Pembridge,' Richard replied thoughtfully. 'A large party of Welsh raiders on the move, he thinks. I suppose I should go and look. A show of force will not come amiss.'

And if nothing else, it would take his mind off the vicious catastrophe. At Northampton, there had been a battle, a desperate clash of arms in which York's army had emerged victorious. King Henry, outmanoeuvred and outnumbered, was now a prisoner in Yorkist hands, his wife and son on the run for their lives. The prospect of the Duke of York becoming King of England haunted Richard's every sleeping and waking moment.

They traversed the local roads with a tight, well-disciplined escort. Nothing. All quiet.

'A figment of our drover's drunken imagination, I suppose,' Richard remarked finally. Rain was beginning to fall and the banked clouds in the west threatened more to come. 'Home, I think. Nothing to be gained by staying out in this. The Welsh are probably long gone if they were here at all.' Yet Richard frowned as uneasy suspicion, almost a premonition, played along his spine. Perhaps it was just too quiet. At a signal the escort pushed their horses into a steady trot along the road.

Ahead, moving slowly towards them, a party of travellers emerged from the murk with supply wagons, a small herd of cattle, a motley array of dogs. It was not the best of places for the two converging bodies to pass as the road narrowed where trees had been allowed to encroach and overhang, bushes thickening the undergrowth. Richard signalled his force to halt and pull aside, urging their horses into the thickets on either side to allow the travellers to pass.

The cattle plodded on with lowered heads and frustrating slowness. Until a fierce barking broke out from the undergrowth to their left. Then a sharp yelp of pain, followed immediately by a deluge of noise, as deafening as hounds on the scent, as the rest of the motley pack abandoned their guard duties and rushed to support their suffering fellow.

'Beware! Ambush! Watch the trees!' Richard raised his voice above the mayhem as recognition blasted through his mind. Why had it taken him so long to see what was happening? Figures on horseback emerged through the trees on both sides of the road whilst arrows from short bows began to fall amongst them as softly as the rain.

There was no room for either attackers or attacked to take up positions on the road as the cattle surged and pushed amongst them. Seeing this, at a silent signal, those who had placed the ambush abandoned any formal plan and withdrew back into the trees. 'That way.' Richard waved his cousin to the right as he drew his sword and plunged into the trees on the left. The soldiers divided into two parties and followed behind, crashing into the dense undergrowth with shouts and the thud of hooves.

And then it was over as quickly as it began. Agile and light of foot, impossible to catch in the overgrown thickets, the ponies and their riders melted away through the dense woodland, leaving Richard no choice but to signal his men back to the road. One of the drovers had taken an arrow through his arm, one of the men-at-arms in the shoulder above his leather jack, neither serious.

'Your Welsh raiders, I suppose. Well, we managed to stop one of them at least.' As they regrouped to push on home, Robert pulled aside into the underbrush, then dismounted to turn over a body, so far overlooked. 'No livery or emblem, so must be Welsh.' Richard joined him, to kneel by the body.

Dark haired, eyes dulled and half-closed in death, the raider was tall and well formed, unlike the usual wiry build of the Welsh.

'I don't know him,' Richard stated.

He would have pushed to his feet when his attention was snagged by a glint of gold. The man's poignard, still attached to his sword belt in a tooled leather scabbard, the hilt highly decorative and chased, set with semi-precious stones, Italian, perhaps, with finely wrought hand guards. Richard bent again, unfastened the fine blade. A memorable piece and valuable far beyond the dagger of any minor knight. Or a Welsh raider.

'What do you think, Rob?' The Malinder troop was once more under way as Richard let the series of events trickle through his mind.

'I don't know.' Robert's grimace expressed his suspicions. 'A chance attack by opportunist thieves?'

'I think not.' Richard's face was grim as he bent to avoid another overhanging branch. He looked at the dagger, tossed it in his hand, the jewels glowing in the wet. Definitely not one of a common thief. 'It was a large force, carefully hidden in a most advantageous place. A true ambush rather than a chance encounter. But whether we or a herd of cattle were the main target...'

'I know where I'd put my money!'

'I wouldn't take the bet. Now, if I were to discover the identity of the owner of this fine weapon…' Richard tucked it into his boot.

'I'd say someone meant you harm, cousin.'

'So would I.'

Richard kicked his stallion into a canter. He would consider it later. When he had time to think. But the unease that this was no chance attack grew. Someone sought his death. Not by chance, but with deliberate intent.

Elizabeth, too, was unsettled.

Richard was uncommunicative, his temper on a knife edge, his patience sparse. It nagged at Elizabeth. Something had happened that he wasn't telling her. She knew of the defeat of the King at Northampton, of course, and of his subsequent imprisonment. That was enough to put a scowl on Richard's face, having York in the ascendant. And perhaps the tensions between them had not quite gone away since her attempt to put an arrow through the black heart of her uncle. But there was something else. Richard was ferociously preoccupied, so much so that it was like living with a permanent thundercloud.

So Elizabeth was unhappy.

It had come to her of late that there was one possibility within her domain that could jolt her lord out of his edgy mood—if he had an heir to fight for, a future to consider not just for himself, but for a son to carry on the Malinder name. It was time she quickened, hence the little bag of walnuts tucked into her belt, since all clever women knew that to carry a walnut in its shell would aid her fertility. It also explained the sprinkle of poppy seeds in her wine. It was simply a matter of time.

As for Richard's part in this plan, she could not fault him. He showed no reluctance to come to her bed. He wanted her. His virility was clear enough. But something was missing, a warmth, an attentiveness. There was a lack of involvement despite his invariable politeness. And that was the problem. Where he had once taken her with searing passion, sometimes with humour, always with consideration for her own pleasure, now he was…well, distant. He would kiss her and hold her and take her in physical union—but it was as if he held his thoughts and reactions in check. As if he feared laying himself open to her by saying too much or showing too much emotion. And from his thoughts and concerns, from the dreams that troubled his sleep and the worries that dug a line between his brows, he blocked her out entirely. Sometimes when his physical needs were sated, he left her, without explanation, to go to his own bedchamber.

Which might not have mattered to the Elizabeth de Lacy who had come from Llanwardine as an unwanted bride. That Elizabeth had entertained no illusion over the marriage other than as a pragmatic arrangement. But it mattered now. Filling a bowl of fragrant herbs to aid calmness of mind, Elizabeth crushed the lavender stalks between her palms as she separated them from their dried flower-heads. Stealthily, on silent feet, unsought and unwanted, love had crept up on her and ambushed her, much as the pungent scent now filled her senses. She remembered admitting it, reluctantly, the day Richard had paid his debt on her victory at the archery butts. Since then love for him, strong and dominant, had imperceptibly stolen in, to fill every little space in her heart and mind so that she could not escape it. It was not just his handsome face or his magnificent body. Not just his care of her, his endless support when she had been grief-stricken over Lewis's death or driven to mindless stupidity against his murderer. Not just his honesty, his sense of justice. Nor his ability to grasp a crisis and turn it to his own advantage. She recalled the near-disaster at the Midsummer Fair with a shudder of horror. Nor even his amazing willingness to let her cry out her grief, soaking his tunic, without a thoroughly masculine withdrawal into embarrassment.

So what was it? She did not know. All she knew was that she loved him. His hard-muscled body combined with his gentle touch. Or the fast race of hands and mouth that set her aflame. He did not love her, of course. Elizabeth's fists tightened further around the bruised stems. But she missed the man who had talked to her. Laughed with her. Awoken her body to a pleasure she could never have guessed at.

'Damn the man!' Elizabeth muttered. She missed the close intimacy that she had begun to take for granted. And her heart ached that Richard should be unhappy whilst she was unable to do anything to help him. How could she when he would not talk to her? Elizabeth ached for her failure to break through the shell of his introspection. Gwladys, lady of all virtues and all talents, would have soothed him with soft words and elegant kisses!

Even now Richard was away from home. He had taken to riding round the Malinder lands, not bothering to tell her where he was going or why. She missed him. She was lonely without him. And desperately restless, for some reason she could not fathom.

Which drove her to make a decision. She would go to Bishop's Pyon. How could Richard object to that? For some reason—again that restlessness—she had a need to return to the place where she had spent her childhood years.

'I shall go to Bishop's Pyon,' she informed Mistress Bringsty. 'And don't tell me that Richard would not approve. Richard is not here to approve or disapprove. I shall go.' And Elizabeth felt a guilty pleasure in her disobedience.

As Ledenshall finally came into view, Richard found it difficult to extricate himself from the dark cloud that seemed to have engulfed him for days. If only it were simply the imprisonment and mental state of the King. True, Henry was past knowing his own name, and his son had yet to reach ten years. There seemed to be nothing to bar the path between the Duke of York and the throne. Could he ever give his allegiance to the Duke of York as King of England? Never! Not this side of the grave or beyond! But for now that was not his main concern. The repercussions of the conflict in the March were far more immediate, where law and order had disintegrated alarmingly. Where, in his own lands, safety and security could no longer be guaranteed.

His gut clenched and he was forced to bite down on the nausea that rose, bitter as bile, as he recalled the scene he and his men had just left. That he had been unable to prevent. The tumbled bodies of a party of innocent travellers, cast into the ditch beside the road. The blood and tangled limbs, women and children as well as their menfolk. Robbed, stripped. Slaughtered. The worthless waste of it all. He had not been there this time when the robbers had struck, so the travellers had paid with their lives. Responsibility pressed heavily on his shoulders.

What if Elizabeth had fallen prey to such vicious despoilers? Richard quickly thrust the vile thought away.

As for the attack by the Welsh raiders… Was it a chance encounter? Or was it a well-laid ambush where the undergrowth encroached on the narrow track, an ambush inadvertently spoiled by the arrival of a herd of cattle? Had he been the target, and if so, whose gold had paid the raiders?

One name persisted in his mind.

But there was no way of knowing, so what purpose in allowing it to sour his mood? Richard cursed himself for a fool. He should have put it all aside days ago. There was Ledenshall before him, familiar, welcoming, and Richard felt a lightening of his spirit, acknowledging that he had allowed himself to be distracted for too long. Better to put aside his fears for the future, hold firm to his authority in the March, and simply wait for events in London to unfold. His own deep reservations over the future king would not affect the clash between York and Lancaster one jot.

First, before anything, he must talk to Elizabeth. As he should have done weeks ago.

A gaudy pheasant rose to wing from the grass verge, causing his stallion to snort and sidestep. As if the russet colouring of the bird had triggered a memory, Richard's mind slid to Gwladys. He could think of no two women more different from each other than Elizabeth and Gwladys. One so beautiful as to steal his breath. The other...

But what a disaster his marriage to Gwladys had turned out to be. Racked by inexplicable fears and nerves that had nothing to do with reality, Gwladys had watched him as a rabbit watched a circling buzzard. Feared him, feared all men perhaps. Had certainly feared and rejected intimate relations between a man and his wife. Bedding her had been a nightmare of an experience for both of them. No matter how gentle, how slow and considerate he had been, despite his own youth and inexperience, Gwladys could hardly bear to have him touch her hand without shivering in distaste, shutting herself away in her own rooms with needlework and music and her prayers. Her connection with his people at Ledenshall was reduced to a minimum. She was as lovely as the gilded statue of the Virgin in the chapel, and just as lacking in animation with her empty smile and blank eyes. Gwladys remained cold and unresponsive. It had been much like bedding a stone statue, Richard recalled, Gwladys cowering against the pillows, the linen clutched to her throat. It would have been laughable if not so painful a memory.

Now Elizabeth was neither cold nor unresponsive. Elizabeth did not shrink from his touch, even when it was only fingertip to fingertip. What a complex woman she had proved to be. Strong-minded, outspoken to an alarming degree, but so vulnerable, touched by the sadness of her past and the cruelties of the present. Gwladys had been beautiful, but

Elizabeth… Before his mind rose a sharp image of her elegant cheekbones, those magnificent night-dark eyes now offset by silken hair in which he could wind his fingers, the softened outline of jaw and chin. Elizabeth was far from unattractive. The picture made him shiver with desire. Suddenly the need to see her, to touch her, was almost overwhelming.

Without questioning the urge, Richard applied his spurs, at the same time pricked by remorse that in recent weeks he had deliberately pushed her away from him so that he would not be drawn to burden her with the worries that gnawed incessantly at his mind. He had proved neither a good husband nor an attentive lover, even knowing that his withdrawal hurt her. The thought of her willingness to accept the demands of his body brought a surprising surge of lust to his loins. It was time he made amends. Elizabeth deserved better than his recent neglect of her. He found himself smiling as he approached the gatehouse.

The smile was wiped from his face when Richard strode into his home to where Master Kilpin bowed him welcome.

'My lord. I thought it might have been the lady—but perhaps she'll stay the night after all. The light is already falling.'

'Where is she?'

'Gone to Bishop's Pyon, my lord.'

'Bishop's Pyon!'

'Master David has gone also, my lord,' Kilpin replied, suddenly wary at the fierce response. 'And Commander Beggard took her with a strong escort.'

'What!' The reply was as sharp as a viper's strike. 'Why in the Devil's own name should she find a need to go to Bishop's Pyon?'

'Well, my lord…'

'The roads are dangerous. If there are a dozen bands of

thieves on the prowl, there are two score. I shall fetch her home.'

Richard rode to Bishop's Pyon with a terrible fear in his heart.

Chapter Fifteen

Elizabeth did not stay overnight at Bishop's Pyon. She did not know why she had wanted to go there in the first place, an inexplicable whim that she could only put down to the fidgety, uneasy mood that drove her, unless it was to relive some of the happier times of childhood when her mother lived. The brief visit gave her no satisfaction, and she was glad to return to Ledenshall. Besides, Richard might be home.

There had been another reason for her desire to be gone from Bishop's Pyon. To her amazement she had found Nicholas Capel there. He had offered no explanation, other than that he was sent there on an errand by Sir John.

He had been polite and respectful. Elizabeth recalled their cursory meeting with a frown between her brows. He had asked after her health. He surveyed her with some deep interest, lingering on her face, her cloak-shrouded figure, from her toes to the crown of her head. It had been hard not to squirm under the blatant appraisal. Thrusting out his hands, he had seized hers before she could resist, his fingers enclosed around her wrists, and searched her face as if he would read something there.

'Master Capel!' She would have pulled her hands away, but he tightened the hold.

'The last time that we met, lady, at Talgarth, I was concerned for your health.' His words were soothing enough. 'I merely wished to satisfy myself that you are restored to the best of health.'

'Yes. I am well. Why should I not be?'

'No reason, lady. My mind is relieved.' He released her.

There was no threat there and yet… The horoscope lingered in her mind. Her flesh crawled. And then David had joined her, putting an end to any personal discussion.

'Your uncle would welcome a visit from you to Talgarth, my lady.'

'Thank you, Master Capel. I'll consider it.'

But she would not. She had nothing to say to Sir John. And, yes, she would be glad to be home at Ledenshall. How strange that she would think of it as home. And that she should feel this deep desire to see Richard waiting for her in the courtyard, his strong hands ready to lift her down from her mare. His smile, for her alone, enhancing his striking features. What had happened in so short a time? There was no other man who had ever touched her senses as he did. No other man could trip her heart and steal her breath, who could inflame her blood with a single look, a single brush of his fingers. No other man had ever stolen her heart other than this marcher lord who held her happiness and contentment in the palm of his hand, who was intent on creating a distance between them, and was at this time God knew where!

She had never loved any man as she loved Richard Malinder. There! She had finally spoken it in bold words, if only within her own head. Elizabeth felt the familiar heat rise to her cheeks at the thought of him holding her in her arms again, kissing her into a miraculous state of joy. Even now she could taste him, scent him, imagine the splay of his fingers on her naked flesh. Her mind lingered unnervingly on the delight she could find with Black Malinder.

And then, as they approached the brow of the rise before the long slope down into Ledenshall, there he was, drawing rein before them. Mud-splattered and sweat-stained, as was his escort, the Malinder pennons lifting sluggishly in the still air. There he was as if her thoughts had magicked his appearance from the shadows.

His brow was black with anger. The muscles of his jaw rigid.

'It's Richard. Come to meet us,' David said unnecessarily at her side.

Elizabeth felt her heart miss a beat. And her breath catch, just as she knew it would. The flush deepened in her cold cheeks as she braced herself for the approaching confrontation.

But Richard simply fell in beside them, so at least the clash of wills was postponed. Beyond a curt acknowledgement, he was clearly in no mood to discuss whatever ill humour rode him and Elizabeth, angling her chin, made no attempt to engage him in conversation. What would be the point? She left it to David.

By the time she reached her chamber, Elizabeth was less sanguine. A half-hour of horseflesh appreciation between her brother and husband had peeled away any tolerance. She stripped off her cloak, her gloves and flung them on the bed. To be all but ignored on the journey home, by both of them. Beneath the chill he had been furious. Beneath the calm discussion with David, anger had bubbled. She had seen it in the tight grip of his fist on the rein, in the cold fire in his eyes. Well, she wouldn't have it. She might have admitted to loving him to distraction, but if she was to have a frank exchange of views with Richard, she was in no mood to be compliant. She was tired and ruffled and in no good temper. First Capel studying her as if she were some strange creature from his magic charts, then Richard riding beside her with a brow as black as thunder, no doubt furious at her decision to travel to Bishop's Pyon. She would have something to say about that when he deigned to present himself.

The door to her chamber opened to admit her serving woman's sturdy figure, carrying a jug and ewer.

'Jane. I'm frozen half to death and weary to the bone.' She tried to push her edgy mood away as Jane poured the hot water. Sat silently as Jane began to prepare a cup of mulled wine, added logs to the fire that had been allowed to burn low. Came to help Elizabeth remove her gown, stockings, rub some warmth into her cold feet and hands. Produced soft slippers and a houppelande that enveloped her in its soft folds from chin to floor, loosely secured with a plaited girdle. Took away her light veil and brushed out her hair, grunting as the silken black length of it at last reached to her shoulders. When the wine was hot and the pungent scent of the spices filled the room, Jane ladled it into a cup.

'Lord Richard, I take it, is not pleased.'

'No. I know not the reason. Our exchange of words so far has been brief.' Elizabeth sipped. 'Whether it be my visiting Bishop's Pyon… But, no, he is not pleased.'

'Hmm.' Jane stood before her, fists on ample hips, beady gaze intent.

Unaware, Elizabeth continued, focusing on the swirl of cinnamon in the wine. 'He won't talk to me. He shuts me out as if I were a servant. Or one of his hounds that gets under his feet. How can I help him if I do not know what the problem is?' It suddenly felt good to release the issues that had been layering silently inside her. 'If he would only tell me…'

On a thought and with narrowed gaze, Jane lifted a candlestick to move it closer. Then stood with it in her hand, her eyes fixed on her mistress's face.

Elizabeth caught the look. 'Now what is it?'

'Let me look at you, lady.' Mistress Bringsty held the candlestick higher to cast light more evenly over Elizabeth's face. The clearly marked brows, the dark eyes a little strained, the oval face, now more comely and rounded, but still with sharply elegant cheekbones. Then she put the candle down and took Elizabeth's hand. Looked long and carefully at the palm, running her fingers over the soft skin, tracing any pattern that she could detect in the lines. 'Well, now...'

'Well, now, what?' Unusually petulant, Elizabeth pulled her hand away. That was the second time this day someone had peered at her as if she were a strange insect in a cup of ale. 'I swear, Jane, I'm in no mood for riddles either.'

'No riddles, my lady.' Mistress Bringsty's face creased in a rare smile. 'It's clear enough to those who can read such things. I wager you've fallen.'

'What?'

'Perhaps it was a good season for walnuts after all.'

'No! It cannot be. I didn't know...'

'Since when do you need to *know* to fall for a child? I can see it in your face. As clear as noonday at Midsummer.'

'No!'

'No point in arguing, mistress. It's done. Early days yet, though.'

'Yes. Early days.' Elizabeth's mind tried to pin down the emotions. Stunned, yes. Shocked. And delighted.

'His lordship might not have been doing much talking, but he appears to have been proficient in other matters.'

Elizabeth pressed her fingers to her lips. Was this the cause of her restlessness? And what would Richard say? Her eyes lifted to her servant were rapier-keen. 'Jane! If it is so... You are to talk to no one about it.'

'Not my place to gossip, my lady.'

Elizabeth angled a glance 'When I want anyone to know—' *when I want* him *to know* '—I'll be the one to say.'

When Jane left, Elizabeth remained in the chair by the fire.

The cat sprang to her lap as if sensing her need for comfort, purring at the soft cloth beneath its paws. Was this not what she wanted? Perhaps. A little warmth grew below her heart to spread and enfold. It was what Richard would want. A Malinder heir. But she would not tell him. Not yet, until it was a reality in her own mind. Until she knew what was in his heart. She spread her fingers over her flat belly and hugged the thought to herself with not a little joy.

But first she and her husband must come to terms.

When Richard entered her room without knocking, he found himself the victim of a direct attack, swift as a sparrow-hawk. Elizabeth rose to her feet, tipping the cat from her lap without compunction, and advanced. Her head was raised, her shoulders braced and spine straight, her arms stiffly at her side. Ready to do battle.

His intentions were not quite clear even to himself as he flung back the door, but the blaze of fear caused by her thoughtless journey, not to mention her damnably stiff-necked refusal to appear in the slightest contrite, goaded him into taking her to task. If he remembered his earlier decision to talk to her, open his heart to her, even accept some comfort from her, it was swatted away as a troublesome horsefly. So he had stayed only to remove his cloak and his sword before taking the stairs with hot urgency, his thoughts tumbling one over the other in justification of his anger. She would not take herself off around the county on a whim. She would not put her life in danger so that all other thoughts were instantly driven from his mind, his heart frozen, a solid lump in his chest. She was his wife, his woman, and he loved her. He had a need to protect her. He could not imagine his existence without her. She had no right to put herself in danger. He loved her, obdurate as she was. When he had seen her ride towards him, all he had wanted to do was sweep her up and carry her home. Until she had raised her chin in sheer defiance.

And still, in spite of that, because of that, he loved her…
Loved her?

No! Love had no place in his emotions. Love weakened a man, compromised his choices. Life with Elizabeth was far simpler if based on respect, affection even.

But his heart thudded against his breast bone. What he felt for Elizabeth was far stronger than affection, far more forceful than a desire to protect. But when had this happened? He had no idea. Richard was still reeling from the shock of that one incontrovertible fact, of that ultimate acknowledgement, when her first words met him, as subtle and conciliatory as a punch to the jaw.

'Before you say anything, I wish to make it clear, Richard. I can go to Bishop's Pyon if I choose, when I choose. I do not need your permission.'

He knew he should mind his temper, bite his tongue. She was his love, was she not? But the latent fear got the better of him. It still had him by the throat. But he would try to remain calm, reasonable, even if she would not. Like hell he would! His reply mirrored his tumultuous thoughts. 'Not if it puts you in danger, lady. You are not free to risk your life and safety as and when you choose. You will do as I say.'

'In danger? I was in no danger!'

'From robbers. Brigands. Any of the riff-raff who swarm over the county in its present state.'

'Surely you trust Simon to escort me.'

'Yes. But are you aware of the target you would make?'

She raised her chin again. A gesture that she thought might just set light to his temper. A wicked impulse urged her on. She was in the mood for lighting a few flames. Elizabeth firmed her mouth against a little smile as she watched her lord struggle for control.

'For God's sake, woman. Are you not aware of the value of your person as a hostage? Or even for the simple matter of robbery. Did you even think about the value of your cloak?

That damned brooch that I was foolish enough to give you. The horseflesh. Law and order hardly exists in the March with the King under armed guard, and with the marauding Welsh thrown into the mix it's impossible to keep travellers safe. And you would deny the existence of danger!'

'Well! I had not thought.' Elizabeth was furious that he was right. Touched by his concern for her.

'When did you ever?' Fury compromised his control so that he felt it slipping through his fingers, so that Richard found himself spilling the words he had determined to keep to himself. To paint for her the horror that faced him when he heard she had gone to Bishop's Pyon alone. 'This day I saw the terrible result of such a robbery not five miles from here, on my own lands. Shall I tell you? Naked bodies in a ditch, innocent travellers, women and children as well as their men, stripped of all dignity, hacked and despoiled to remove jewellery. Robbed of their lives. That's what I feared for you.'

Her heart clutched. But she would not back down. Here was no cold distancing, no deliberate stepping back. Ripe fury vibrated, his eyes alive with it, his whole body primed for action. As if he would spring forwards, a hunting cat on its quarry. They faced each other, focused and hissing as cats on the stable roof, whilst her own animal, coward that she was tonight, retreated to crouch beneath a rush chair. The air in the room positively crackled. Where had seduction got her? Now defiance! This was far better for causing a conflagration. Even though she might tremble at the outcome, even though she might be consumed by it.

'You will not put yourself in danger,' Richard continued, face vividly ablaze. 'I expect you, as my wife, to be discreet. You don't know the meaning of the word discretion. The Malinder's Black Vixen is the talk of the March.'

His control was now balancing on the narrowest of edges. Elizabeth sensed it. 'I shall do as I please.' That should do it. She waited, breath held.

Richard swooped, hands gripping her shoulders. 'No, you will not. Not when it puts you in danger. Not when your loyalties conflict with mine.' He shook her, but was still sufficiently in command, just about, to temper his strength.

'Ah, so that's it.' She frowned. 'Did you think I was going to join my uncle, to engage in Yorkist plots against you with my de Lacy family?'

'No. Of course not—'

'How completely unwarranted!' So where was fairness now? 'How dare you dishonour me.'

'Be silent—'

'I will not!' She wrenched herself from his grasp to sweep across the room, from where, at a safe distance, she turned to glare. 'I have had enough silence from you these past days. It's time you talked to me and told me what is making you as ill tempered and edgy as an autumn wasp amidst a glut of apples.'

'Elizabeth, I warn you. I'll not tolerate—'

'Will you not, Richard?' Elizabeth stalked back across the room, took hold of the furred neckline of her lord's tunic, tugged and kissed him full on the mouth. 'Will you not? What is it you will not tolerate?' Again she took his mouth with hers.

It took them both aback.

Elizabeth recovered first and spoke what was in her mind. What had she to lose? 'I care about you. I care that you are troubled and unhappy. I hate that you are distracted and preoccupied. I hate that you shut me out as if we mean nothing to each other, even if it is only that we share a bed and disagree over who should wear the crown.'

She kissed him again. Fast and fierce. 'So, what have you to say now?'

'Ah…very little.' His thoughts had scattered into the air. 'Elizabeth…'

'Richard!' She scowled at him, still not satisfied.

And Richard found himself transfixed by the brilliance of her eyes, and was suddenly speaking the words and thoughts that had distilled in his heart on his ride back to Ledenshall. That had driven him to unreasonable fury when he discovered her absence.

'Do you not realise that I love you?' *How should you. When I did not even know it myself?* 'That the thought of losing you or allowing harm to come to you destroys me. It's not your politics or your family allegiance that drives me to intemperance. I care not whether you are Yorkist or Lancastrian. If you were attacked, harmed, I would be wounded, too. If you were killed—living without you would be too painful to contemplate. I love you…' It was unnerving to hear it spoken aloud into the silent room. Unnerving to watch her response.

'Ah, Richard…'

He could read nothing in her face, which became carefully guarded. She touched her tongue to lips gone suddenly dry. He closed his hands firmly over hers, held them wrapped close. 'I love you, Elizabeth. Why I should find a need to love a woman so opinionated and wilful, I have no idea.'

'The same reason I should love a man who is arrogant and dominant and would command my obedience, I suppose.'

He heard her reply, lethal to the heart. Took a moment to take in so astonishing an avowal of love. Much as his had been for her. But Elizabeth again recovered the faster. She huffed a breath, her exasperation more evident than her professed love. He still did not seem to take her meaning. Why was he so *slow*? So she would make it plain enough, to hammer a nail into a plank of wood!

'I love you, Richard Malinder, God help me! I dare you to remain silent now.' She shook her head. 'You fool, Richard. You beloved fool!'

And then she was in his arms and they were closed fast

around her. Who moved first was unclear, but the outcome was the same.

'I am filthy.'

'I don't care. So am I.'

They tumbled to the bed.

'I was afraid for you. I could not bear to lose you. I love you.'

'Show me. Show me now!'

'I can do that.'

Minds played little part in what followed, only touch, demand answering demand. Only an unspeakable need, a fire to burn hot between them, to scorch and consume all their differences. Desperate kisses, a fast race of hands, a furious dragging away of garments until there was nothing to separate them. Elizabeth's hands, smooth as silk on chest and belly, over hips, wrapping around his hard erection, all but robbed him of control.

'No…! Not yet!' A harsh intake of air as he struggled to command his body.

Capturing her wrists, Richard pinioned them above her head as his mouth ravaged hers, his tongue seeking and discovering that dark, inner sweetness. Then, anticipating that same hot sweetness between her thighs, and because he could resist her no longer, with one thrust he entered her, hard, sure.

'Richard…' Elizabeth's voice hitched on a ragged breath, her body arching in demand as sensation bloomed to make her shiver on the edge.

'Watch me, Elizabeth. Stay with me.' The kiss he placed on her lips was all tenderness, all delicacy, despite the tumult that had brought them to this moment.

'Yes.' She gasped as he began to move within her, to fill and own, and she shuddered beneath his weight, his urgency. 'I know who you are, Richard.' She returned the gentle caress in something akin to awe.

'As I know you.'

It was the last softness, the last words between them for some time. Richard proceeded to drive them both to mindless oblivion before burying his face into her newly grown hair.

Breathing settled, blood cooled. Their minds took longer to recover, stunned at the explosion of passion that had swept all before it, carried them with it. Until the underlying scents tickled Elizabeth's senses. She wrinkled her nose. Dust and horse, leather. It was not unpleasant, but she now thought longingly of scented water. Even so she had no desire to move, so turned her cheek against Richard's chest, enjoying the sensation of his heart beating strongly beneath her ear.

'I love you, Elizabeth. I could worship the ground you step on. Why did it take me so long to see it?' Richard lifted her more firmly against him as his mind took control from his body once more. He had lived with her, argued with her, God knows he had disagreed with her. And at some point he had simply fallen in love with her. Cradling her face between his palms, he took in every beloved feature. How had he not seen her beauty beside Gwladys, who had blinded and wounded him against other women? And there she was all the time, hair silken soft against him, eyes dark, mysteriously enchanting. A beauty all her own. Why had he not seen it, acknowledged it, until now? Her delicious curves, firm yet soft. Seductively smooth under his hands, his mouth.

'Because you did not want me,' Elizabeth answered gruffly, truthfully.

'I don't think I knew what I wanted. But now I do.'

'I didn't match up to Gwladys.' Elizabeth sighed. 'You can't deny it.'

'No. You are nothing like her, thank God!' Richard placed his fingers lightly on her lips when they parted to ask. 'No. No more about Gwladys tonight. Have I told you how beautiful you are?'

'No.' She would have looked away if he had allowed it. 'No one ever has. And I was a poor thing when I came to you.'

He touched her mouth with his own, whisper soft. 'Then it is for me to tell you. You shine as the sun on my horizon. You glitter as the most costly of all my jewels. You are more precious than all my lands, all my estates. You are my whole life.'

Elizabeth could not reply, too full of emotion, satisfied to lie beside him and drift for a little time in a sea of immeasurable contentment. So they loved each other. A miracle, as bright and precious as her Book of Hours. One that she could not quite believe—but had he not said the words? So had she. Had he not proved it with his body, that hot possession? As she had responded. Elizabeth felt the deep flush stain her skin at the knowledge of her response. She tucked the delight away to take out and study, to think about later. But the business was not done. She would not quite let the Lord of Ledenshall off the hook yet, even if he could worship the ground she stepped on.

Had he really said that?

'Richard—tell me why Henry's defeat troubles you so. Why you cannot—*will not*—support York, if we have to accept a Yorkist Plantagenet king.'

'Hmm?'

Elizabeth prodded his ribs, achieving an instant wince. 'I need to know.'

'When did you ever not?' he murmured. 'I thought you were asleep. I was.' He stirred enough to plant a slide of kisses along her shoulder. 'But now I'm not,' he murmured, his breath warm against her neck.

'Richard!' She shivered, was tempted to abandon every plan but the one clearly in his mind—but set her will to resist. 'Richard—will you tell me? What troubles you. Why is York an anathema to you as king in place of Henry? Both can claim royal blood.'

Richard groaned. 'I see love hasn't mellowed you.' But he curtailed his kisses. And because it was in his mind and because something had loosened round his heart, he told her the whole. His despair over Henry's instability, his inability to rule the country. The wanton destruction of law and order in his own lands. All the concerns that had made such uncomfortable travelling companions on his ride through the March. All of which she knew. But then, what she had no presentiment of, he told her of the Duke of York's outrageous actions after the battle at St Albans, laying it all out for her to examine and judge. When Richard Plantagenet, the then Duke, had ordered the execution of Sir Thomas Malinder, Richard's father, ordering the striking of his head from his body in bloody retribution.

'There was no need for my father to die,' he finished. 'He could have been imprisoned, ransomed, as were the other Lancastrian leaders. Instead he was dispatched like any common criminal. It was a political murder to remove a rival in the March. Vindictive and bloody. I cannot forgive it, but forgive me for shutting you out. It's a habit—keeping my thoughts close—not sharing them.'

'I'll forgive you—but only if you don't do it again.' Elizabeth kept the moment light, even as it touched her heart that he should share so personal a burden of bitter residue of loss and grief with her. She stroked a hand across Richard's chest, as if she could smooth out the rough edges for him and make the future plain. The old Duke had been killed at Wakefield back in December, his title inherited by his seventeen-year-old son, Edward, Earl of March. 'I think we can only wait and let it play out. Perhaps Edward, the new Duke, will be an easier man to follow.'

'Perhaps he will.'

Richard captured her hand, to press his mouth to her palm in a wave of gratitude. Elizabeth understood. Why had he held back for so long? But he would not tell her of the ambush set for him. Nor of his suspicions of its instigator. They were still uncertain, and now was not the time to burden his new love with such fears for his safety.

Chapter Sixteen

Yuletide festivities. Elizabeth was now certain. She carried a child. She had said nothing yet, as too often a child was lost before its existence was even recognised, but her monthly courses had stopped and although she suffered from no unpleasant or obvious symptoms, thanks to an infusion of sweet balm leaves steeped in wine, she *knew*.

'Did I not say so?' Jane smirked as she helped her mistress into a sumptuous gown of jewel-like amethyst brocade with oversleeves to sweep the floor in luxurious extravagance, lacing the low-necked bodice, looping the beaded girdle. And Elizabeth forgave her. It was a very precious knowledge and she could not but rejoice. So, she decided, it could be in the way of a Twelfth Night gift for her lord. It pleased her to wait a little longer and to anticipate his pleasure.

At the feast, they drank, exchanged cups, drank again, lips claiming the imprint of the other's lips in deliberate possession, as eyes held and expressed every emotion they did not put into words. A loving cup such as was never shared at their wedding feast.

Then, leaving those who would to drink and roister until dawn, they withdrew to their chamber. Elizabeth poured the wine and came to sit beside him, bringing with her the pewter goblets and a carved and inlaid box, smiling as he raised his brows in query.

'I have a Twelfth Night gift for you, my lord.' She smoothed her hand over the fine wood of the box on her lap.

'Have you now? And what might that be, my lady?'

'When we were wed you gave me gifts. I wanted to give you something. As a symbol of my love.'

With a brush of lips against her hair, Richard took it from her, opened the ornate lid. Turned back the soft velvet wrapping and lifted out, to sit on the palm of his hand, a little ivory chess piece, cunningly carved into the shape of a knight astride his horse, arms raised to grasp sword and lance and shield. Perhaps, looking at the intricately worked mail coat and carved folds of a linen surcoat, a crusader from years past. It was beautiful and a mere herald for the exquisite castles and bishops and pawns that followed to be lined up on the table at his side.

'They're magnificent.' Richard turned the figure of the king in his hand, complete with crown and sword and staff of office, his robes swirling in stiff folds to his feet. 'York or Lancaster, do you suppose?'

Elizabeth sighed and leaned against him. 'In truth, I don't know. And at this moment—dare I admit it?—I don't know that I care.'

'What a conformable wife you are tonight!' He placed the king next to his stiff-backed ivory queen with her severe and unsmiling expression. 'Now, what should I give you in return, my wife?'

'You've already given me a gift.' Her lashes hid her smug complacence from him for a little time yet. But not much longer. She burned to speak out.

'Apart from the cloak and the brooch. I gave you those before I came to love you.' His arms slid smoothly round her so that she fit against his hip.

'That's not my meaning.' She eased her dry throat with a sip of wine, put down the cup. Then looked up, gaze open on his and steady. 'You have given me a child. I carry your heir, Richard.' The emotion built as she saw the realisation of her words strike home, to his very heart. Her smile lit her face with joy, an inner glow that brought a flush and a sparkle, as if she had won a victory in battle.

'A child!' There it was in his face. The delight. Then the quick concern for her safety. How she loved him for that. 'How long…? How long have you known?'

'Ha! I swear Jane told me within a week!'

'A witch's prediction?'

'No.' The clasp of her hands on his soothed and reassured. 'She's skilled in reading the signs. But now I am sure. My body tells me. Three months, I would say.'

He turned her so that they were facing. 'Since I can't think of the words to say to you, I think I must kiss you.' And did. Pouring into the meeting of lips all the tenderness and fierce possessiveness he felt for her and their unborn child.

'You'll have an heir before the end of the summer,' she whispered when she could.

And then nothing would do but for him to take her to bed and repeat the relevant act all over again. Elizabeth felt she could never be happier. Surely the future would smile on them.

The future scowled in the form of a royal messenger, a hastily delivered document, driving Richard into immediate action.

'Elizabeth. I have to go. There's to be a battle and I'm summoned to join the Queen, in the name of the King, with any force I can muster.' He was suddenly swamped with the logistics of travel with armed retainers over water-logged roads. Until he realised that Elizabeth had not replied. He looked up from the parchment. A deliberate smile. 'I'll not die, I promise. I'll be back before you know it.'

'You can't know that. I'll pray for your safety.' Face strained, she walked to stand close. The little knot of anxiety that had been present since the first days of their marriage, and even after the bright glory of their love for each other, still remained firmly lodged, a piece of grit in a pearl. This was not the best of times to ask, but she knew she must. Selfish it might be, but there might never be another opportunity. Ask Lord Malinder, Jane had said, so she would. 'Richard—will you tell me one thing before you go?'

'Anything.' He could not read the stillness in her face.

She bit her lip, could not meet his eyes for fear of what she might see there. 'I know it's foolish but—tell me about Gwladys. You never speak of her.'

She could sense his wariness. 'What do you want to know?'

Elizabeth frowned. 'Did you love her? Does she still hold a place in your heart?'

Of course. Carelessly, he had not thought, had not even considered the possibility. That Elizabeth, in her vulnerability when she had first arrived from Llanwardine, had lived with this fear that his heart remained in Gwladys's keeping. Richard discarded the letter to draw her close, so that he might rest his brow against hers with a little sigh.

'Did you love her?' Elizabeth repeated.

'Love her? No. I did not.'

'I thought you loved her,' Elizabeth stated gruffly, 'loved her too much to love me. She was very beautiful.'

'Elizabeth! Have I not said that I love you?' Richard stroked her hair, letting it fall and curl through his fingers. 'You need not fear Gwladys. She is not some wraith who demands my loyalty, who will haunt and step on the edge of your gown whenever you turn your back.'

'I didn't know. Gwladys seemed to be a forbidden subject.'

Elizabeth waited and he knew he would have to explain. So he did, as simply as he could, struggling to prevent the old hurt from resurfacing.

'Gwladys was lovely beyond question. But any intimacies in marriage terrified her. She put up with my demands because she saw it as my right, but there was no joy in it for her. She shrank from me, hated every minute of it—which made me feel like an uncivilised barbarian. I tried to be gentle, considerate. It did not make much difference—I doubt the lady could see the difference between a seduction or a rape. She felt only relief if I did not come to her bed. My only consolation was that she would probably reject any man, no matter whose arms held her. But I was very young and there was always that doubt…that *I* was the problem.'

'Oh.' Elizabeth could think of nothing to soothe so deep and personal a wound. Her eyes darkened at the sadness and silently cursed the lovely Gwladys for the pain she had unwittingly inflicted. Then sharpened. 'I remember. When you first took me to bed. When I flinched when you would have stroked my hair—or lack of it. I was embarrassed.'

His lips twisted in wry pain. 'And I thought—well, you can guess what I thought when it seemed you did not wish to be touched. I could not bear it again. I had known Gwladys for ever, since we were children, you see.' Sliding his hands down her arms, Richard drew Elizabeth by the hand to sit with him in the window-seat where the sun gilded and warmed them both. 'I thought we had a close friendship, certainly enough affection to pass for love in what was considered by our families as a desirable marriage. I was wrong. Even the friendship died. Gwladys gradually retired into her own world of embroidery and prayers. She fulfilled her duties as my wife and Lady of Ledenshall without question, but only what need

demanded. After she quickened with my child—I no longer
went to her bed. It was a relief for her and for me.'

Elizabeth bowed her head at the pain she had resurrected.
'I am sorry to have raised the spectre.'

'As I am sorry it troubled you. I suppose I should have
told you long ago.' Raising her chin with his hand, he gently
wiped a suspicion of a tear from her cheek with the pad of
his thumb. 'Don't fear her, Elizabeth. You have all my heart.
My love and my respect. Do you still not know that?'

'I do know it.' Her smile was brilliant and he saw the
leap of desire in her eyes. '*I* do not flinch from you, dear
Richard!'

'I am aware.' She felt the rumble of a laugh deep in his
chest as he pressed his lips against her temple. 'As *you* should
be aware, my Amazon—that you are more beautiful to me
than any woman, past or future.'

The remaining sliver of ice in Elizabeth's heart, that whisper of doubt that she was not worthy of his love, dissolved
into joy. There was no one in Richard's mind but her.

The day of Richard's departure arrived. Elizabeth woke. It
was still early with only enough grey light to create shadowed
outlines in the still room. At some time in the night she had
turned to Richard and his arm, although lax in sleep, was
curved round her to hold her close. Her hand, which she had
spread against his chest, made her aware of the slow rise and
fall of his breathing. Turning her head gently so as not to
wake him, she could make out the clean profile, the fan of
dark lashes against his cheek, the ruffled fall of dark hair.
Wished for the light to brighten so that she could see more
clearly, could study his face without his being aware and
fix this moment securely in her mind. Considered and then
rejected the temptation to stroke the dark wave where it lay
on the pillow. It mattered. Heart-breakingly it mattered. For

today he would take his retainers and ride to inevitable battle
in the name of the imprisoned king. Death or glory.

The darkness paled further. Elizabeth revelled in the
warmth, his closeness, breathing in his scent, the imprint of
his flesh on hers. Oh, how she loved him. And the miracle
of it was that he loved her. And even more of a miracle that
Gwladys no longer haunted her. The icy jealousy around her
heart had quite melted away. Perhaps if King Henry was
restored to his throne, then Richard could come home and
they could try to live with some semblance of normality. But
God knew when she would see him again. She could not even
think of any other alternative. Unable to resist any longer,
she lifted her hand to touch the silk of his hair, then with a
finger to trace the outline of his lips. And felt them curve in
response.

'So you are awake,' he murmured, turning his face into
the soft angle between her neck and shoulder, pressing light
kisses there.

'Yes.'

'I can hear you thinking.'

'Only how much I love you,' she murmured in delight that
he was awake. 'I shall miss you, dear Richard.'

Drawing her close to savour her smooth skin and the sharp
perfume of herbs in her hair once again before he left her,
Richard allowed himself to be steeped in her. Held her so that
she might experience the strength of his desire for her once
more. So that she stretched, sighing, as he slid so perfectly
inside her. And Richard deliberately controlled the pace as
they rocked together in the warm sanctuary that was their
own. Gentle, tender, with none of the scorching passion that
sometimes consumed them when they came together, it was
a long, slow loving, to remain with them when the days and
miles stretched between them. Until Elizabeth shuddered
against him, driving him into his own dark surrender. Until
both lay with heightened breathing, but content at the last.

She wrapped her arms around him as if she would still hold him, yet knowing that she must not. It was the burden of women to wait and fill their hands and minds so that they would not contemplate the dread outcome of battle.

As if he could read her mind, Richard pushed himself to his elbows so that he could look down into her face. His was serious, the lines strongly marked. 'I need you to hold the castle for me, Elizabeth. In my name and that of my heir. To protect my people and my land. Will you do it?'

'With all my heart, my dear love—' A hammering at the door cut off her words.

'My lord, my lord…' Such was the tone, and the voice very young, that Richard leapt from the bed, stopping only to snatch a robe for modesty's sake before he opened the door to one of the kitchen lads.

'Master Beggard sent me, my lord.' The child was out of breath, his eyes wide with shock and excitement. 'He says to come at once. We are beset.'

'Beset? What's wrong?'

'A force, my lord. Master Beggard says to tell his lordship it's not friendly, by God!'

'Did he now? Tell him I'm on my way.' The lad sped off.

'What is it?' Elizabeth asked anxiously, suddenly remembering a previous occasion when Richard had been summoned from her side to the tragedy of Lewis.

'I don't know. But I soon shall.'

The battlement walk provided a perfect vantage point from which to view the problem. Richard leaned beside his commander with narrowed eyes. Before the castle, already deploying around the walls in both directions, was a considerable force of men-at-arms and archers. Baggage wagons could be seen where a camp was being set up. There was no pretence at taking the inhabitants of the castle by surprise. Orders were shouted, curses floated on the damp air, as men jostled and manoeuvred equipment into place or unloaded baggage animals. It was a formidable force, prepared to stay.

'A siege, my lord?' Richard felt an echo of the amazement in Simon's voice.

'Must be. They're digging in.'

Robert joined them, alerted by the commotion and the growing noise.

'Visitors. And not with good intentions towards us.' His laugh was sharp, humourless. 'Who in God's name would set up a siege in February, and when the situation between York and Lancaster is at so crucial a juncture?'

'I don't know.' Richard scanned the scene again, taking in the other obvious omission. 'What do you notice, Rob?'

'Apart from a large, well-organised force intent on taking your castle?'

'Look at them!'

'Ah!' Robert nodded. 'Faceless and nameless.'

But it was Simon Beggard who spoke the thought. 'There's no livery, my lord. No standards, no pennons, no herald—or not that I can see. We don't know who comes against us.'

'And, I wager, we're to be deliberately kept in ignorance,' Richard replied. 'So who would come against us in this manner? It'll take them months to reduce us to surrender. We're well stocked with provisions and our water supply is secure. What in God's name are they thinking of? They must know I won't negotiate.'

'Well, there's your answer.' Robert pointed to the road where horses approached, slowly, ponderously, dragging heavy wheels behind them. 'Whoever it is has no intention of negotiating terms with you either.' The horses dragged behind them four large cannon. 'You've a powerful enemy, Richard,' he stated. 'Someone who intends to blast a hole in your castle wall and simply walk through.'

Richard watched as the cannon were dragged into position, their purpose horrifyingly apparent. Someone, hiding behind deliberate anonymity, intended to destroy the castle wall. And since no herald summoned them with traditional courtesy to a parley before the attack began, the besiegers were not interested in offering terms of surrender.

The inhabitants of Ledenshall were soon rattled by the first crash of a cannon ball. Followed by another and then another. An hour later the stonework was beginning to suffer damage. The final outcome could not have been more obvious.

'So what do we do?' Robert demanded, unaware of the grey coating to his red brows. 'We can't just sit here and wait to be battered into submission.'

Richard saw the outcome etched clearly in his mind. The wall would gradually sink and collapse under the barrage, vertical crevasses opening wide. The Malinder men-at-arms would fight to the bitter end to defend Ledenshall, of that he had no doubt, but ultimately? Surrender. Capture. Death.

'We are pinned here like rats in a trap with terriers waiting for the chance to snap our necks in two,' he observed dispassionately.

There was no way out of Ledenshall without meeting deadly resistance.

Apart, that is, from the easily overlooked, completely overgrown postern gate.

On Richard's orders, the men met around the table in the Great Hall. He could have drawn his detailed plan of action into the dust on the surface before him.

'We're in danger.' He let his gaze rest on each face. No point in pretending otherwise, but his voice was calm, his manner exuding confidence. When a missile thwacked against the first-floor level of the keep above their heads, he did not even flinch. 'If we sit here, we shall be at worst dead, at best prisoners. This is my plan. We'll make use of the postern—at the first hint of dawn when men are at their most susceptible. Rob, you and Simon will remain here and keep up the resistance, for what good it is, as if we were all still trapped. Begin a fire attack to draw all attention and open the main gates as if a sortie is planned. It'll distract attention from the ditch by the copse where the postern opens out.'

Richard waited until he had received a reluctant nod of acceptance from Robert. 'It's my intention to get the women out of here. There's no indication that we shall be granted free passage if the wall falls, so I think we must presume that we shall not. I'll deliver the women to safety—and then I shall ride to my estates to collect an armed force. Then I'll return to raise the siege. Four, five days at the most, by my reckoning.'

'Where will you get horses?' Robert asked.

'At the inn in the village—again our only hope. I'll try to get a man out during the hours of darkness to give notice of our needs.'

'What about me?' David asked. His fingers tightened into fists on the table, his dark eyes fixed on Richard, part challenge, part plea.

'Of course.' Richard had already taken the pride of the de Lacy heir into consideration. How to get him out of danger without denying his abilities? 'You will disguise yourself as a peasant and will come with me. I'll need some support if we're to get the women away.'

David nodded, a quick smile, the disguise appealing to his sense of adventure. 'I'll do it.'

'Good lad! I thought you might argue the point. Now I'll go and break the news!'

'I won't go! I won't leave you here!' In the solar Elizabeth faced him, full of ripe fury that he should send her away.

'I am not *asking* you, Elizabeth.' He set his jaw, tried for calm. He had expected this, had he not? 'This is an order. And you are not leaving me here. I am coming with you.'

It had no noticeable effect. 'I'll not be shuffled off to safety.

I'll stay with you and fight against whoever dares to attack our home. Against whoever dares to put your life in danger.' Despite everything, he had to admire her battle spirit, but now was not the time.

'Listen, my foolish one.' He dragged her away from the vulnerable window opening to the centre of the room and forced her to sit and listen, keeping hold of her hands. 'Look at me and listen.' He waited until she did so, only then aware of the glitter of unshed tears in her eyes. 'We don't know the purpose of this attack. We don't know that the usual rules apply because there appear to be no rules, that if I am prepared to negotiate or even surrender, you'll be allowed to go free. We can't hold out indefinitely against their firepower. Someone is very determined on our defeat, so I expect no quarter. This plan—it will be a near-run thing, but I think the balance is on our side. I have to know that you are safe. Once you are removed from here and in a place of safety, then that is one less problem on my mind. I have my men to consider and my people at Ledenshall. If nothing else, think of that.'

His words were clear and simply stated. They cut cleanly to Elizabeth's brain, to her conscience, through the underlying uncertainty and the fear. And of course he had not said anything that she had not worked out for herself. But she could not give in. Could not leave him to whatever fate held for him.

Richard saw her refusal written in her face.

'I love you, Elizabeth—you are my life. Your safety is always, will always be, my greatest concern.' He grasped her shoulders and shook her gently. 'And if something should happen to me, and God grant that it does not, the child you carry will ensure the continuation of the Malinder inheritance.' How could she stand against so stark a truth? 'I'll leave you somewhere in safety and then collect a force from my own tenants so that I can return and raise the siege. It's the only way—the obvious way. You have to see the sense of it.'

And she did. 'I am afraid,' she admitted as she leaned against him for a moment, her forehead against his shoulder.

'I know. But you are also very brave. You will do exactly what needs to be done. As a Malinder and a de Lacy.'

He could not have said better. Now she looked up, face pale but determined. 'Tell me what I need to do.'

'I need to take you somewhere safe. I haven't decided where…'

'Talgarth? I won't go!'

'No! Not Talgarth.' If his rejection was sharper than he had intended, she did not notice.

A glint dispelled the fear in her eyes. 'I know where you can take me. I know where we shall be safe. But you must promise to rescue me.'

'Of course I will rescue you.' Richard kissed her with quick fire, with utmost tenderness, then stood to lift and push into her hands a pile of instantly recognisable clothing.

'Put these on.' He grunted a laugh. 'If we're to travel the wilds of the country against an unknown enemy, we'll take every precaution. You can dress as a lad with my blessing.'

Chapter Seventeen

The night was dark with low cloud sweeping in on a chill wind and intermittent rain, perfect for those planning escape. During the darkest hours just after midnight, two men, separately, slipped through the postern to make their way through the lines, avoiding watch fires and sentries. There was no outbreak of sound to indicate a capture.

Richard took a breath in relief.

Just before dawn, with the faintest glimmer of lighter sky in the east, a little group gathered in the courtyard in a motley selection of borrowed clothes, but all enveloped in dark cloaks, hoods drawn up. Richard in plain gear would travel as a town worthy. Beneath his cloak was strapped sword and poignard. Elizabeth, in male attire, and David with a dagger in his belt and boot, would pass well enough as grooms. Mistress Bringsty robed herself as a merchant's widow. As long as no one looked too closely, all they would see was a small party intent on travel, well garbed against the weather.

At the end Richard clasped Robert's hand. 'Make a good show of force, Rob. We depend on it if we're to bring this off.'

And then they were gone, one after the other, Richard

leading, David bringing up the rear, into the rainswept grey light.

Luck was with them as they slipped through the outposts. Dark cloaks, heavy cloud, a sudden fast shower of rain. At the crucial moment a hail of fire arrows winged their way from Ledenshall's battlements towards the cannon to draw all eyes, enough to distract the sentries. The fleeing group heard the groan and grind of the massive gates of the castle being opened, as if a sortie were planned, with harsh shouts, the clatter of hooves and a blast or two of a herald's trumpet. Richard lifted his head in appreciation. Robert had planned well. Richard forced his mind away from the safety of his home, his family, to the urgency of the mission before him.

Then they were at the inn where three horses were already saddled.

Jane Bringsty was urged on to one, David on another. Elizabeth placed her foot on Richard's to be pulled to ride astride behind him. They were gone, fleeing before the noise and the glow of flames over the castle, where Robert's archers were doing good work.

Llanwardine at last. Pitch-black, the nuns retired to their hard pallets. The walls of the Priory loomed dark above them. No lights were evident, but they drew their horses to a halt at the main door and slid to the ground.

Elizabeth groaned as her shrieking muscles took the strain when she landed on her feet. What an impossibly long journey it had seemed. More than once she had found herself drifting in and out of sleep, her arms clasped round Richard's waist, her cheek pillowed against the rough cloth of his shoulders. Holding to his warmth and his nearness, his strength of body and will, her mind wove through images, unsettling and unnerving, finding it impossible to escape until she could not distinguish reality from dreams.

'Who would have thought that I would rejoice to return here?' Elizabeth murmured.

Richard reached up to ring the bell for admittance. They heard it echo within, but there was no sign of habitation, still no lights. Impatiently, he rang again and now there were approaching footsteps.

A small barred window within the massive door opened. Richard stepped forwards. 'We are travellers benighted, who would claim hospitality from the Priory. We mean you no harm. I am Malinder of Ledenshall. I have two women here with me. They are in need of a place of safety to rest.'

They heard the turn of a key and the rattle of a chain as the door was opened to release the glow of a lantern. There stood the Lady Prioress herself, holding the lamp high to cast light on to the travellers. Her eyes travelled over the little group, then returned to Elizabeth as she pushed back the hood of her cloak.

'You said I should come, if I were in trouble,' Elizabeth explained.

'And you are welcome.'

The Lady Prioress opened the door wide and invited them into sanctuary.

They snatched a heart-wrenching moment of privacy. Despite their rough clothing, they dominated the small room, a magnificent pair, as they stood together in the bare parlour, illuminating it with the heat and vibrancy that ran between them. They were made for each other without doubt.

'Farewell, Elizabeth. God keep you.'

'Keep safe, Richard.'

Both robbed of suitable words, both engulfed in nameless fears for the future. There was every chance that they might not meet again. Their hands clasped tight, their eyes taking in every beloved detail of the other's face, until Richard bent his head and, soft as a promise, claimed his wife's lips.

At first they were cold and rigid beneath his, unresponsive through fear, then warming, softening, opening to his insistent pressure.

What to say?

'I'll come back for you.'

'Yes.' Her fingers clutched tighter. 'I have nothing to give you to aid your safekeeping.'

'I need nothing. All I need is to know that you'll be safe from harm here.'

'And the child.'

'Yes. But, most importantly, yourself. If I should die…' He laid his fingers on her lips when she would have rejected such a thought. 'If I should die, raise the child as I would wish it, as my heir. You can hold the power until the child is of age.'

'I will.' Her eyes glinted, but he knew she would not weep. 'Now you must go.'

Only time for one final salute between them. One final kiss, mouth against mouth in a desperate statement of loss. Of love and impossible passion. Everything he could not say, Richard poured into it so that he would remember the taste of her as he rode away. And she would remember him.

'You have all my love. I cannot bear it, Richard…'

'As you have mine. Be brave, Elizabeth. My love, my heart. My life.'

And then he was gone. Leaving her alone, her heart full of love, her mind full of fear.

Richard swept through the March to summon Malinder tenants to his aid. Marching as fast as they could towards Ledenshall, scouts were sent out ahead, returning with the news that the besiegers must have had their own sources of information. Word of the approaching Malinder force had reached them so that at some time in the night they had melted away, leaving nothing to mark their assault but a series of ugly fortifications and four brass-bound cannon. As the Malinder

standard and pennons heralded their approach over the crest
of the hill, Robert and Simon Beggard were already outside
the wall, inspecting its imminent collapse in one section.

'Good timing, Richard.' Robert's face lit with a broad
smile. 'Better late then never.' The cousins clasped hands
with no need to say more.

Richard eyed the widening fissures, kicked his boot against
a pile of rubble at his feet, already assessing the need for
repairs. 'They did not want to be seen.'

'No, they did not.' Robert fixed him with his bright gaze.
'Any guesses?'

'I think so.'

With time for reflection on the long ride, there was only
one name that returned again and again to Richard's mind
as the source of all evil. He might not know why, but he was
certain he knew who. There was only one man in the March
who could command such a force other than himself. So far,
without real proof, Richard had stood by the letter of the law.
But Elizabeth had been put in danger of her life. His home
had come under attack. He could no longer sit by and do
nothing.

The rest of the day was spent in shoring up the wall whilst
Richard took stock of the damage. It could be worse. A section of the wall would have to be rebuilt, although the foundations themselves appeared sturdy enough. The kitchens,
where David had immediately run bread and meat to ground,
as well as the stables, would need total reconstruction, but
the main structure of the keep and living accommodations
was intact. At least Elizabeth would have a home to return
to. Robert stood at Richard's side, both contemplating the
damage. Exhaustion stamped their faces.

'Another day and that section would have collapsed
inwards.' Robert pointed, acknowledging what they both

knew. It was a near-run thing. 'We couldn't have held the castle longer.'

'You have my gratitude, Rob.' Richard glanced away from the destruction, his decision made at last. It was a lot to ask of any man, but he would ask it. 'I would ask a favour of you.'

'Another?' Robert groaned as he leaned against the parapet, rubbing his face on his sleeve. 'I was planning on going home.'

'De Lacy is involved in this,' Richard stated. 'It *has* to be de Lacy. If I asked it, would you and your retainers ride with me against him?'

Robert never did reply. The hooves of a small approaching force on the road drew—and kept—their attention.

'We have a visitor,' remarked Richard in level tones. 'And, by the pennons, it's a de Lacy.'

At Llanwardine, surrounded and cut off from the world by the long ridges of the Black Mountains, time hung heavy for Elizabeth. She made the best of the unappealing food and bleak accommodation. At least it offered sanctuary.

But it was the not knowing that scraped at nerves and stalked her through the long watches of the night. At Ledenshall it would have been possible to bury her worries, if only for a few short hours, in some necessary activity. At Llanwardine, in the cold fastness of February when even the vegetable plot was abandoned, she was thrown back on her own strength and her courage to hold fast to a distant hope.

No visitors. No news.

And Elizabeth, in her borrowed nun-like robes, went to kneel in the Priory church where she would never have dreamed she would find comfort. The vast, arched spaces and the silence helped her to empty her mind of the terror that gripped her, helped her to think rationally. There she petitioned the Virgin in her cool serenity for Richard's safety.

All she could do was wait. And pray that her black habit was not some dreadful presentiment for the future.

'Aunt Ellen!' David gasped, echoing Richard's astonishment. 'What are *you* doing here?'

Ellen de Lacy made no move to enter the small parlour where she was invited, but simply stood there on the threshold in an unnatural stillness, wrapped around in a cloak muddied around the hem. From what could be seen beneath the sweep of her hood, her usually impassive face was pale and her lips firmly set. Her unexpected presence here at Ledenshall stunned Richard, then something suddenly slithered queasily in his gut. It could mean nothing but ill.

'David. And Richard.' She gave a little sigh. 'Thank God. They told me I would find you here.'

Richard reacted at last, but cautiously, hanging on to a hope that his fears were unfounded. 'Ellen—you should not be here with so small an escort. It's too dangerous, as things are.' The prospect of an unaccompanied woman of gentle blood being alone in the March appalled him. Then, as practical considerations took over, he took hold of her arm and drew her gently into the room, aware of a fragile quality beneath her determination. When she unclasped her cloak he took it from her and pushed her to sit in a chair beside the fire. 'You must excuse the lack of comfort. We've experienced some turmoil…'

'No matter…' Ellen swept it away with an impatient hand, her eyes all for Richard. 'I need to talk to *you*, Richard.' Her expression was suddenly imprinted with a wretchedness that tightened her lips and drew lines at the outer corner of her eyes, and her hand grasped his wrist like a claw. Surprised by such emotion, Richard now saw how drained and tired she looked. 'I have thought about this long and hard. I almost lost my nerve coming here…'

Ellen fell silent as David returned with cups and wine,

accepted one, but did not drink. Instead she began to speak, hesitantly at first, but then her voice growing stronger. 'I know some of what's happened at Talgarth. I watch. I listen. I listen at doors, God help me! Do you see what I have been driven to? Such behaviour in my own home! It is not beneath me to go through papers, searching for God knows what! Locked boxes. Drawers and chests. Even to question servants.' Unknown fears gripped her. Putting aside the cup, her hands clasped and unclasped in her lap until Richard drew up a stool, sat and took possession of them, to still them. He held her fingers gently but firmly in his as she stated finally, 'I should be ashamed, but I am not.'

'Tell me what you know, Ellen. Tell me what brings you here.'

'Yes. Yes, of course.' She closed her eyes for a moment as if to focus her strength. Then began, her voice firm. 'You know about Lewis's death.' She made of it a statement of fact rather than a question, her eyes moving from Richard to David and back again.

He had not expected so open an approach. 'We know about the jewellery that you sent to Elizabeth. And the pieces you gave to David. You said that they were in Sir John's possession.'

'Yes. In his room. I stole them.' Her eyes were wide, as if shocked at her admission, but without regret. 'I can think of only one reason for them to be there. Sir John must have known where they came from, the identity of their owner. And so he must know whose sword struck Lewis down. It would be Gilbert de Burcher. I *know* it was. And then David was kept from contact with Elizabeth and from you when you came to Talgarth with the hawk.' David nodded in agreement when Ellen's eyes slid to his. 'That was Capel's doing. He has a clever hand with herbs and simples.'

'So we suspect that Sir John had a hand in Lewis's death.' Richard gentled his voice as he might to a restive mare. 'But why would he carry out so monstrous an act? Lewis was his nephew and as suitable an heir as any man could ask for.'

'You must think I have lost my wits.' On what was alarmingly close to a sob, Ellen's gaze burned into Richard's as if it were in her power to force him to see and accept the truth. 'It's got to be power, land, ambition… My lord is driven by ambition. A desire to rule the whole of the central March, with no rivalry, with no interference. You can't imagine of what he is capable. And Capel has a hand in it.' For a long moment she lapsed into uncomfortable silence.

'Go on…'

Ellen blinked. 'He wants your death too, Richard.'

'Mine!' There it was, stated openly. The suspicion that had been riding him since the ambush. But Richard frowned. 'Can I believe that?'

'Why not? Think of this. He was keen for your marriage to a de Lacy. When Maude died he was quick to put forward Elizabeth. If Elizabeth carries your heir, and if you conveniently die, leaving her alone and unprotected, who would take care of the grieving widow and her child? Sir John, of course, her concerned uncle. Who would rule the Malinder estates in the infant's name? John de Lacy. Who would be prepared to plot and manipulate until such a position of power had been achieved?' She raised her eyes to Richard's once more and did not need to say more.

'Ellen,' Richard asked slowly, 'does Sir John know that Elizabeth already carries my child?'

'Oh, yes. Master Capel has extraordinary gifts. He says that she will carry the babe to term and it will be a son.' The sneer sat oddly on the lady's soft features, but was more striking for that. 'He can read the signs of the health of the body, of the state of nature, of the past and the future. I swear he has sold his soul and is in league with the Devil himself. And uses his powers to further Sir John's desires—as well as his own.

With evil divination the man was able to recognise Elizabeth's condition. He knows—without doubt he knows.'

'But Sir John's plotting rests on one point.' Richard's mind had homed in on it in Ellen's impassioned words, picked it up, and was working furiously on its implications. 'That I die.'

'Of course. Why not? He killed Lewis, did he not? For some reason, it became necessary to dispose of Lewis. Why not you also, if he considered it necessary?' Her nails dug deeper into his hands, imprinting crescents into his skin. 'Has your life been threatened, Richard? Have there been no recent occurrences to put you on your guard? I think there have.'

He thought about it. As he had thought about nothing other in past hours, past days. It was impossible to deny.

Ellen began to lose patience. 'Tell me about the siege, Richard.'

That got his attention. 'What do you know of that?'

'You would be amazed at what I know. Men are inclined to overlook the presence of a quiet woman who goes about her affairs and makes no comment on what goes on under her nose. As if she were a fool or witless. I am neither! I will tell you about the siege of Ledenshall if you need to be convinced of my integrity. Men without livery. A well-organised attack. No offer of terms or parley because there was never any intention to allow you to escape with your life. And four cannon to batter down your walls. Those same cannons which spent at least two nights in the courtyard at Talgarth on their journey to Ledenshall.'

Richard released a breath as Ellen effectively drew back the curtain to reveal what must undoubtedly be the truth. 'So Sir John was behind the siege.' As he had suspected.

'Of course he was. Easy enough for him to acquire knights and soldiers to fight without livery.'

'But a siege?' Richard still found it difficult to accept. 'Would Sir John attempt so extreme an attack?'

'Yes. Sir John is beyond moderation. A successful siege

would have given him Ledenshall, as well as control of you and Elizabeth, all in one action.'

'So…I can see his planning,' Richard mused. 'How my death would be to his advantage in the March. De Lacy would be pre-eminent. But that rests on the presumption that Elizabeth would hand over her authority as Lady of Ledenshall. That she would willingly hand over the care and upbringing of her child. She'll never do it.' But Richard was horribly aware of what Ellen would reply. A heavy weight of anger began to ball in his gut, began to smoulder.

'And you think Sir John does not know that? Do you truly believe that Sir John is not prepared for resistance from Elizabeth?' Ellen spat her disgust. 'He will destroy any opposition with as little compunction as I would wring a fowl's neck to make a chicken broth.'

'You say he would harm Elizabeth? Are we talking death here?' Richard asked the question he could already answer. The threat was real. Richard's mind was already travelling the road to Llanwardine, to where the defenceless nuns held his most precious possession.

'If necessary, I believe he would. He would not be squeamish if he could achieve his vision of power through one little act of murder. Lewis's blood is already on his hands. What would be one more life—or two?' Lady Ellen's hands tightened around her own cup. She had not yet finished. 'Sir John also has a band of Welsh raiders at his beck and call. I think they were sent against you.'

'Yes. They were.' In some ways it was a relief to admit it. 'But why Lewis?' he asked, returning to the one point that did not fit the puzzle.

'I don't know.' Ellen wrinkled her nose. 'Lewis was a fine young man. I like to think that it was because he refused to go along with my lord's plans. Sir John made a mistake and took Lewis in some part into his confidence. I think—I hope—that Lewis would have threatened to tell Elizabeth—and you. If that were so, Lewis could not be allowed to live, could he? Whereas you, David…' she glanced across, eyes full of compassion '…might be a more conformable heir, young enough to be moulded into Sir John's own image.'

David, standing silently through all this, looked as if he had been struck on the head with a mace.

'And since my lord managed to turn the responsibility of Lewis's death on to *your* shoulders—' Ellen shifted her gaze back to Richard '—no one bothered to even question the true source of the deed. No one would question Sir John, mourning his heir as he did, as if his heart were broken.' She twisted her face away. 'Sir John has no heart to break, as I well know. I cannot bear the knowledge. I had to speak out.'

'So he accused me of Lewis's death.' For Richard the pieces continued to fall into the pattern as pieces into a complicated mosaic in the royal palace at Westminster. 'You have had much to tolerate.' Richard raised Ellen's fingers to his lips in sympathy, marvelling at the inner strength, the sheer courage of the lady to whom he had never given much time or consideration.

But Ellen drew her hands away from the brief caress. 'Richard! We waste time here. You must go to Elizabeth. It's imperative. She's in great danger.'

'No, no. You are mistaken.' Richard would have pressed her to sit again. 'I know where she is. She's safe.'

'*No.*' Ellen's renewed grip on his arm intensified. 'Don't you dare to humour me! She is *not* safe at all. I know where she is. At Llanwardine.' Richard's brows rose. He glanced across at David, who shook his head in denial. He was not the source of the information. Ellen ignored the silent interchange. 'And I think that Sir John has gone there to—to take her back to Talgarth.' She ended on a whisper. 'To take her under duress if she refuses to go willingly.'

'But Sir John does not know…' Richard frowned at Ellen

as her words drove home. 'Ellen…how do *you* know where Elizabeth is?'

'Capel discovered it. It is never wise to underestimate Nicholas Capel, you see.' Lady Ellen shook her head and added, quite calmly, 'I fear him. I hate him. He knows, although I see that you still have doubts.' Her smile was sad, but not without understanding.

Not enough doubts were still lodged in Richard's mind to prevent him sending David to saddle the horses, giving Richard a final opportunity to ask the question that was burning in his brain.

'Ellen—why would you do this?'

She looked down at her bone-white fingers, clenched into fists, and he thought she would not answer. Yet when she lifted her face it held a clear conviction and she spoke at last calmly and from the heart.

'Humiliation can be a very strong motive. My marriage would seem to be one to give satisfaction and comfort to both parties. The perfect match to unite estates in the March.' Her lips twisted with pain. 'But I could not carry a living child to term. I have been made to acknowledge that failure every day of my life since I married Sir John. It became worse when Maude died… So it is vengeance, you could say—no more than the reaction of a bitter, neglected wife, if you would. And I could have loved him… But I know too much and I'll bear no more on my conscience.'

Ellen stood, gathered up her cloak from where it lay over the ladder-back of her chair. 'I see the love that is possible between you and Elizabeth. It is a splendid thing, outshining everything around it. Even when you were both intent on denying it, and each other.' She gave a half-laugh. 'I wish it were for me. But it can never be.'

'Where will you go now?' Richard asked.

'Home. To Talgarth. Where other should I go?'

Ellen allowed Richard to place the cloak around her shoulders and then walked to the door, where Richard stopped to collect his own cloak and weapons from the court cupboard, inadvertently dislodging a dagger, that he had all but forgotten, to clatter against the wood, slide and fall. With excellent reflexes, Richard put out his hand to catch it before it hit the floor. Ellen froze, her attention caught, and stretched out her hand to touch his wrist.

'This. This dagger.' She turned his hand and took from it the jewel-encrusted poignard, lifting it to inspect the workmanship in the candlelight.

'What of it?' Richard frowned down at the weapon now clasped in Ellen's fist, at her close inspection of it. 'Do you know it?'

'Yes. I know who owns it. I would ask how it comes to be in your possession, Richard.'

'Tell me what you know of it first.'

'A fine piece, but well worn.' She smoothed her fingers over the scabbard. 'If you draw the dagger from its sheath—' she handed it over to allow him to do so '—there's a deep notch towards the point of the blade. Shall I tell you how it got there?' He drew the knife. True enough. 'It was used against an opponent in battle. It struck the edge of the knight's breastplate and did not kill as it was intended. It almost cost the owner his own life. I have heard the tale often over a tankard of ale.' She hesitated. 'At Talgarth.'

Richard ran his thumb over the disfigured blade. It was the final nail in Sir John's coffin, hammered in by pure chance.

'So who owned it?'

'Thomas Morgan. A Welsh knight from Builth. One of Sir John's retainers. How do you come by it?'

'It belonged to a man who tried to ambush me,' Richard replied softly as his fingers clenched around the chased grip.

Ellen's answering smile was wry. 'So, Richard Malinder. Do I have to give you any more evidence? What a pity that

Elizabeth's arrow at the Midsummer Fair did not find its mark.'

But Richard was already opening the door, striding down the stair.

With a handful of picked men-at-arms, Richard Malinder once more rode through the night to Llanwardine, with Robert who would not be left behind. He thought he would know every inch of that rough and pot-holed track. They rode in tense silence, pushing their mounts. Richard's tired muscles complained, but he drove them on. Elizabeth was unaware of the danger. Elizabeth believed herself to be safe. Dread rode at his shoulder, a heavy presence that shadowed his every move. He tried, without success, to block from his mind the bloody image of what might await him at Llanwardine.

Chapter Eighteen

Holy Mother. Blessed Virgin. In your mercy, keep Richard safe.

Weaving through Elizabeth's anguished prayers, the voice of the Prioress rang clear and true as she sang the service of Compline, the final office of the day, the sisters kneeling in the choir stalls making the responses.

Keep Richard safe. Let him return to me. Preserve him from his enemies.

Her mind tripped over the request again and again, as beads on a rosary, asking nothing for herself. Except that Richard should return to her. And she added, on a guilty afterthought, safety for David and Robert.

Behind her hovered Jane Bringsty, aware of Elizabeth's every move with the keen focus of a hawk guarding its young. For there was death in the images that came to her mind through the incense. Through her dreams and the casting of the cards which she did nightly in secret. Grim and dark, a man loomed and threatened. The clothes were unclear, the face undefined, elusive as Welsh mist. Her one certainty was that death would be brought amongst them.

Jane hunched against the cold, quelling her frustrations.

What use these old women with their scratchy voices, their empty Latin, shut away in this desolate valley? What use was it if the signs were shown to her, yet she could not read them? Her sight used to be clear enough, but now the future was unreadable, doused in that same thick mist, thicker as the hours passed. Was it her own skills, waning with age? All she could do was be on her guard, even in this place of enclosing walls and rigid rules and the freezing tranquillity enough to stultify the soul.

But tonight there appeared to be no threat. She allowed her gaze to drift over the elderly nuns, the elegant figure of the Prioress and back, as ever to Elizabeth de Lacy—now Malinder—before her. So strong, so determined. Mistress Bringsty made no attempt to participate in the devotions, but would watch over her mistress on whom the waiting and inactivity was becoming more of a burden with every passing day. She would watch over Elizabeth until death robbed her of breath.

The prayers began again. Jane sighed loudly.

The service was over and the nuns began to file out, the stronger helping the more infirm. In the dank February cold, they gathered at the foot of the night stair to take their candles to light them to bed. There was a stir amongst them. Elizabeth deliberately held back, aware only of urgent whispering, the black cowls nodding and fluttering in the draughts. The Prioress turned to Elizabeth.

'We have guests. They wish to speak with you.'

Elizabeth swallowed against her heart leaping to her throat, only one question on her lips. 'Is it Richard?'

'No, my dear. It is not. I will accompany you.' She laid a hand on Elizabeth's arm, but her glance was towards Mistress Bringsty in unusual collusion. 'We will both accompany you. Remember that you are not alone. Have courage, sister.'

But Elizabeth could feel nothing but dread. Not Richard?

Who knew she was here other than Richard and her brother? Who would come for her here? And if another had come, was the news they brought of the worst?

She could never have guessed the identity of the impatient guests who awaited her in the parlour. They had not sat and were not at ease, had not put aside their travelling garments and were keen to be gone. They turned to the opening door as one. Sir John de Lacy. Gilbert de Burcher, the Talgarth commander. Nicholas Capel.

'Sir John.' Elizabeth drew her tongue over suddenly dry lips. 'What brings you to Llanwardine, Uncle?'

But her attention was for Nicholas Capel. Her eyes slid to where he stood beside the door. It was as if he dominated the scene, as if he, habitually black-cloaked and stern-faced, held the ultimate authority in that little room. How had this happened? In that moment Sir John de Lacy seemed pale and powerless in comparison.

Master Capel bowed low before her. She could not fault him there, but fear crawled along her skin. Elizabeth felt Jane stiffen behind her, a low growl in her throat, was aware of the Prioress at her right hand, making one subtle step closer to her. It was impossible to ignore the unsettling aura around this man, although there was nothing of disrespect or threat in his manner. Grave and formal, he bowed before the three women, but his eyes and greeting were for Elizabeth.

'My Lady Malinder. We are relieved to find you here.' The few candles that had been brought to the parlour flickered and overlaid his features with shadow.

Elizabeth dragged her eyes from him, to address Sir John directly. 'Why are you here?' she repeated. Fear licked unpleasantly over her skin. One thought uppermost. How did he *know* she was here?

Sir John approached. It could have been sympathy she saw in his face. His voice was soft with understanding and compassion. Yet she felt Capel's bright inquisitive gaze compelling her to glance towards him again. There was no compassion there, whatever his words.

'There's no way to break this news in a kindly manner, Elizabeth,' Sir John said brusquely. 'It's Malinder. He is wounded—when he returned to the siege.'

'No! Not Richard!' Her lips outlined the words soundlessly as she looked from one to the other. Richard dead? Hurt? Not possible. Rejecting all logic, holding to instinct, Elizabeth's mind resisted. How could she not have known, in her heart, if Richard were hurt? Surely it was all a mistake.

'He lives still, my lady, at Ledenshall,' Capel intervened smoothly. 'But a severe wound. Sir John thought you should join him there. You must come with us.'

Elizabeth fought against the icy blackness threatening to close in on her senses. Simply breathing became sheer effort. If Richard was wounded and near death... Her mind was filled with the image that almost forced her to her knees, so that there was only one choice that she could make. 'Yes. Of course I must go to him.'

She felt Sir John take her hand in his, speaking to her as if she were a child. 'We have a strong escort to ensure your safety. We should be there some time before noon if we travel now. We have brought a horse for you to ride and will see to all your needs. We should leave immediately.' All she could see and hear was the urgency, the concern and the smothering layers of sympathy. All she could imagine was Richard lying at Ledenshall in pain with death approaching, blood on his breast and in his hair. In her waking dream it was as if she could perceive death itself standing by his bed, dark robes spread wide, ready to envelop. She fought against faintness and swayed... Then Elizabeth felt Jane Bringsty's fingers close tightly around her forearm and she blinked, forcing herself back into her mind to think, aware that she was fighting through a barrier of impenetrable heaviness. 'Shall we be in time?' Her words came to her ears from a great distance.

'I hope so, my lady. I pray that it will be so,' Capel replied. He never took his eyes from her face, as if willing her to believe. To obey. She knew it, yet could not resist him. 'But as Sir John says, you should be there at Lord Malinder's side. It would be unwise to linger here.'

Again Elizabeth found herself seduced by those smooth accents and the heavy concern, thick and cloying as sweet honey. They wound themselves around her senses. 'Yes, of course I must go with you, as you say. Immediately.'

Then there was Jane's quiet but insistent voice in her ear, pulling her back from a dark brink. 'Don't listen to him. Who's to say its true, that your lord is hurt? And who would Master Capel be praying to, do you suppose? The Devil himself, I'd say. I don't like it, my lady.' Jane tugged on her sleeve.

'I must go to him.' Elizabeth shook off the nuisance.

But Jane held tight. 'It's not right! Listen to me, mistress.'

'Richard is hurt.' It was the only thought in her mind, bringing the terrible visions closer again. He was near to death. Why was she still standing here discussing what she should do, when his blood was staining the linen on their bed?

'I don't like it,' Jane repeated, now grasping a fold of Elizabeth's skirts.

Elizabeth twitched her garment away and was already moving to the door. And then they were in the cloisters, cold air striking their senses. Elizabeth stumbled, breathed the air, heard the Prioress's anxious concern. 'Why not wait until daybreak?'

And Elizabeth hesitated. One thought breaking through. *Who's to say it's true?* Could she trust Sir John? Could she trust Nicholas Capel? She knew in her heart she could not.

As if sensing her resistance, Sir John was with her, urging her forwards. 'It would not be wise to delay. We leave now.'

'Yes. I have said I will come with you.'

And Nicholas Capel smiled.

Elizabeth saw the curl of the thin lips, the gleam in the dark eyes. Saw the glow of victory. At that moment, Elizabeth knew it was all wrong. In this strange, shadowed holy place, everything was *wrong*. As if the world had tipped on its side, upset by a strong will with wicked purpose. Nor was she the only one to sense it. When the Prioress stepped in front of Sir John, hands raised to halt his progress, he drew his sword with a snarl.

'Get out of my way, woman.'

'I will not. I question your honesty in this, Sir John.'

It seemed that he considered the wisdom of striking her to the floor. Elizabeth waited with breath held, hardly able to grasp this terrible turn of events. With a grunt Sir John changed his grip and with a sweep of the flat of the blade he struck the Prioress a heavy blow against her arm and side. There was force behind it, enough to shatter fragile bones. The Prioress cried out and fell to her knees.

'You were warned, Madam Prioress. Keep out of my way.' He spun on his heel to address his commander, all subtlety abandoned. 'Take her,' he ordered.

'Yes, my lord.' Gilbert de Burcher seized Elizabeth's arm and began to drag her to the door, impervious to her attempts to kick and claw and scratch. For the events of the past minutes had awakened her to the real danger in which she stood. This was deliberate abduction and could yet end in bloodshed. Was Richard wounded or was this an excuse to take her from this sanctuary? What did Sir John intend for her and her unborn child? Cold fury rose to give Elizabeth strength to fight. She had no one to call on, nothing to fortify herself but her own determination to resist. She fought against Sir Gilbert's hold, fuelled by sheer desperation. She would never give in, never allow the Malinder heir to be taken into Sir John's power.

Sir John's patience was at an end. He sheathed his sword, pushed Jane Bringsty unceremoniously out of the way and grasped Elizabeth with both hands around her forearms. He shook her, pushed his face close to hers.

'Save your breath,' he snarled, 'and your strength for the long ride. I'll carry you to the horse if I have to. There's no rescue for you here. I'll treat you with consideration, but don't push me too far.' And he thrust her into de Burcher's arms. 'Now, move!'

Elizabeth found herself hauled inexorably across the cloister.

'No. I'll not go with you!' Elizabeth struggled against the cruel hands, raked her nails down de Burcher's cheek. Blood welled, dripped.

'Bitch! Vixen! You're well named.' De Burcher lifted a hand, clad in a heavy leather gauntlet, and Elizabeth knew that he would strike her. But she would not flinch. She stood her ground and waited for the blow to fall.

'I advise you not to strike my wife. Take your hands from her or, before God, my sword will let your blood.'

Richard!

Elizabeth froze in Gilbert de Burcher's grip, her attention stripped from the painful vice of his hands around her arm. She twisted against the hard grip to face the door. Richard! Not wounded. Not dying in blood at Ledenshall. But here, miraculously, at Llanwardine. She did not bother to question how or why, but simply allowed herself that flood of intense relief to thaw the cold dread. The Holy Mother had answered her prayers. Surely Richard's coming would put an end to this scene of horror. All would now be put right.

At the grim command, softly spoken but with a chilling threat, all eyes were drawn to the arched doorway. Two figures stood there beneath the carved lintel, indistinct in the shadows, but for Elizabeth there was no mistaking the tall figure, the imperious command. Light glimmered along the length of the sword already in his hand. Robert, equally alert with weapons to hand, came to stand at his side.

'Take your hands from my wife,' Richard repeated when de Burcher made no move to do so. The order appeared perfectly reasonable, a request even, but no one could ignore the light in his face as he paced slowly forwards. Cold fury coated a blaze of wrath. With one hand he broke the clasp on his cloak and cast the garment aside.

'Malinder. So you are come.' Sir John's face creased in a satisfied smile. 'I did not expect you. But why not? Why not finish it all here? All my plans coming to perfect fruition at once. It couldn't be better.' He turned to de Burcher, who still clasped Elizabeth close. 'Leave the girl. Kill him.'

Richard raised his sword. 'What's this, Sir John? A cur to carry out your orders? Are you afraid to face me yourself?'

'I have no fear of you,' Sir John snapped. 'And even a cur can kill.'

And Elizabeth found herself pushed unceremoniously out of the way as de Burcher turned, sword drawn and threatening, to face Richard and carry out Sir John's orders. All Elizabeth desired was to move into the shelter of Richard's arms, to touch him and know for herself that he was solid and alive, not a vision of her overwrought imagination, but this was not the time.

'Elizabeth.' One word, expressing all Richard's concern for her.

'I am quite safe,' she replied softly.

'Unharmed?' Low, tense.

Elizabeth nodded and their gaze held for one precious minute, speaking everything between them. Thus reassured, Richard turned his attention back to his opponent who already circled, the point of his sword raised in aggression, his other hand gripping his dagger. Elizabeth kept her distance, retreated one step, then another. To distract him now would only hinder him. But she could not take her eyes from him.

Richard watched Gilbert de Burcher, breathing deeply, exerting the last vestiges of control over his temper, his blood so hot, so full of anger, that it would seem impossible to face this man with icy deliberation and clear judgement. His first sight on entering the cloister had wiped his mind clear of any thought but to punish the man who ill treated her. Gilbert de Burcher, dragging his wife against her will, one hand pinioning her wrists, an arm around her body to all but lift her from the floor. Yet control was of the essence against this formidable soldier who was now under orders to take his life. This same man who had been paid off to kill Lewis de Lacy.

'You will answer for your actions towards my wife, de Burcher.' At last his breathing and temper answered to his will. 'And for the death of her brother.'

'Lewis, is it? And what proof do you have of that?' The snarled response was immediate, the lips curled in derision. 'Come then, my lord Malinder. Let us see who will gain the upper hand.' The smile became a smirk.

Richard was ready as de Burcher lunged forwards, feet agile for so heavy a man, and the personal battle between the two was joined. Attack, retreat. Thrust, parry. Pursue and feint. Both hampered by moving shadows and uneven surface, both intent on victory, because both were aware that defeat would bring death. The swords, heavy enough to crush a skull, to shatter bone, rose and fell with the loud clang of metal on metal, whilst the daggers flashed to search out weak points, careless defence. The protagonists were well matched with muscle and sinew sleek and firm from constant use, much of a height, similar breadth of shoulder. Worthy opponents.

Elizabeth watched with breathless horror, unable to admire Richard's skill, unable to think anything beyond the worst of outcomes, so evenly matched as they were. Both bloodied, both answering blow with blow. She pressed her hands to her mouth when de Burcher's sword ripped through Richard's sleeve into flesh. Felt the pain in her own body when Richard winced with an indrawn breath before leaping forwards into another attack.

Until hope, the tiniest flame, began to flutter in her breast. Richard was fighting with a disciplined rage now perfectly channelled, waging a tireless and implacable assault driven by a need for revenge, his face a graven mask. His sword beat at Sir Gilbert's, the dagger flashed, lured and tasted blood. Elizabeth knew there would be no forgiveness here, no final mercy for the defeated.

Yet the contest continued for what seemed an eternity, unreal and macabre in the cloister of Llanwardine Priory with an audience of bent and elderly Brides of Christ, over the grassy garth, under the ribbed vaulting. Nothing but the thud and shuffle of booted feet, grunts of effort, the laboured breath, the hiss of pain as honed steel met flesh.

The end had to come. Exhaustion took its toll and the broken edge of a raised flagstone. De Burcher lost his footing, for a blink of an eye, but it was enough to distract and Richard Malinder took advantage with a feint, a lethal lunge. The final thrust took de Burcher in the chest below the ribcage, the poignard angling upwards to pierce the heart. He fell like a stone.

Robert knelt to turn the prone figure.

'He is dead.'

'I know. It was my intention.' Breathing laboured, sweat streaking his face. Blood dripped from a deep slash to Richard's forearm. The fires of Hell only died from his eyes when Robert touched his arm, bringing him back to the present and unfinished business.

All eyes on the deadly conflict, no one had taken note of Nicholas Capel, the necromancer. No one saw him as he drew a dagger from his sleeve and stealthily advanced. Not until he stood in the midst of the watchers, his blade glinting in the fitful light.

Of everyone there, Jane Bringsty was the nearest to the grim figure with the dagger. A band squeezed around her heart. The darkness round Master Capel was far greater and more intense than that of his black garments. Here was the source of the wickedness, the dark power that had muffled her skills, of that she was certain. But who would he attack? Elizabeth? All Jane's visions crystallised into one shining certainty in her mind. Of course it was Elizabeth. Had her dreams and cards, her scrying, not told her so? Here was the dark man who would be a threat to her mistress, who would prove to be her sworn enemy. His dagger would take her life. But it must not be! Elizabeth and the child must not be harmed. Without thought, Jane flung herself forwards to impede, to deflect the blade, only to have the necromancer, startled, wheel round in defence. They came together, the small, stout figure attempting to grab the wrist of the tall, powerful man.

It would always be an unequal struggle and the element of surprise was not enough. Whether by chance or intent, the knife's point turned and slid silently, with a terrible smoothness, between her ribs. Jane Bringsty fell to the floor at Nicholas Capel's feet as Robert, too late, too slow in his movements, pulled the man away.

Jane!

Elizabeth fell to her knees beside her serving woman, her friend, her loving companion, uncomprehending of this final turn of fate in the aftermath of all the other horrors of the night.

'Jane. Jane,' she cried, stricken by the total vulnerability of the crumpled figure, the shrunken features which *in extremis* revealed her age. 'This can't be.' Elizabeth tried to call her back as her hands sought to discover the wound, but she knew immediately she could do nothing. The wound was fatal, even though Jane's eyelids fluttered open. A pure effort of will. Blood stained the pale lips as she coughed. Too much blood. The blade had pierced the lung, for which there was no remedy, even within Mistress Bringsty's skills.

Now Richard was beside them, kneeling likewise, using his strength to help Elizabeth to lift Jane to lean against him as her serving woman breathed shallowly in agony and choked in her own blood. When their eyes met it was in acknowledgement of what they both knew. Elizabeth read the truth, the compassion, that brought tears to her cheeks.

Jane's fingers dug hard into Elizabeth's hand. 'I saw death,' she gasped as Elizabeth still tried ineffectually to staunch the blood with her skirts. 'But the truth was hidden from me. I thought it was your death I had seen in the cards. Perhaps it was my own after all…' Jane twisted her face away as the pain gripped harder.

'You saved my life, Jane.' Gently Elizabeth wiped the blood from her mouth and cheek, bent to kiss the hollow of her temple. 'You have always loved and cared for me. As I have loved you.'

'You were the child I never had.' It was an effort for her to speak, to move, but she pulled Elizabeth closer to whisper, 'Take care of the babe. Teach him what he needs to know.'

'I will.'

The Prioress had come to kneel beside them, holding her injured arm against the dark folds of her habit.

'Please…' Jane showed her teeth in what was not a smile. 'I know about death. Do me the courtesy of not praying over me.' Dry humour touched her eyes even in the face of such tragedy, before the pain once more laid claim and she groaned with the power of it. 'It will do neither of us any good. I shall die—and you will surely fail in your petition to God for mercy.'

Ignoring the blood and her own discomfort, Isabel de Lacy

leaned to kiss Jane Bringsty on the forehead in a final blessing. 'Then I will not pray for you.' Although she did in her heart. 'But I will wish you a safe passage, Jane Bringsty.'

'My thanks. You would have protected us. You would have saved my mistress.' Jane's voice and breathing grew more laboured.

'I would save any soul from the grip of evil—and without doubt evil was present this night. Be at peace, sister. Whatever our differences, we were at one in the end.'

'A nun and a cunning woman? Who would believe it?'

The soft laugh ended on a cough. And it was over.

Chapter Nineteen

The breathless stillness was rent by the harsh rasp of a sword drawn from its scabbard. Richard rose to his feet, lifting Elizabeth with him, to find Sir John de Lacy grim-faced, weapon grasped in his hand.

'You have killed my commander, Malinder,' he snarled. 'But you have not won yet. Nor will you.'

Elizabeth found herself clamped firmly to Richard's side as he faced her uncle. His face might be weary, his wounds bloody, but there was no doubting his defiance. 'What do you intend now, de Lacy? Do you kill me now? Or do you take us both to Talgarth? To engineer my death most conveniently in one of your dungeons there, whilst you keep Elizabeth safe and under surveillance until the child is born?'

'Why, yes.' De Lacy's smile broadened to show his teeth. 'I can think of no better plan.'

Elizabeth stiffened within the shelter of Richard's arm. Could she believe this, a cool admittance of deceit and bloody murder? And was this a threat to her own freedom? What did Richard know that she did not? She glanced up at his rigid features, but his attention was all for Sir John.

'You can't stop me, Malinder. My men-at-arms will escort you.' Sir John raised the tip of his sword in overt threat.

'No, de Lacy. You're wrong. It won't hold together any longer.' It amazed Elizabeth how calm Richard could remain under such provocation. 'The events of this night, the skeins of duplicity, are already unravelling. Too many people know or suspect. So you think no one will question a handful of too-convenient deaths? You will have to silence Lady Isabel, I think. Sir Robert too. And you will have to kill me if you wish to seize control over my child. I will resist you with every drop of blood in my body. I will never hand him over to your guardianship. And nor will Elizabeth.'

'Richard...!' Elizabeth could not believe what she was hearing.

'It will be your choice, of course.' Sir John's smile slipped into a grimace since it was no longer needed. The reply cold and callous. 'No one will be allowed to speak against me. At this moment I hold you—all of you—in the palm of my hand.' He held his hand open before him, then squeezed his fingers tightly together into a fist, as if to crush whatever might be in his grasp.

'And David?' Richard asked evenly. 'Are you so certain that he will be the willing ally—which Lewis would not? If he resists, must he die too?'

'Leave David to me. He's young. He'll know his best interests—I will show him the glory of his inheritance. He will rival every Marcher family in the extent of his estates.' Sir John barked a harsh laugh as he swept the matter away as of little account with a confident sweeping gesture. 'Nothing can halt the progression of events now.' He turned his attention to Elizabeth. 'But first I should see to your comfort, my dear niece.'

'I don't understand...' she whispered.

'Your uncle,' Richard said, fury vibrating through him, into her own body, 'has a well-planned campaign. He has followed it since before we were wed. To kill me and take possession of all the Malinder lands through my heir.'

'Is that true?' Even though she asked, she knew it was. She fought to take a breath. 'And you expect me to accept your hospitality, Uncle, whilst you plot Richard's death? I'll never do it. I will broadcast your sins to the world first.'

Sir John merely looked on, considering, icy cold with a terrible confidence, as unconcerned as if she were a small girl intent on some childish piece of defiance, of temper, of rejection of what was good for her. Confidence oozed from every inch of his body, victory in his proud stance.

'Lewis threatened the same when he saw my reasoning,' he remarked. 'I had no choice but to remove him. It should be a warning to you, Elizabeth.'

Elizabeth gasped at the brutal admission.

'No one will believe you, my obstinate niece, even if you do find someone to listen to your woes. A woman's sickness, brought on by the sudden and unexpected death of her lord in a Welsh ambush. If it comes to the ears of anyone, it will be cast aside as nothing but the ramblings of a disordered mind. Besides, you make too much of it. Your are and were a de Lacy before you were ever a Malinder. Where is your loyalty, girl? You will come with me to Talgarth. When the child is born, we will rule the Malinder lands together.'

Shivering, Elizabeth dared not look at Richard, fearing her own weakness if she allowed herself to contemplate his death, if she thought of the blood that was even now dripping from his arm to the floor. But she could not stand by and allow this. Could not allow her uncle to have his way. She could bargain. In that moment she knew that she would give her life if there was no alternative. But there was one chance....

'Sir John!' Pulling away from Richard's grasp, she stepped to face him, and push aside the point of the sword, forcing him to look at her. 'Can we not come to some agreement? Will you not make a bargain with me? In return for my lord's life,

I will return to you all my dower lands. They are not insubstantial—they would increase your holdings in the central
March. Would that not be enough?'

'Such loyalty, Elizabeth. You amaze me,' de Lacy sneered.
'No, they are not insubstantial. They were, after all, the bait
for the rat, to make it impossible for Malinder to refuse your
hand in marriage. But such a small parcel of land compared
with the whole extent of the Malinder lands. Mine for the
taking, in the name of your child.'

'You will have to take my life, too.' She had known it was
a futile gesture all along.

'Then so be it. Meanwhile, Elizabeth, as I said, no one will
believe your feverish rantings of threats to your life.'

'They would believe me, I think.'

The quiet words, dropping like rose petals on to summer
grass, fell into the screaming tension. The slide of soft shoes
on stone paving. Everyone turned. Ellen de Lacy walked
calmly forwards across the cloister until she stood beside her
husband. She pushed back her hood from her veil and folded
her hands before her. Those ignorant of the proceedings would
see her as the perfect submissive wife.

'Sir John,' Lady Ellen said, 'I think you should release your
niece, allow her to go her own way.' She took in the players in
the scene. 'And Lord Richard too. If any harm comes to them,
I will speak of what I know. Any denial from you would bear
no weight. There are too many here who know the truth.'

'Ellen. This is no concern of yours! What are you doing
here?' A façade of concern touched Sir John's features, but
blood drained from his face to leave him ashen in the candlelight. 'You should be at Talgarth.'

Ellen's amazingly serene smile remained in place. 'I have
not been at Talgarth for some days, my lord. I found a need
to make a visit to Ledenshall. And, so it seems, I have a need
to be here also.' Head tilted, she looked at him. Took a step
back when he would have grasped her hand. 'I have to salve

my conscience, my lord. I have secrets that I have kept when I should not. I have prayed about this and I need to put it right. I think the state of my immortal soul might depend on it.'

Sir John continued to bluster. 'Your immortal soul? What nonsense is this? What can possibly trouble your mind?' Again he stretched out his hand to her, expecting her to acknowledge the gesture.

But Ellen drew back her skirts as if she feared contamination. 'I know about Lewis,' she stated clearly. 'And I know about the scheme to draw in Elizabeth, worked out between you, my lord, and that man—that creature—whom you would call your adviser. I knew Richard's life was in danger. So I have spoken of it.'

'To whom?' Suddenly de Lacy was still; a heavy line was dug between his brows. 'Who would listen to you?' he demanded, using all his authority to impose his will on this woman who had never in their marriage stood against him.

'I would.' A young voice gruff with emotion.

For behind her, in the shadowed arches, stood David.

Elizabeth at last felt a tremor of hope begin beneath her heart, felt it swell as she heard de Lacy draw in a breath, the confident arrogance overlaid for the first time with doubt. Surely this would be the end of it. But too soon. In instinctive reply, de Lacy lifted his sword, a bright flash of metal to claim every disbelieving eye. Against whom would he use it?

It was David who spoke, a resonant voice of reason. 'No, Sir John. You cannot. Think of what you are about, Uncle. Do you want more blood on your hands?'

But Sir John's reply was for his wife. 'Ellen. You should have trusted me.'

'I could not. All the lies. What were you thinking? And Lewis… You killed Lewis. You must not be allowed to harm Elizabeth.'

'You have destroyed me.'

'You destroyed yourself.'

Sir John looked around the hostile onlookers as if for the first time he realised the enormity of what he had done. The tip of his blade fell. Elizabeth felt Richard's muscles tighten as his hand clenched around his own sword. She was in no doubt that he would use it to protect her, but she could stand no more.

'Richard.' She waited until he turned his eyes to hers. 'Let him go. We all know his guilt. There has been too much bloodshed here tonight. No more, I beg you.'

She saw the battle in Richard's face. Saw the desire for revenge. And at the end, with gratitude, saw the reason, the compassionate judgement. He bowed his head. 'Very well, my wife. It shall be as you wish. Sir John de Lacy's blood will not be on my hands.'

Sir John sheathed his sword and strode out into the night.

Of Nicholas Capel, alive or dead, there was no sign.

Elizabeth simply stood and looked around her. It was impossible to take in, her thoughts scattered by this whirlwind of unspeakable brutality after so long a period of stagnant inactivity and waiting. And now, as in the eye of the storm, the winds that had brought lies and violence and death to Llanwardine had died away to an uncanny stillness. At her feet lay the mortal remains of the woman who had given her the one certainty in her life, who had wrapped her around with reassurance and comfort and counsel. Perhaps not always wise or honest counsel, certainly not tolerant, but always to protect and nurture. She would have faced death for Elizabeth de Lacy. As she had in the end. It was too difficult to take in, a cold hard weight in the centre of her chest.

Around her the nuns went silently about their business to care for the dead, to minister to their wounded Prioress. How strange. She blinked as tears stung at last. That the near-destruction of her marriage, her life, had not come from the hostility of York against Lancaster, but from her own blood. All Sir John's plotting to achieve the death of Richard. Even, it seemed, her own if she refused to comply. All to get possession of a Malinder heir. And if the influence had been that of Nicholas Capel, who had followed some devious desire of his own, still that did not absolve her uncle from his heinous sin.

And there was Richard Malinder, the centre of her world. He filled her horizon. And he was looking at her as if she filled his. Then they were alone in the cloister and the charged atmosphere dispersed around them into a brittle tranquillity, although the blood-stained paving stones bore testimony to the outrages committed there. The single candle left to them cast a pale flickering circle as the rest of the cloister was doused in darkness. For a little time their own private world.

They stood and looked at each other, reading with their minds as well as their eyes. Elizabeth saw the impossibly disordered hair, the lines of weariness that ran between nose and mouth from long riding over hard ground, to come to her rescue. There was blood on his clothes, on his sleeve, his bloodied sword was still in his hand. But the handsome features and the fierce gleam in his gaze were all that she loved and wanted. He had fought for her and killed the man who would have harmed her. He had come back for her. He had stood for her against her uncle. And in the end he had had the strength not to take another life.

For him, Elizabeth, in her severe habit and linen veil, looked too much like the rebellious nun who had arrived at Ledenshall a year ago to take up a position which she anticipated with little joy. Except that now she was his wife and he knew her, loved her. Saw the beauty in her. Would give his life for her.

They had been apart too long. Placing his sword on the floor at his feet, he opened his arms and she stepped into them. It was so simple. His arms enclosed around her and she leaned against him with a sigh from the depths of her soul.

'Thank God you are safe. I have prayed for this moment.' Elizabeth's forehead rested against his shoulder and she breathed in the sweat and dust, the sharp metallic tang of blood, the knowledge and wonder that at last he had returned to her filling her lungs, racing through her blood until her body shivered at the miracle of it.

'You are well. Unhurt. And the child.' It was a statement, to reassure himself. He could see it in her face, feel it in her body pressed close to his. The acceptance surged through him in a tidal wave of relief enough to cause him to breathe deep and turn his face into the soft folds of her veil. Then, on a thought, a desperate ploy to lighten the mood that threatened to unman him in emotion, he lifted his head, with a wry smile. 'You haven't let them cut your hair again?'

A faint laugh was all the answer he needed. Her arms crept slowly around him, her fingers savouring every inch, to hold him closer yet.

'I can feel that you have not wasted away this time.' His hands moved softly over her ribs, the sleek covering of flesh beneath the coarse wool.

'No—because I knew you would come for me.' Her breath was sweet against his face. 'It was a sanctuary—not a prison for the rest of my life. But oh, Richard!—it has been hard to wait in ignorance and uncertainty. When Sir John told me you were dying…' When a shudder ran through her body, he held on so that they stood silently in the shadows, one single entity with no division between them.

'I love you, Elizabeth.' He murmured the words against her lips and it was all she needed to hear.

'And I love you.'

'Look up.' And when she obeyed he took her mouth in a kiss of such tenderness, such sweetness, such contrast to the blood and death about them, that her heart trembled. And the tears at last came. He tasted them, understood, and held her so that he could see her face and wipe them away with his fingers.

'I'm sorry I could not save her.'

'I loved her. Jane was the only mother I ever knew.'

'Then I owe her a great debt for watching over my wife for me.'

'First she loved my mother and then she loved me and cared for me my whole life, when no one else cared…' She could not go on, but wept bitterly for all the memories and the loss, Richard allowing her the healing outpouring of grief in the security of his arms.

Eventually she was calm again. Sighed against him as she remembered.

'Jane saved my life. She took the blade that she thought was meant for me. She was wrong, wasn't she? I see it now.'

'Yes.' Richard smoothed the damp hair from her cheeks. 'She thought your life was in danger, but it was not so. She would not have known. Capel's blade was not intended for you, Elizabeth. You were central to your uncle's plan and always have been since he released you from Llanwardine. Capel would have used the dagger against me, or anyone who stood in the way of his success, but your present health—and that of the child you carry—was vitally important to the de Lacy future.'

Richard drew her to the stone ledge that provided a sheltered seat around the cloister where the nuns would read and take their leisure hour, where the shadows were darkest as seemed most appropriate, and told her the tale of deceit and unscrupulous plottings. He kept her hands enclosed in his as he separated and recounted the strands of the complicated tapestry from Ellen's revelations, his own knowledge of past events, Lewis's role in the tragedy. Seeing how well it fit as he spoke it aloud. Weaving together a whole that would damn Sir John de Lacy as a man of blood and treachery.

'So I would be a means to an end. Have always been so—to consolidate my uncle's hold on the March. Our child who would inherit the Malinder land would give him the means to absorb your land into his.' She turned her face against him as thoughts raced through her mind, quick to see the implications. 'But of necessity your life would be forfeit.'

'Yes.' He moved his hands to bracelet her wrists, feeling the firm pulse of her blood beneath his grasp, taking comfort from it.

'And mine too.' She looked up, eyes wide. 'Once the child was born. If I resisted him.'

'Yes. You would not be allowed to reject his guardianship.' At the thought, the rage returned, diamond bright. Unknowingly his grip tightened until Elizabeth squirmed and protested. 'Forgive me.' He immediately loosened his fingers, raised her wrists to his lips. 'I find it impossible to contemplate it without...' But he could not speak it. 'Perhaps Sir John thought he could persuade you to be amenable.'

'Then he does not know me! And David would replace Lewis, would be the chosen heir, could be moulded to ask no questions, but accept my uncle's orders. Which Lewis would not.'

'Undoubtedly. Except that he did not know David very well either. David is very like his sister with a mind of his own.'

She thought for a little while, then covered her face with her hands, although her voice was strong. 'It shames me, Richard. That such an outcome should have been in his mind when he offered me as your wife. And you accepted me in all ignorance that he plotted your downfall—your death.'

'There's no shame. You were an innocent weapon to be used against me. There's no blame on your shoulders.' Reaching out, he lifted her chin, so that she must look at him. 'As you see, I have come to no harm.' At last he rose from the cold stone, drew her hand through his arm to lead her from the cloister. 'Do you wish to leave Jane here?'

'No. I think she is too restless a spirit for this place,' Elizabeth replied after only a moment's thought. 'What would she think of nuns lighting candles around her and praying over her? I think she would rather rest at Ledenshall.'

'I shall arrange it.'

Grief took hold again, and an intense gratitude that Richard was *here*. She continued to lean into the shelter of his embrace. 'I can't believe that you are here,' she murmured. 'He said you were near death.'

His lips on hers, warm, tender beyond bearing, confirmed the life force that beat beneath the palms she spread against his chest, which echoed her own raised pulse as she sank into his reassurance.

'Where can I stay until dawn?' he asked as intense weariness finally bit.

'Come with me.' She took his hand, recovered the candle and led him from the cloisters to her own room, closing the door after them. 'This is the best I can offer.' A ghost of a laugh stirred the dank air, her breath coming in little puffs of moisture. 'The holy sisters would be horrified if they knew I had brought you here, but I will not be parted.'

She saw the room, little more than a cell, through Richard's eyes. The stone walls with their slimy gleam of damp, the bare flagged floor, the single unglazed window that let in the cold night air. The narrow bed and the lack of all furnishings, other than a crude crucifix fixed on the wall—nothing to offer any comfort to the chance guest.

Richard's quick grimace said it all. 'A penance in itself! And that bed, if we are to share it, is as narrow as a coffin.' He hissed a breath at his clumsy words. 'Ah! Elizabeth, forgive me…'

She placed her fingers over his mouth, then her own lips before pulling him to the bed where they stretched together in a supreme discomfort that neither would have refused. More precious than the most sumptuous of bedchambers,

more acceptable than the softest of mattresses, the smooth-
est of linens, the hard pallet provided all they needed. Fully
clothed, their body heat as Richard held Elizabeth close in
his arms, her head on his breast, made magnificent compen-
sation for the thin covering. By mutual decision they left the
candle burning until it guttered, as if to keep at bay the images
that might encroach with the dark. Whispered words of love,
a quiet acceptance of what had almost destroyed them, an
inseparable closeness of mind and body, it was the sweetest
and saddest of reconciliations, but finally a strange contentment wrapped them round. The visions of death and murder,
of headlong fearful flight through the night, gradually ebbed
away. Until they were silent, content to simply be together
after all that had separated them.

Richard kept watch until dawn. Perhaps Elizabeth slept
a little, until the ringing of the Priory bell for Prime stirred
them into a new awareness of each other. Without a word
they moved together in a very necessary healing. Soft kisses,
soft sighs, the minimal removal of garments to reaffirm their
love. A slow slide of hands, a catch of breath the only sound
in the little room. Lifting her above him, Richard lowered her,
filled her, owned her, gave all his tenderness to her, whilst
Elizabeth took him in, surrounding him with her body and
her love, her gaze never leaving his, drowning in the love she
saw in his face for her. Breath ragged, completely involved in
their own small world within the four walls of the cell, they
rocked together in the gentlest of rhythms until it was done.

Her words, finally, against his mouth expressed both their
desires.

'Take me home, Richard. Take me to Ledenshall.'

Epilogue

Every surface was covered with a thick layer of dust. They breathed it. Ate and drank it, the bed linen scratchy with it. Yet they were home and it lifted Elizabeth's heart.

Ellen was at Talgarth under David's watchful eye. Sir John was in London, petitioning the new Yorkist King, young Edward, for justice. Nicholas Capel had vanished, without trace. Elizabeth shivered as if a cloud had obscured the sun. His crimes, and those of Sir John, were beyond penance. As for the future...she turned her mind from it. The scrying dish had not been used since Jane's death.

Voices in the distance informed her where Richard would be. The shattered stonework and sinking foundations of the massive wall took much of his attention. When it was not focused on her. Elizabeth understood how hard he had to try not to cushion her with care, and loved him for it. Her lips curved, complacent as a cat in a sunbeam, at the anticipation of the gleam in his eye when he looked at her.

On the battlement walk, Richard rolled up the plan for new buildings and looked across to where Elizabeth had come to stand at the top of the steps outside the Great Hall, her skirts blown against her thickening waistline as she raised a hand to hold her veil back, a very feminine gesture. Immediately he went to her. The threats to her freedom, even to her life, were still too vivid to be easily cast off. Losing her was more than his mind could contemplate.

'What are you doing?'

'Do you need to ask? I can sign my name in the dust on every surface!'

His mouth was firm on hers, his hand possessively gentle on the swell of her belly, but knowing better than to suggest that she rest as he brushed the cobwebs from her sleeve.

'Don't worry. David will make an excellent Lord of Talgarth,' he assured her, sensing the shadow that still lingered in her mind.

'I know.'

Richard drew her close, an arm around her waist so that she fit neatly against him, resting his cheek against her frisky veiling, content for that sun-filled moment to stand and look towards the activity where the stone blocks were being chipped and shaped. Until a familiar feline figure wound round their feet, down the steps and across the courtyard to the stables. Ears alert, her sides bulged and rippled under soft fur.

'Another with offspring on her mind,' Richard remarked drily.

'Perhaps one of them will have the gift.' Elizabeth laughed softly as the cat disappeared round the stable door. 'I hope the kittens are better tempered than their mother.'

'Amen to that. And I think my Black Vixen is content too.'

'Dear Richard. More than content.' Her words expressing all the love that was between them.

'My lord.' Below, Simon Beggard raised his hand as they began to hoist a large block with rope and pulley.

Richard lifted Elizabeth's hand from where it was tucked within his arm and rubbed his lips over her fingertips, still tempted to linger in the sun. The future was suddenly full of promise. Time would tell what manner of man Edward of York, their new King, would be. A better man than his father, he admitted, and perhaps a king who would bring peace to a war-torn country.

'You are needed.' Elizabeth sighed, nudged him gently.

'Later, then.' Richard ran down the steps to discuss the finer points of wall construction.

The Malinder heir kicking in her belly, her heart unfurling with an intense happiness, Elizabeth remained on the top step and watched him.

* * * * *

*Harlequin Presents®️ is thrilled
to introduce the first installment of
an epic tale of passion and drama by*
**USA TODAY *Bestselling Author*
Penny Jordan*!**

*When buttoned-up Giselle first meets
the devastatingly handsome Saul Parenti,
the heat between them is explosive....*

"LET ME GET THIS STRAIGHT. Are you actually suggesting that I would stoop to that kind of game playing?"

Saul came out from behind his desk and walked toward her. Giselle could smell his hot male scent and it was making her dizzy, igniting a low, dull, pulsing ache that was taking over her whole body.

Giselle defended her suspicions. "You don't want me here."

"No," Saul agreed, "I don't."

And then he did what he had sworn he would not do, cursing himself beneath his breath as he reached for her, pulling her fiercely into his arms and kissing her with all the pent-up fury she had aroused in him from the moment he had first seen her.

Giselle certainly *wanted* to resist him. But the hand she raised to push him away developed a will of its own and was sliding along his bare arm beneath the sleeve of his shirt, and the body that should have been arching away from him was instead melting into him.

Beneath the pressure of his kiss he could feel and taste her gasp of undeniable response to him. He wanted to devour her, take her and drive them both until they were equally satiated—even whilst the anger within him that she should make him feel that way roared and burned its resentment of his need.

She was helpless, Giselle recognized, totally unable to withstand the storm lashing at her, able only to cling to the man who was the cause of it and pray that she would survive.

Somewhere else in the building a door banged. The sound exploded into the sensual tension that had enclosed them, driving them apart. Saul's chest was rising and falling as he fought for control; Giselle's whole body was trembling.

Without a word she turned and ran.

Find out what happens when Saul and Giselle succumb to their irresistible desire in

THE RELUCTANT SURRENDER

Available January 2011 from Harlequin Presents®

HARLEQUIN®

A Romance

FOR EVERY MOOD™

Spotlight on
Classic

Quintessential, modern love stories
that are romance at its finest.

See the next page
to enjoy a sneak peek from
the Harlequin Presents® series.

MARGARET WAY

Wealthy Australian, Secret Son

Rohan was Charlotte's shining white knight
until he disappeared—before she had
the chance to tell him she was pregnant.

But when Rohan returns years later as
a self-made millionaire, could the blond,
blue-eyed little boy and Charlotte's heart
keep him from leaving again?

Available January 2011

Love Inspired ®

Bestselling author

JILLIAN HART

brings readers another heartwarming story
from

the

GRANGER FAMILY RANCH

To fulfill a sick boy's wish, rodeo star Tucker Granger surprises
little Owen in the hospital. And no one is more surprised than
single mother Sierra Baker. But somehow Tucker ropes her heart
and fills it with hope. Hope that this country girl and her son
can lasso the roaming bronc rider into their family forever.

Look for

His Country Girl

*Available January
wherever books are sold.*

REQUEST YOUR FREE BOOKS!

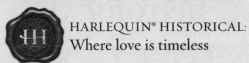

HARLEQUIN® HISTORICAL:
Where love is timeless

2 FREE NOVELS PLUS 2 **FREE GIFTS!**

YES! Please send me 2 FREE Harlequin® Historical novels and my 2 FREE gifts (gifts are worth about $10). After receiving them, if I don't wish to receive any more books, I can return the shipping statement marked "cancel." If I don't cancel, I will receive 6 brand-new novels every month and be billed just $4.94 per book in the U.S. or $5.49 per book in Canada. That's a saving of 20% off the cover price! It's quite a bargain! Shipping and handling is just 50¢ per book.* I understand that accepting the 2 free books and gifts places me under no obligation to buy anything. I can always return a shipment and cancel at any time. Even if I never buy another book from Harlequin, the two free books and gifts are mine to keep forever.

246/349 HDN E5L4

Name _____ (PLEASE PRINT)

Address _____ Apt. #

City _____ State/Prov. _____ Zip/Postal Code

Signature (if under 18, a parent or guardian must sign)

Mail to the **Harlequin Reader Service:**
IN U.S.A.: P.O. Box 1867, Buffalo, NY 14240-1867
IN CANADA: P.O. Box 609, Fort Erie, Ontario L2A 5X3

Not valid for current subscribers to Harlequin Historical books.

Want to try two free books from another line?
Call 1-800-873-8635 or visit www.morefreebooks.com.

* Terms and prices subject to change without notice. Prices do not include applicable taxes. N.Y. residents add applicable sales tax. Canadian residents will be charged applicable provincial taxes and GST. Offer not valid in Quebec. This offer is limited to one order per household. All orders subject to approval. Credit or debit balances in a customer's account(s) may be offset by any other outstanding balance owed by or to the customer. Please allow 4 to 6 weeks for delivery. Offer available while quantities last.

Your Privacy: Harlequin Books is committed to protecting your privacy. Our Privacy Policy is available online at www.eHarlequin.com or upon request from the Reader Service. From time to time we make our lists of customers available to reputable third parties who may have a product or service of interest to you. If you would prefer we not share your name and address, please check here. ☐

Help us get it right—We strive for accurate, respectful and relevant communications. To clarify or modify your communication preferences, visit us at www.ReaderService.com/consumerschoice.

HH10R

COMING NEXT MONTH FROM

HARLEQUIN®
HISTORICAL

Available December 28, 2010.

- **WHIRLWIND REUNION**
  by **Debra Cowan**
  (Western)

- **TAKEN BY THE WICKED RAKE**
  by **Christine Merrill**
  (Regency)
  Book 8 in the *Silk & Scandal* miniseries

- **THE ADMIRAL'S PENNILESS BRIDE**
  by **Carla Kelly**
  (Regency)

- **IN THE LAIRD'S BED**
  by **Joanne Rock**
  (Medieval)